MY BONES AND MY FLUTE

ALSO BY EDGAR MITTELHOLZER

Creole Chips
Corentyne Thunder
A Morning at the Office
Shadows Move Among Them
Children of Kaywana
The Weather in Middenshot
The Life and Death of Sylvia
The Adding Machine
The Harrowing of Hubertus
My Bones and My Flute
Of Trees and the Sea
A Tale of Three Places
With a Carib Eye (nf)
Kaywana Blood
The Weather Family
A Tinkling in the Twilight
The Mad MacMullochs (as H. Austin Woodsley)
Eltonsbrody
Latticed Echoes
The Piling of Clouds
Thunder Returning
The Wounded and the Worried
A Swarthy Boy (nf)
Uncle Paul
The Aloneness of Mrs Chatham
The Jilkington Drama

EDGAR MITTELHOLZER

MY BONES AND MY FLUTE

A Ghost Story

In the Old-fashioned Manner

INTRODUCTION BY KENNETH RAMCHAND

PEEPAL TREE

First published in Great Britain in 1955
by Martin Secker and Warburg Limited
This new edition published in 2015
Reprinted in 2022

Peepal Tree Press Ltd
17 King's Avenue
Leeds LS6 1QS
England

ISBN13 Print: 9781845232955

Printed in the United Kingdom by Severn,
Gloucester, on responsibly sourced paper

KENNETH RAMCHAND

INTRODUCTION

1. A SUCCESSFUL GHOST STORY

My Bones and My Flute (1955) is different from every other Mittelholzer novel. Its difference begins with the circumstance that it is narrated in the first person by a figure who is both a main character deeply implicated in the action of the novel, and a narrator committed to sticking to the facts and telling the truth. The narrating character is called Milton Woodsley.[1]

It is a ghost story or a tale of the supernatural. As with many ghost stories, there are related elements of horror and mystery. It was recognized as an outstanding example of the genre when it first came out in 1955. For frightening you and keeping you in suspense, and for making you jumpy when you hear certain sounds or smell certain smells in the night, or in the bush, there is no better Caribbean tale. For making you wonder in vacant or pensive moods if there *are* entities and presences and shadows moving among us that our notion of "reality" denies too stubbornly, there is not a more suggestive text. In his BBC *Caribbean Voices* review of November 1955, V.S. Naipaul said that "We believe in it implicitly while we are reading it",[2] but as will be seen, Mittelholzer doesn't only want you to believe the story while you are reading it. He wants to leave you accepting the supernatural.

The dreadful and increasingly fantastic happenings in this novel and the contagious tension and hysteria of the main characters are all roused by a ghost. Everything turns and twists around the ghost. The ghost first manifests, innocently enough, as the sound of a flute in the distance. It has been inadvertently activated when a very live human being handles a two-hundred-year-old parchment rescued from a perished Dutch plantation in the Berbice jungle.

The author of the manuscript is Jan Pieter Voorman, once owner of Goed de Vries, an eighteenth century plantation in which he has never been much interested. He is really an artist, convinced that no one values his efforts. He is obsessed with extending the range of the flute beyond known limits, and he has made the reckless mistake of invoking the instruments of darkness to help him further his overreaching ambition (p. 228).[3] He commits suicide at the time of the Berbice Rebellion of 1763 as a rampant slave army approaches and just as the dark forces he has unleashed begin to claim him as their own. It is the ghost of Mynheer Voorman that plays the importuning flute.

Mynheer Voorman writes on March 4, 1763, the day of his suicide, that he will never rest "till the day that my bones and my flute are found and interred with Christian rites". He places "a curse and a plague" upon anyone who touches the parchment: his "roaming presence will pester him or them unto death unless my wishes are carried out" (p. 75).

The manuscript comes into the hands of Mr Nevinson a member of an old respectable commercial family with "Coloured" blood[4] but looking white enough to be considered white. He is managing director of the Berbice Timber and Balata Company, and he is given the canister containing the parchment on one of his visits to the Company's interior station. He takes charge of this historic document, having turned part of his home into a museum of Dutch and Amerindian relics, with a library of maps, letters, books and historical documents. (The narrating character Milton Woodsley enjoys the atmosphere, the "old-book scent" and "the restful gloom that always lurked in the spaces between these dark mahogany bookcases" where companionable and "benign jumbies seemed to crouch" (p. 55)). As an amateur historian and antiquary, Mr Nevinson – according to Milton a cultivated and composed citizen – is enthusiastic about Guyanese history especially "such matters as slave uprisings in the eighteenth century and the doings of the old Dutch settlers" (p. 54).

Contact with the parchment turns Mr Nevinson's hobby into a

deeper involvement. It brings history as a living force into the conventional lives of the Nevinson family, a privileged family living comfortably enough in New Amsterdam, then a small respectable colonial town, though located, ominously if it cared to imagine, on the edge of the jungle and at the mouth of a huge river.[5]

According to Nevinson's daughter Jessie, as she tells Milton: "Since he came back from that trip last month, he's been very nervy and jumpy – and sort of excited inside, as if he has a secret he's afraid we might discover" (p. 60). Whilst Milton appreciates Jessie's feminine charms, he is not inclined to think of her as having much of a brain, but it is her insight that allows the narrator to prime the reader with the opening sentence of the novel: "We must have been well over halfway to our destination when I received the first hint that there might be some other reason behind Mr Nevinson's invitation to me to spend time with him and his family up the Berbice" (p. 51).

Mr Nevinson cannot help going back to the bush where he was given the canister, and he takes the unusual step of bringing his wife and his daughter, and inviting the more than willing painter, Milton Woodsley, to come with them to the cottage. He offers Milton a commission to paint some jungle scenes to adorn the Company's head office in New Amsterdam.

The cottage is located in a clearing on ground that was part of the abandoned Goed de Vries plantation. Conventional ghost stories tend to have a haunted house, and this cottage is it. When the steamer arrives at Goed de Vries at twenty minutes to six on that fateful Wednesday evening, Milton, as narrator, reflects on the life of the past: "I found myself smiling as I tried to imagine what Goed de Vries must have looked like two centuries ago when it was a flourishing plantation under the Dutch. All that jungle that loomed beyond the clearing must have been culti-vated terrain." He imagines the plantation house, the "rows and rows of logies for the accommodation of the slaves", the bells or the horn summoning slaves from the fields, and the administer-ing of the day's punishments on "many a naked black body secured in the stocks" (p. 84). This is a ghost story but its social and historical underpinnings play a structural role.

The novel relates how the beleaguered Nevinson party endure

the nerve-racking haunting of the cottage by the shades of the past, battle the inner and outer forces that would prevent them from leaving the cottage to carry out Mynheer Voorman's wishes, and eventually make their seemingly purgatorial way through a phantasmagorical jungle landscape till they arrive at the place where the bones and flute of the Dutchman are buried. The story is riveting enough as it unwinds. The mystery and the mounting horror are in the sensuous details. Which is why, even if you have read the novel fifty times, knowing the story does not prevent you from being frightened.

2. Reception of the Novel

West Indian reviewers seem to have had no difficulties swallowing Mittelholzer's brew. According to A. J. Seymour in *Kyk-Over-Al*, it is "a great success because of its relative simplicity and its compulsive power born of the author's skill to lead the reader's attention from one page to another in pity and terror."[6] W. Therold Barnes finds that "the increasing menace of unknown forces is expertly paced, and, in spite of our foreknowledge from the introductory note that all will come through unscathed, the suspense is maintained admirably." Barnes ends his review in *Bim* 23 thus: "For the lover of ghost stories, old-fashioned or otherwise, here is one which he cannot afford to leave out of his collection."[7] In his BBC *Caribbean Voices* review of November 1955, V.S. Naipaul praises Mittelholzer's "masterly" narrative art, and his ability to "capture a mood and recreate an incident without strain." Naipaul confirms that the story is "tantalizingly unfolded, with skilful variations in pace and mood." He recognizes that Mittelholzer has the gift that cannot be taught or learnt of "fertility and invention", and in summary pronounces that "Mittelholzer has set out to tell a ghost story, and he tells a rattling good one."[8] Rattling.

Thirty years later, the verdict was unchanged. In his introduction to the Longman Caribbean Writers edition of 1986, Mark McWatt praises Mittelholzer for displaying in the novel "a thorough knowledge of the fictional conventions of the supernatural story"; and he describes the many forms that manifestations of the supernatural take in the novel, pointing out that they appeal "to as many of the senses as possible", and that they become "progressively more terrifying as we move towards the novel's climax."[9] Reviewers in Britain, too, were taken by this novel, invoking distinguished practitioners of horror, mystery and the supernatural like Sheridan Le Fanu, Edgar Allan Poe and M.R. James.[10]

Mittelholzer would have expected the reference to more familiar practitioners. In telling Milton Woodsley about the parchment and the flute, Mr Nevinson apologises for being about to relate a tale "that is going to sound like something out of Edgar Allan Poe – or that other writer, M.R. James" (p. 75). When Mr Nevinson discloses that in addition to hearing the flute he has now begun to see a misshapen creature more beast than man, Milton reflects that in other circumstances he would have laughed at him outright and told him he was seeing creatures invented by M.R. James and even using the language of the famous author of *Ghost Stories of an Antiquary*.[11] Milton finds out soon afterwards that Mr Nevinson had brought with him "several volumes, fictional and otherwise, that treated of supernatural matters" (p. 138). Later, Milton laughs at himself for speaking in "the tone of voice I imagined Sherlock Holmes or that character of Poe's, Dupin, might have used" (p. 173). Mittelholzer was aware of the kind of book he wanted to write and he knew the classical writers in the tradition. He was not trying to imitate them but he would stand on their shoulders when it would benefit his original invention to do so.

It is no wonder that sixty years after its first publication, the work has continued to fasten its bony grip on those who ritually reread it, on new readers whom they initiate, and on some who have just chanced upon it.

3. A LITERARY MYSTERY

Everybody enjoys *My Bones and My Flute*. For those who have read other Mittelholzer books, this one is often their favourite. When critical assessments are delivered, however, *My Bones and My Flute* is not listed as among the most "important" or "significant".

Some raise up the Kaywana trilogy, some look to *Shadows Move Among Them*, and, in a letter dated 15th June 1962 in a private collection "Letters from Mittelholzer to Ruth Wilkinson (circa March 1941-15th June 1962)", Mittelholzer himself chooses his penultimate novel, *The Aloneness of Mrs Chatham*: "It's my most important novel to date, for in it I've expressed what I feel not only about contemporary society but also about my beliefs in the Occult (Yoga)."[12]

Mittelholzer's selection of *The Aloneness of Mrs Chatham* was made in 1962 at a time when his feelings about the state of contemporary society and the struggles in his own mind were paramount. In the same year he made a distinction between his serious novels and the "more or less lightweight attempts at fantasy, or comedy or mystery or the supernatural" when he wanted to take a holiday from "seriousness".[13] Included among the lightweights are the delightful *Of Trees and the Sea*, *My Bones and My Flute*, and the not bad at all *The Weather Family*, *A Tinkling in the Twilight* and *Eltonsbrody*.

This introduction does not accept the distinction between the serious and the lightweight, and it does not subscribe to the view that the only content is surface or easily-seen content. How can you say a book is your favourite and then say or imply that it is not all that significant? How does one come to terms with the discrepancy between the "responsible" critical attitude to *My Bones* and one's spontaneous response?

To this reader, *My Bones and My Flute* is Mittelholzer's most enjoyable and best-written novel, and his most important one. There are so many pages in this book that touch on metaphysical issues, on consciousness, and on the nature of time and reality that it can't be looked at as just a ghost story. We can note briefly at this point that it is compounded out of a number of well-known Mittelholzer interests, such as early Guyanese history; the Guyanese landscape, especially river and jungle; the supernatural; heightened mental states; death and the meaning of life and human aspiration; social and economic arrangements; and behaviours reflecting race and colour. His proclaimed interests in sex and religion are present too, but like most of the items listed the treatment does not extend to thematic exploration. What is unique about *My Bones and My*

Flute is the fusion or boundarylessness of the different kinds of material in it. Which is another way of saying that it is about everything under the sun at one and the same time.

4. BEFORE AND AFTER *MY BONES AND MY FLUTE*

My Bones and My Flute does not come up when Mittelholzer's later novels are discussed, and little is said about it when the early novels, mostly set in Guyana and the Caribbean region, are reviewed. This seems to call for a comparison of *My Bones* with the novels published before it, and those published after.

a. Before

Seven novels, a collection of sketches *Creole Chips* (1937), and a novella originally entitled "Immoral Fable" but published as *The Adding Machine* in 1954 are listed in the Mittelholzer Bibliography as having been published before *My Bones and My Flute*.[14]

There is a problem here. It is obvious that dates of publication cannot indicate when a work was conceived, or when a first draft was ready, or if further drafts were produced until the final manuscript was submitted. It is often the case that a book is published long after it went the rounds seeking publication. This is especially so in the case of Mittelholzer who had the habit in the early part of his career of working on two or three books at the same time, or beginning a new one while waiting on submitted manuscripts to be published. In Chapter 2 of her dissertation, Juanita Westmaas quotes a passage from a Mittelholzer letter to Frank Collymore, dated April 26th, 1946, which tells about the progress of *My Bones and My Flute* and also suggests that in 1946 *Shadows Move Among Them* (1951) had already been started: "I'm doing something I really enjoy – a novel set on the Berbice River (the locale of SHADOWS); it is a ghost story but with sharply delineated characters and lavish atmospheric effects (in the old-fashioned manner). It's really a revision of something I did years ago [in 1944] and is called MY BONES AND MY FLUTE". Westmaas also cites two letters of 1954 written to Carl van Vechten informing Van Vechten that he was finalizing *My Bones and My Flute* and repeating that a first version of *My Bones* was originally written in 1944.

We can draw from Westmaas's research that nearly all of Mittelholzer's novels with a Caribbean setting were conceived, written or almost completely written in the 1940s period, except for *The Weather Family*, *Latticed Echoes* and *Thunder Returning*.

The situation we have then is that while the 1944 version of *My Bones* was just sitting there or being tinkered with as the letters referred to above indicate, Mittelholzer was exploring the themes and expressing the ideas for which he was to become known, sometimes notorious, when the novels were eventually published between 1951 and 1957. It is remarkable that little or none of the content and attitudes of the works in process between 1944 and 1954 (including *The Mad MacMullochs* published 1959 but completed 1953) managed to seep into *My Bones and My Flute*.

Creole Chips (1937) and *Corentyne Thunder* (1941) are the only books that can be said with certainty to have been written and published before *My Bones*. It is interesting to see how it relates to these two works. In *My Bones*, Milton Woodsley eventually allows Jessie to accompany him on his visit below deck to those whom her class would consider "the rabble of the lower deck", on their journey up river. He is greeted amicably: "The second mate and I were already acquainted. He was one of my barbers' shop companions in debate" (p. 65). Earlier, Milton describes how he rejects the attempts of his kin to use their influence to advance his career in commerce. "From that day I was regarded by the respectable people of New Amsterdam as an eccentric crank who would 'get nowhere in life'. I became renowned for the bad company I kept. I talked philosophy in barbers' shops with bus drivers and stevedores and porters – people far below me in class; I was a disgrace to my family" (p. 53). Edgar Mittelholzer speaks in his autobiographical *A Swarthy Boy* (1963)[15] about "crawling out of the mollycoddling mire" in which his mother and repressed aunts were trying to keep him for his own good. He was allowed at last to have his hair cut at a barber shop in town rather than at home, and to him: "It seemed more manly, and one met interesting characters while one waited. The chatter, too, was worthwhile listening to" (*A Swarthy Boy*, pp.101-102).

The grounding with ordinary people that Mittelholzer attributes to the fictional Milton Woodsley appears in the self-published *Creole Chips* (1937) where Mittelholzer writes with the wit, humour, amusement and tolerance that are also to be found in *My Bones*. The same balanced attitude to people appears in the other definitely pre-*Bones* work *Corentyne Thunder*. Like *My Bones*, this first novel (which I appreciate and value more today than I did forty-five years ago) feels the immensity of the cosmos, the puniness of man, and the spirit residing in nature and landscape, whilst it also savours the presentness of the material world in which people toil and have their being, the tension between flesh and spirit, the ambition for success and the longing for happiness. Mittelholzer manages somehow to use the convention of omniscient author to articulate the thoughts and feelings of his peasant characters without falling too much to the temptation to offer perspectives not arising naturally from the scene. In short, there is no preachiness in *Corentyne Thunder*. In the closing scene, we don't have to be told that Beena accepts the fact of death, the mystery of a Universe that does not cease, and the burden of human beings to honour with courage their belonging to the creation:

> She looked all about her. No, nothing had changed at all. Surely, the savannah must know that Ramgollal was dead and that there were pebbles and pieces of dried mud lying scattered on the floor in the mud-house. It looked so untroubled, so flat and at peace as though nothing at all had happened. And the sky too, and the wind, the sunshine – all untroubled, the same as they had been yesterday and all the days before: the sky blue, the wind cool, the sun red because it was low in the west.
>
> Ramgollal was dead but the whole Corentyne remained just the same.
>
> The frog behind the mud-house squeaked again. Yes, she had better go at once and drive the cows into the pen for the night. It was getting late.[16]

The social and cultural awareness, and the consciousness of race, colour and class shown in *Creole Chips* and *Corentyne Thunder* are also part of the solid base anchoring the incredible story and events in *My Bones and My Flute*.

Before the publication of *My Bones* in 1955 Mittelholzer had also published seventeen short stories in *Bim*[17] (some repeated in *Caribbean Voices*) and another five in *Caribbean Voices* that were not published in *Bim*.[18]Nearly all the short stories are set in Barbados, Trinidad, England and British Guiana. They are peopled by all ethnic groups, classes, and types: Indians in "We Know Not Whom to Mourn", absurd and pretentious middle-class people in "Mr Jones of Port of Spain", working people including the unemployed; predators as in the comedy of "Miss Clarke is Dying", trickster types like Samlal in the story of that name; psychologically disturbed persons and groups as in "The Cruel Fate of Karl and Pierre" and "Something Fishy"; spinsters and widows, artists and reclusive types.[19]

Mittelholzer professed not to like the short story form but many of these stories are worthwhile for their own sake. A few are of particular interest because they deal in psychic phenomena, the paranormal, hysteria, and a whole range of abnormal states. They give a glimpse of some of the things that were going around in the author's head at the time when he had just written *My Bones*. In "Breakdown" the stranded passengers, strangers to the area where their car has broken down, have no doubt they have seen a man who the villagers know to be recently dead.[20] In the somewhat frightening "The Paw-Paw Tree", a "rank vegetable odour" emanates from a tree planted over a Dutchman's grave; a dried leaf turns into a brown withered hand then turns into a leaf again; the sleeping and dreaming narrator is only saved from being smothered by the withered hand when his friends see it climbing on his face.[21] In "Sorrow Dam and Mr Millbank", the retiring Mr Millbank works quietly to remove himself from deathlike existence in an office in New Amsterdam to live in a house he builds in the countryside among country people with manners and community spirit.[22] The satire against New Amsterdam in this story is of a piece with the satire in *My Bones*.

Mittelholzer's early interest in unusual mental states and emotional conditions can be seen in three stories, "The Cruel Fate of Karl and Pierre", "The Burglar", and "The Sibilant and the Lost". In "The Burglar"[23] a mental outpatient has regular delusions of a burglar coming to rob him. He narrates one of these delusional encounters in which he practices the most sadistic kind of torture on the man from a nearby slum, taking deliberate pride in his lack of compassion and his vicious inhumanity. Of special interest, too, is the 1950 short story "The Sibilant and the Lost"[24], again narrated by a madman. This narrator has made a pact with "Them" and his relationship with these forces leads him to think that he should "liquidate" his son. Earlier in the story, in a vein usually associated with the later novels, though here unequivocally the rantings of a madman, he condemns his wife and the authorities for being so weak as to allow him to live. As he tells his doctor: "A terrible thing [...] when people grow too liberal-minded. Too over-mellow with humanity. The criminal and the mentally unfit ought to be liquidated quietly and without pain – for their own good and for the good of the community. [...] Today people think it kind – oh what a fine thing! To be lenient with a criminal. No death penalty. Not even a little flogging. But in reality they're not being kind; they're being weak. And the weak go under." At the end, the narrator confesses to his doctor about the pact he has made with the unidentified "Them": *They* have come for me, doctor. But no pity. I want none, I tell you. I merit none. [...] I'm lost, doctor. Sibilant and lost." It is interesting that on p. 90 of *My Bones*, a description of the river contains both words: "The river made a soft sucking at the shrubs that bordered the bank – a secretive sibilance that, somehow, seemed even more remote and lost than the whirr and hum of the insects." The short story is gripping and readers of *My Bones* will recognise that the narrator of this story has transgressed further than the repentant and frightened Mynheer Voorman.

Along with these stories we can look at a kind of meditation entitled "Romantic Promenade: A Divertissement in Minor Chords".[25] In this piece, Mittelholzer tells about a pastime peculiar to his "solitary moments in the open air – that of endowing trees or buildings with a living intelligence and human emotions". Looking at a gnarled giant tree with a spread of branches sheltering an area over an acre he muses on the way in which landscape is not only what it looks like on the surface, but is also a medium in which actual and spiritual history are embedded: "Who can tell what varied segments of history, wide and narrow, the sapling had not garnered to itself and aloofly smiled upon throughout the decades that had converted it into this majestic colossus? Who can guess what dreams and memories are not simmering even at this instant deep within those tight-packed rings of wood that go to form a trunk?" This kind of intuition allows Mittelholzer to use landscape and history in *My Bones* to create atmosphere and mystery and preserve the shadows of every form of life.

b. After

It is standard practice in Mittelholzer criticism to argue that in the very latest works – *A Tinkling in the Twilight* (1959), *The Piling of Clouds* (1961), *The Wounded and the Worried* (1962), *Uncle Paul* (1963), *The Aloneness of Mrs Chatham* (1965) and the *The Jilkington Drama* (1965) – Mittelholzer uses mouthpieces, some of them bearing a resemblance to the actual Edgar Mittelholzer, to deliver pungent opinions on social, religious and political matters and on the prevailing "liberal" attitudes that encourage human "vermin" at the expense of their victims. These works are all set in England, and the sense of life is not strong in them. Other "essays" appear on death, suicide, sex and religion in a rotting society; the need for strength as against weakness in social and personal life; on the occult, and alternative spiritual practices like yoga and Buddhism. Neither in method, content, or manner does one see any hint of these later novels in *My Bones*; nor on the contrary does one see any of *My Bones'* sane balance in these late books.

Of the other novels published after *My Bones*, three are set in Barbados, three in British Guiana, and one encompasses Trinidad, England and St Lucia.[26] Whilst there is little connection between *My Bones* and these novels in theme, in all of them landscape and nature have a strong presence. The gruesome *Eltonsbrody* (1960), which is closest in genre to *My Bones*, and which according to Westmaas existed in an early draft by 1945, uses these elements to enhance its horror effects, but comparison only serves to highlight how unique and how nearly perfect *My Bones* is.

Two of the later novels *Latticed Echoes* (1960) and *Thunder Returning* (1961), set in British Guiana, are notable for Mittelholzer's experimenting with leitmotifs placed in the narrative and tuned to suggest particular people, moods, and events in the novels. The leitmotif novels drew some attention to themselves, though it is generally held that the experiment was not successful. Nevertheless, this is an opportunity to point out that Mittelholzer was a novelist's novelist, always trying something new with the novel form, but not always as ostentatiously as in the leitmotif novels. This introduction will argue that despite the evocation of an "old-fashioned manner", *My Bones* is Mittelholzer's most experimental and avant garde novel.

Another significant difference that emerges when we compare *My Bones and My Flute* with the novels published after it concerns sex and religion. In *Edgar Mittelholzer: The Man and His Work* (1968), A.J. Seymour quotes from a letter of the early 1950s in which Mittleholzer declares: "Yes, Arthur, you'll come to learn that sex and religion are my themes as a writer. I hold strong views on these two subjects and in everything I write you will note that I shall touch on them. In some works I shall emphasise them heavily, in others I shall introduce them as background accompaniment, but they will always be there."[27] They are not background in *The Mad MacMullochs* and *Shadows Move Among Them*.

5. SEX AND RELIGION IN *THE MAD MACMULLOCHS* AND *SHADOWS MOVE AMONG THEM*

The themes of sex and religion are emphasised heavily in two Utopian novels in which Mittelholzer sets up model communes. In *The Mad MacMullochs*,[28] which though completed in 1953 was not published until 1959, having spent a long time looking for a willing publisher (Westmaas), the setting is Barbados where Mittelholzer creates a sexually liberated nudist commune. This is a settlement in which life is organised in such a way as to challenge the deadening effects of the social, political and economic arrangements and sexual repression of conventional societies, including Barbados.

The other Utopian novel, *Shadows Move Among Them* (1951) was published before *My Bones* but it is convenient to look at it here. The action takes place in Berkelhoost a commune established in the deep dark jungle up the Berbice River, a place full of shadows and influences, teeming with "passionate, cruel spirits" and bristling with "the residual effluvia of past violence". This is virtually the same setting as *My Bones* and, just as in the later novel, landscape and history flow in and out of each other. Sex is quite prominent in *Shadows*, but the greater emphasis is on religion. The leader of the commune, Reverend Harmston, satirizes the superstitious character of orthodox Christianity and its inability to adapt to change in the world, and he fills the shells and empty forms of the old to shape a new religion equipped with its own creed and called "The Brethren of Christ the Man". In addition to their concerns with sex and religion, both Utopian novels contain sharp critiques of the evils of Western civilization, though in both of them there is a degree of irony over the tight control the leaders have over members of the commune.[29]

The group in the haunted cottage in *My Bones* is not a commune, Mr Nevinson shows no sign of dictatorial tendencies, and whilst the novel's critique of New Amsterdam society may be read as a satire on a mimic colonial middle-class nurtured on Western influences, *My Bones* does not indulge in broadsides against Western civilization. The commercial outlook, the small-mindedness and philistinism of New Amsterdam are the objects of subtle comedy and potent but good-tempered satire rather than rabid pillory.

6. SEX AND MARRIAGE IN *MY BONES AND MY FLUTE*

Nowhere in Mittelholzer's writing is sex handled so lightly and delicately as in *My Bones*. There is no agonizing over it, no scenes of lust or sexual passion, and not a hint of a rant anywhere that there is a problem with sex in modern societies. According to Milton he was "violently in love" with Mrs Nevinson when he was ten years old (p. 58), and even now he makes the harmless confession that "her gay roguish laugh never failed to quicken my heartbeats (I believe I must still have been in love with her)" (p. 68). In drawing attention to the mark of the flute on Mrs Nevinson's leg he is most circumspect: "People with nasty minds will probably explain it differently but so far as I know, it was by sheer accident that my gaze happened to pause on Mrs Nevinson's unstockinged legs" (p. 133). Later on, Mrs Nevinson makes a risqué joke about hard candles as against soft candles, and there is a reference to female hygiene (p. 169) which, coming when it does, helps to relieve tension for a minute or so. Milton's activities in looking through the women's bedroom window to monitor events inside the room could be construed as a form of voyeurism, but this text is free of anything that could be construed as slackness or pornography.

Since Mittelholzer had every opportunity to insert more sex and different kinds of sex in *My Bones* when he was getting it ready for publication in 1953-54, but did not do so, we have to assume that what was in the 1944 draft of the novel suited his purposes.

There is one moment in the novel where the reader understands that Mittelholzer is aware of the problematic nature of relationships between men and women, but the presentation makes it clear that it is not to his purpose to go into the subject in this book. Mrs Nevinson has just intruded upon a conversation between Milton and Mr Nevinson, and Milton observes that the husband is not pleased:

> I could see that Mr Nevinson resented her intrusion. Normally his attitude to her is one of affectionate tolerance. I had long ago discovered that while he did not share her passionate love of company and her craving for the more harmless pleasures of the world – for he is of the ascetic self-contained type – he never censured her for being what she was, but merely let her go her way while he went his own. This policy, I knew, did not always work successfully – there were sometimes long periods of coldness between them – but on the whole, they were a sensible couple and seemed to have learnt how to avoid major disasters affecting their relationship. I had no fear about their ever separating or finding themselves in the divorce court (p. 80).

The comfortableness of the Nevinson partnership invites a comparison with the partnership of the Voormans, the flute-playing Dutchman and his discontented wife. Mynheer Voorman writes: "This colony depresses her, and, moreover, my flute-playing annoys her. She places no value on my researches. What is it to her whether I add three more keys to the flute? My ambitions as an inventor of a flute of wide range mean nothing to her" (p. 228).

The last item in this reflection on sex in *My Bones* is the most important, which is to note that an understated love story is threaded through the harrowing tale. Milton Woodsley sees himself falling in love with Jessie and in the postscript to the novel he discloses that he is married to Jessie. He expects her to be satisfied that there has been a "conclusion" to the mystery, "but Jessie has, I fear, a rather poor appreciation of the value of words (having been married to her for over seventeen years, I can take these liberties on paper), so it may be well for me to state that I have no intention whatever of attempting a solution" (p. 227). The love story that comes to a conclusion with their marriage is presaged most noticeably in the verbal sparring between the couple that goes on throughout the book (pp. 61, 64, 66, 68, 70, 151, 171). Its threading through the novel is one of the strands of "reality" that Mittelholzer uses as binding for the ghost story.

Mittelholzer allows Milton's own words to show him up as a male chauvinist. His patronising attitudes, based on his feeling that women are the weaker vessels, are clearly indicated by Mittelholzer whose implied critique is being inscribed a decade or so before a feminist agenda became part of Caribbean consciousness. However we take this, it is the love story that stands out. In a telling paragraph Milton confesses: "Watching her now sitting beside me in the little craft as the outboard motor spluttered harshly and sent a trail of foam through the black water in our wake, I felt a distinct tenderness towards her. She looked so furtive and frightened despite the air of light-hearted indifference she tried to assume" (p. 106). On the journey back to the cottage after finding the body of the Amerindian woman who has been lured to her death and marked by the flute, Milton continues to be aware of Jessie: "She sat close to me in the boat, and looked so pale and frightened that I was tempted to put my arm around her to console her" (p. 113). When Jessie shows her disturbance at Mrs Nevinson's nightmare (the flute pulls her, and a bony hand grips her arm from behind), Milton confides to the reader, "The expression on her face fanned alive in me one of those strong impulses I had been having of late to hold her and pet her. It was so strong on this particular instance that

I had to ask myself whether it could be that I was falling in love" (p. 136). When he is truly hooked, Milton talks to his diary (in vain, it turns out) about checking up on himself: "Felt really soft about her myself, and sorry I tackled her about her weakness. Really believe developing a soft spot for her, in spite of resolutions to desist from falling in love. Must pull up. Won't do, this" (p. 182).

We are prepared for this love story within the ghost story by the brilliant exchanges that take place when Jessie pursues Milton to his retreat away from the rest of the passengers on the steamer. Mittelholzer's social comedy, his tolerance of and amusement by human foibles, his ability to write witty dialogue and his power to impress a character's character and personality with swift touches are all in evidence here. The reader should read this episode to see a light, bright, sparkling, gender-attuned Mittelholzer who slowly disappears out of his work and who only emerges again in the delightful *Of Trees and the Sea* (1956). The short sample below suggests a more focused Jessie than the helpless one Milton is drawn to, and the exchanges reveal that both characters have sized up each other and know where things will end:

> After lunch I returned aft with my book, but this time I was not to be left undisturbed. I heard footsteps and glanced up to see Jessie approaching. She stopped near my chair, peered with mild curiosity at the book in my lap and said: 'Poems, I suppose.'
>
> I nodded gravely in confirmation. 'Yes, poems.'
>
> 'I could have bet anything on it.'
>
> I did not rise to offer her my chair, but this in no way discouraged her. My chair stood near a locker in which, I believe, life-belts were stored. She gave me an amused look and seated herself on this locker (p. 58).

When the conversation is about to move in a different groove, Mittelholzer signals what is going on by having a ukulele-strumming passenger on the lower deck sing "in a crude but melodious voice, *If you were the only girl in the world*" (p. 61).

There is a kind of innocence and intuition in this early novel that makes me wish Mittelholzer had not developed so many explicit ideas about society and the world.

There isn't a theme of religion as such in *My Bones* though there is considerable mockery in Milton's description of his grandmother's fanatical religious attitudes. He tells us that although she had a generous heart and a rich imagination, the imagination was misdirected, with the result that she had "the ability to produce terror in small boys like myself with her vivid and convincing word-picture of what would happen to mankind on the Day of Judgment" when the unrighteous would be "cast into Eternal Flames with Satan and his Black Angels!" Milton jokes that he has no fear because he is convinced that when the Day comes, his grandmother's saintly tutelage will guarantee his being numbered among the Righteous "who would [...] be herded comfortably in That Place of Milk and Honey High Above" (p. 105). Milton also tells us that "at the age of nineteen I succeeded in ridding my scheme of thought of all my former religious fears relating to the perils of the hereafter" (p. 104).

Milton's grandmother's religious fanaticism runs very close to Mittelholzer's account of his grandmother Le Blanc's religious teachings, of hell and brimstone, milk and honey, in *A Swarthy Boy* (1963):

> So strong were her beliefs, and so confident in manner was she, that she spun about me an atmosphere of security. Nothing, I felt, could possibly go wrong when she was present. The heavenly Guardian Angels she told us were on our side, and though Satan's Black Angels might be hovering up in the darkness of the rafters, I could fall asleep at night with the complete assurance of protection from Grandma and the Guardian Angels (p. 47).

Noticing that among the passengers going up the Berbice River on the *Arawana* were an Anglican priest and his wife, Milton discloses that his people were "staunch Anglicans – as I myself, indeed used to be in the days before I began to think for myself" (p. 57). There is enough here for us to conclude that Milton's attitude to organised religion is similar to Mittelholzer's, but in the novel he allows Milton to participate without demur in the burial of Voorman's bones and flute according to Christian rites. Indeed, in the narrator's commentary on the episode, Mittelholzer allows Milton to speak as one who finds nothing at which to scoff. This brings us to a little crux. There is no religious theme as such in *My Bones*, but the action of the novel is motivated by the religious despair of Jan Pieter Voorman: "I shall never rest till the day that my bones and my flute are found and interred with Christian rites" (p. 74). He lays a curse on the person or persons who touch his parchment: they will be pestered unto death unless they carry out his wishes so that his soul may find peace.

In his manuscripts, Voorman defiantly proclaims that he is not of the Reformed Church to which his wife and her uncle belong: "I do not care, I say. Hail Mary! My candles shall burn. My statue of Mary shall stand." When the sinister forces with whom he has bargained call insistently to claim his soul, he avows that although errant, "I am at heart still a Christian. My church is my rock…"

In his last hours he sees himself "sinking deeper into the Gloom", facing catastrophe: "I am a thwarted, craven soul, a human tottering on the edge of ultimate darkness. To whom, to what, must I turn for salvation?" He is on his knees "beseeching the saints of heaven to intercede". If they don't intercede, however, all is not lost. It is for him to ensure that his body is not desecrated by the slave soldiers. Whenever his bones and flute are discovered and given Christian burial, despite his suicide, his soul will be saved.[30]

The Mittelholzer of *My Bones* sets these things down without contempt or intellectual arrogance. He even allows Milton to describe the group setting forth to find the bones and flute and give them Christian burial as a "sacred religious procession"(p. 212).

8. A NOVEL ABOUT WRITING A NOVEL

One of the first things noticed on opening *My Bones* is that it begins with an Introductory Note, and closes with a Postscript. The first is signed by Milton Woodsley, with an address "New Amsterdam, British Guiana", and it is dated July 1954. But the front cover and the title page advertise that the author of *My Bones* is Edgar Mittelholzer; and we know that the novel was finalised in Barbados in 1954 where Mittelholzer was living at the time. We also know that Mittelholzer did not go to New Amsterdam in 1954 or 1955. In *With a Carib Eye* he records: "In February of 1956 when, having mastered my nightmare neurosis, I visited New Amsterdam after an absence of fifteen years (I escaped in March 1941), I found it still as pretty a sight from mid-estuary but as peacefully dismal as ever" (p. 137).

What we can take from this little diversion is that Mittelholzer is playing. He is pretending that Milton Woodsley is the author. But every reader knows that both the Introductory Note and the Postscript are parts of the novel, inserted not by the purported author Milton Woodsley but by Edgar Mittelholzer. When Mittelholzer allows Milton, writing in 1954 to tell us on page 227 that he has been married to Jessie for over seventeen years, we know that a deliberate attempt is being made by Mittelholzer (married in Trinidad to Roma Halfhide in 1942) to reserve the right not to be identified with his fictional character.

Mittelholzer was always an experimenter. His fiddling or flute-playing with form puts *My Bones* ahead of its time as a Caribbean novel. His deployment of Milton Woodsley in overlapping roles as purported author, as narrator, and as an idiosyncratic character involved in the action gives a complex form to the novel that involves the reader in the process of putting the story together.

Milton makes a number of apparently unstudied comments on convincingness, language, and fidelity to the facts. It doesn't matter too much that in some of these comments narrator and purported author are not separable. What is pertinent is that in an era when the figure of the "unreliable" narrator has become a commonplace of fiction writing and academic discussion of the novel, this does not appear to have been Mittelholzer's motive for creating Milton Woodsley as a narrating character. Why I say this, I will go on to show.

9. MILTON THE NARRATOR

Milton's conscientiousness and his circumspect attitude as narrator can be seen throughout. I am isolating for the purposes of illustration three such moments. Having affirmed (p. 115) that "In writing this narrative it is upon my diary that that I have depended chiefly", Milton is careful to explain that just as the diary cannot include everything that happened, so in the writing-up there has to be a principle of selection: "Were I to attempt to give a detailed day-to-day account of everything that happened to us and the sensations we experienced during the two weeks we spent at Goed de Vries, this record would begin to assume the proportions of *The Golden Bough*. I shall have to limit myself, therefore, to narrating only those incidents I consider to be of outstanding significance and interest. This does not mean, how-ever, that I shall fail in my duty as a chronicler and omit mention of vital details" (p. 135). In the second illustration on p. 168, Milton refers to his commitment to maintaining chronological order and to amalgamating the bare diary notes into narrative form, then has to apologise to the reader for making a slight deviation from chronology this time. In the third illustration on p. 181 he begs the reader not to think that he is departing from his promise to write up his notes in polished form, but says he has to "quote briefly from the scribblings…" He explains to the reader that: "My purpose in giving you this glimpse into my diary is to illustrate the state of our nervous and mental balance during the hours that preceded the experiment, and to do this without having recourse to long and wordy descriptions" (p. 182). Then he goes back to the polished method of narration.

We have comments like these from the narrator on the techni-cal difficulties of putting his material on paper and on the likelihood of it being considered outlandish ("a story like this is not the kind of thing any normal civilized person would care to go rushing into print" (p. 201)). There are frequent addresses to the reader in which he admits that if he were told what he is telling them, he too would find it hard to credit. He insists on what he has seen and felt, however, and banks on the reader giving credence to the feelings and emotions he is describing. The frank admission of difficulties, and the personal appeals to the reader are crucial. They add to the texture that makes *My Bones* a dramatic and gripping novel, at the same time as they make it a thankfully accessible novel about the writing of a novel.

This work of 1954 is in effect a meta-novel of a unique kind: it is accessible; it has a strong story, vivid characters, sharply described incidents, and a sense of place and of life, ingredients that seem to be missing in some modern (or post-modern) meta-novels and the theorizing about them that became fashionable decades later.

10. MITTELHOLZERIAN PLOYS

A ghost story has to be credible. It will not work if it does not induce the reader to suspend his disbelief. The fantastic happenings in the book seem to be a mix of science fiction and the supernatural: the sound of the flute; bodiless physicality; grey masses that turn into greyish furry things with claws; smells off the river and jungle that could be noxious chemicals manufactured in a laboratory; psychedelic lights and colours flashing from primordial creatures with a hint of the human but the malevolence of the inhuman; bodies being charged into by fuzzy creatures moving like battery-driven toys and diabolic shapes pulsing in the air. At the end is the incredible "bubble of twilight", like a spacecraft that drives the group with an "incomprehensible compulsion" to the spot they are looking for – all this accompanied by rumblings and tumblings in the atmosphere.

In addition to the "Introductory Note" and the "Postscript", Mittelholzer deploys a number of devices calculated to create suspense, and to immerse readers sensuously in these happenings, in spite of their "better" judgments. Every artistic ploy in this work is done in the service of credibility. But be warned. Mittelholzer will accept a suspension of disbelief while the reader is experiencing the work but, as previously suggested, he has the grand ambition of inducing the reader to believe in the existence of the supernatural.

Mittelholzer moves with all the studied cunning and opportunism of a grandmaster. Some of the strategies are obvious enough. Most of the chapters end with a shock or surprise, not bringing closure but pulling the expectant reader into the next chapter. We can bank on the recurrence of the flute, but only more or less. Haunting by the flute begins for each person from the time when he first touches the manuscript, and since they all touch it at different times, the reader has to accommodate different degrees of haunting at the same time. The pattern becomes more complicated and shocking when other manifestations begin to appear along with the flute. Mrs Nevinson's dream of horrors happening to her in the day alternates with Jessie's nightmares. Whatever the manifestation, each is part of a sequence building to a crescendo, and the reader feels the relentless march, not able to guess where it will go. The reader has to hear, smell and see the manifestations and suffer the disturbance of the characters.

When the level-headed Mr Nevinson hears the flute and then sees "a hazy human figure hovering near the veranda door", a great fear takes possession of him. He tells Milton:

> "When I gripped your arm I did so because I had the most overpowering desire to follow that spectral figure outside into the darkness. I *had* to grip you. After a while, it began to move. I saw it gradually shifting outside and I wanted to follow it. Within those few seconds it became an obsession. It took all my will to resist. And it may sound a sensational thing to say, but I knew without doubt that it was calling me to my death" (p. 103).

Again and again, Mittelholzer writes up scenes like this to frighten and involve the reader. They are located first in the feelings of his characters rather than in external manifestations, though such manifestations come to play an increasingly salient role in the narrative. Credibility is his aim, and if he can persuade you at the sensuous level the work is more than half-done.

There are strategic narrations by characters other than Milton to vary and consolidate the burden of the narrative. There is Mr Nevinson's account of his dealings with the Dutchman's parchment (pp. 72-75); Mrs Nevinson's account of her first nightmare (e.g. pp. 135-136); "desperate" and raw quotations from Milton's diary (pp. 181-182) and well-placed insertions from texts written by Mynheer Voorman with commentaries by Mr Nevinson (pp. 74-75, and by Milton (pp. 115-116 and 228-231).

The descriptions of unusual happenings attempt to bypass the rational barrier by appealing to the senses: sight (deep dark colours, monstrous shapes and mysterious shapelessnesses, the print of the flute on flesh); sound (bird, beast, frog, baboon, gurgles, whispers, something falling in the water); smells (rot, fermentation, musky emanations) and textures (slime, slush, fuzz, furriness). The case for the truth of these sensuous renderings of strange phenomena is made by the interventions of the earnest narrator appealing to the reader, offering explanations, conceding that yes, he can see how incredible it sounds, but how to doubt what has come home to your senses?

Accurate and sensuous descriptions of landscape are a staple in Mittelholzer's writing. They are crucial in *My Bones*. There is the sensuous passage on page 156 that begins "The early morning mists had not yet dispersed entirely..." and ending "...the splash of a corial going past would disrupt the silence". In this passage and others like it, we are not just dealing with a writer who loves the Guyana landscape and all it holds. Here, the accuracy of such descriptions leaves the landscape open to be a source of unseen entities and strange shapes and colours, depending on what the person describing wants to charge it with and, of course, what the responsive reader brings to it.

In other passages, the landscape is still described in its own observable physical terms, but Mittelholzer uses Milton's sensibility to express intuitions and misgivings, to describe his sense of entities beyond the surface, and to make them feel real to the reader. Landscape and nature become a timeless medium, containing the life of the now as well as traces of other nows and other lives in the past. A good illustration can be found on page 92, where we see the night, the river and the fireflies, hear the frogs and the baboons, the insects and the rustling of the shrubs, feel the texture of the silence swooping back into place, and scent "the musty old-leaf scent of the centuries". Milton is located in the here and now, but he cannot deny the emanations that his temperament and sensibility are responsive to: "I had the sensation of being able to see and hear and touch the essence of the scene – the night itself, the intimate spirit of trees and water" (p. 92).

We are in the hands of an artist who makes every chirrup of a frog, the river's soft sibilance, even the drop of a palm berry in the water count. Landscape is indeed a presence helping to create atmosphere, but there is more to the bursts of such descriptions scattered through the text (pp. 61, 69-70, 83-84, 88-90, 113 and more). Each description seems like a signal sounding out the significance of the event being described, almost as if, already, Mittelholzer is drifting towards what he would attempt more self-consciously in those later novels written in the leitmotif manner.

Mittelholzer's use of landscape and nature in *My Bones* helps to anchor the novel in a familiar if sometimes exotic reality, but it is also the slipway into encounters with other realities that are no less real than our familiar realities. There are other means by which Mittelholzer makes his incredible world credible.

11. SOURCES: UP THE BERBICE RIVER

In February 1933, Edgar Mittelholzer made a trip on the river steamer *Arawana* to visit his uncle, Bishop Duggin who owned a cottage at a place called Coomaka a hundred miles up the Berbice River. The steamer journey and the two weeks spent at Coomaka are described in *With a Carib Eye* some twenty-five years after the trip. Uncle Bishop was the husband of Mittelholzer's Aunt Bertha and the group in the cottage also included a girl – Mittelholzer's fifteen year old cousin-in-law. All we find out about her is that she was not keen on playing bridge but was happy enough to operate the gramophone. Nothing sensational or even exciting seems to have happened in the two weeks. Mittelholzer did some exploring during the day, and the evenings were spent playing bridge. However the cottage, surrounded on three sides by jungle and on the fourth by the dark river, the sawmill and the rafts of greenheart and mora one hundred yards downriver, obviously shaped the invention in *My Bones and My Flute*.

His activities included making the short trip to Tacama, a station halfway between Coomaka and the steamer terminus at Paradise. Tacama is where the Rupununi cattle trail ends, and stock wait there to be herded onto the steamer. At Tacama, Mittelholzer frightened himself by teasing the blue-black spiders living in the middle of the wild pines beyond the swizzle-stick trees. This episode from 1933 is made more sinister in the short story called "Tacama" where the narrator gets a lash from the spirit of place. In the landscape of Tacama, Mittlholzer's narrator reports, the silence seemed "Wicked. Tried to wrap me in a winding sheet".[31]

The river journey as described in *With a Carib Eye* is full of interest for readers of *My Bones*. Mittelholzer's thrill as he began the trip in 1933 was "the thrill of one about to penetrate into a territory of ghosts – the ghosts of the eighteenth century Dutchmen and their slaves who had peopled the banks of the Berbice for over a hundred miles up" (p. 159). His head is also full of the fighting connected with the violent events associated with the uprising of the slaves in Berbice in 1763 and the abandonment of the capital Fort Nassau by the retreating Dutch settlers. Milton's imagining of Goed de Vries and the perished Dutch plantations in *My Bones* (pp. 83-84) is a version of what Mittelholzer describes on page 162 of *With a Carib Eye*.

In the description found in *With a Carib Eye*, history and landscape are inseparable. History was "concealed in every mysterious opening amidst the glittering greens that overhung the rapidly darkening river" (p. 160). Some of the descriptions confirm that Coomaka and the surrounding space, "spongy with the humus of long years" are the genesis of the world of *My Bones*: "It is always twilight amidst the trees, and the silence can be frightening. It seems as though a hundred hidden eyes are fixed upon you, and that a hundred creatures have purposely paused in their occupations to camouflage themselves amongst the tangled branches overhead and peer down at you" (*Carib Eye*, p. 166).

The actual experience of the 1933 trip no doubt contributes to our sense of the reality of the history, ecology and geography of *My Bones*, and forms the solid material base out of which the happenings and beings of that novel emerge. Mittelholzer's working of the journey of 1933 into the novel of 1955 includes a foregrounding of the town of New Amsterdam at the beginning. The invention of five characters, including the narrating character Milton Woodsley, came from his imagination.

12. THE CHARACTERS: A SPECTRUM

Milton is the main character in *My Bones and My Flute* – unless someone up above or down below wants to make a case for the ghost! He is fully involved in all the actions in the book and he interacts in significant ways with all the other important characters. It is through Milton that the several levels of meaning in the book are disclosed, and it is his developing character that equips him to narrate the story and win the confidence and trust of the reader. The other characters of note in the book are Mr Nevinson, Mrs Nevinson, and their daughter Jessie, who ends up marrying Milton as she probably had in mind from early. These characters are well-developed and interesting, but their functions are not as important as that of Milton as actor in and teller of the story.

In two economical paragraphs on page 52, Mittelholzer carefully gives the pedigree of both Milton and Mr Nevinson: both come from old "Coloured" families, and both are able to trace their ancestors "back to the late eighteenth century, at which time the Nevinsons and the Woodsleys had not yet acquired the strain of negro slave blood that runs in them today." Before looking at the Nevinsons and Milton Woodsley as individuals it is important for our understanding of the book to consider the ethnic group with which Mittelholzer pointedly identifies them.

This group of White or near-White characters belongs to the privileged group in the society. In a stern paragraph in *A Swarthy Boy*, Mittelholzer declares that "it was people of my own class – people of coloured admixture but of fair or olive complexions" who were the dispensers of prejudice against East Indians, poor Portuguese, Chinese immigrants, some plantation overseers ('white riff-raff') and the descendants of Africans who had been enslaved for over two hundred years" (*Swarthy Boy*, p. 155).

Outside of the White/Coloured group in the novel is Rayburn, the African Guyanese caretaker of the cottage at Goed de Vries. Minor characters include the second mate of the *Arawana* who Milton claims as one of his barber's shop companions; Patoir, described as a Bufianda (of mixed Amerindian-Negro ethnicity), who bequeaths the canister to Mr Nevinson; Patoir's Amerindian paramour Matilda, who is the first person in the novel to die because of the flute, and the cook Timmykins (Timothy) who is sitting on the steps when the party return to Goed de Vries after interring the bones and the flute of the Dutchman according to Christian rites. Mittelholzer's sense of the divisions in West

Indian societies based upon genocide, slavery, indentureship and colonialism informs the plot of *My Bones*. From the careful selection and disposition of the characters as members of different ethnic groups it is possible to trace an allegory in which Mittelholzer offers a social vision of healing and reconciliation.

12. A Trace of Allegory

In this allegory, the key figure is Rayburn. When we first see him, he is "a solitary figure standing on the pier" at Goed de Vries. Rayburn smiles and raises his hat respectfully, as does the cook Timmykins. We know that ghost story or no ghost story, Mittelholzer is alive to manifestations of divisiveness in every facet of his society. On being introduced to Rayburn by Mr Nevinson as "Mr Milton Woodsley", Milton extends his hand: "He took it, shook it briefly and released it as though it were a chunk of hot metal – and this despite the firmness of my own grip. Naturally, he could not know that I was accustomed to shaking the hands of such people as porters and stevedores and other 'low-class persons'; he must have expected from me just the cool, patronizing smile and nod of a middle-class young man" (p. 86).

Milton may have overcome his society's prejudices, but Rayburn's instinct was right. When the suggestion is made by Mr Nevinson that Rayburn should sleep upstairs with them as a guard over him when the flute comes to lure him to his death, Mrs Nevinson refuses instantly. For her "the situation isn't so desperate that we must have that black man hanging round us in the house here every moment of the day" (p. 123). Even when she herself is in danger, at a later stage in the haunting, Milton reports that Mrs Nevinson was adamant that the position was not so desperate "that we had to sacrifice our dignity to the extent of having a black man rubbing shoulders with us as though he were an equal" (p. 132). Eventually, with Jessie and Mr Nevinson unable to resist the call of the flute, Mrs Nevinson recognizes the need for reinforcement. According to Milton, "The events of that morning brought matters to a head concerning Mrs Nevinson's foolish prejudices. She agreed, when we tackled her, that things

32

had got to a point where we would have to 'forget our dignity and call in the help of Rayburn'" (p. 146). From this point the narrator is meticulous in his documentation of the big and small ways in which the resourceful Rayburn, the character most able to weather shock, holds them together and helps them to retain their sanity. When the party travels up river in pursuit of the sound of the flute, it is Rayburn who is sitting in the bows (like Wilson Harris's bowman Vigilance in *Palace of the Peacock*) (p. 154), and when the time comes to bury the bones and the flute, "the battered-looking Anglican prayer book from which Mr Nevinson read the burial service belonged to Rayburn."

The purgatory through which the inheritors of the plantation order must pass; the humanity that knows the torment of the planter and gives him his rest; the peace that comes when the pilgrimage is guided by the one who has suffered most and has the most to forgive: all of these are stations in Mittelholzer's allegory. When the bones and the flute are buried, all are blessed for the moment by a vision of what is possible in the divided and self-repressing society to which they belong. "We knew that never had we experienced such peace as the peace in the twilight clearing" (p. 225). Seeing a connection between this ending and the visionary conclusion of Wilson Harris' *Palace of the Peacock* (1960) is by no means fanciful.

13. SOCIAL CRITICISM

The main characters in the novel may be seen as figures in an allegory, but they are also part of a material society which Mittelholzer wants to portray and criticise. Milton's character and experience as a member of New Amsterdam society are used to effect this criticism. After Milton asserts that "Mr Nevinson was no small town philistine who treated artists with a simpering patronage" and acknowledges him as "one who genuinely wished me well in my career as an artist" (p. 52), the novel turns to satirize the town and society of New Amsterdam for its commercialist mind, its philistinism, and its inability to accommodate any behaviour that is less than respectable or is not in keeping with its place in the accepted scheme of race, class and colour. A critique of New Amsterdam as a dead and suffocating place is to be found in the short story "Sorrow Dam and Mr Millbank" referred to above, and in *With a Carib Eye*, where Mittelholzer describes a recurring nightmare in which he returns to New Amsterdam for a visit after many years and is seized with panic: he is trapped and lost and will never get out again (pp.134-135).

In the novel, the town is intolerant and dismissive of anyone whose way of being is different from theirs. Milton's contacts have engineered him a job as a sales assistant in a hardware store. After "three months in the gloom of nail barrels and shelves of hinges and hasps and staples" he is offered an "opening" that could lead to a high position in the firm. Milton puzzles everybody by declaring that he does not want an office job, but wants to be a painter (p. 53). As noted above, Milton sums up his fate briefly and without rancour as being labelled a crank who keeps bad company and is the disgrace of his family.

On the edge of river and jungle, New Amsterdam feels none of that immensity. It has long forgotten the day when ocean-going ships came and went freely. It lacks self-knowledge and lives a superficial life. This critique of New Amsterdam occurs early in the novel but the reader is not allowed to forget that the spiritually closed-up town is an objectification of the condition of the people in it. After a week of hauntings at Goed de Vries, Mrs Nevinson announces her intention to abandon life in the disturbing interior and return to civilised life in New Amsterdam. Milton and Mr Nevinson eventually persuade her that there is protection in being together, and that "a solution must be found to our problems before we returned to New Amsterdam. To leave Goed de Vries and go back to our homes in town would signify defeat, and added to our ignominy, we would still have this uncanny curse attached to us" (p. 149). The evocation of New Amsterdam is part of the process in the novel by which the town dwellers are liberated into greater self-knowledge and greater understanding of things beyond their ken. Bringing New Amsterdam into focus through Milton's experience of it and attaching the tale to a solid social reality also serves credibility, the *sine qua non* of a ghost story.

Characterisation is one of Mittelholzer's great strengths in *My Bones*. He makes Milton, Mr Nevinson, Mrs Nevinson and Jessie idiosyncratic. He brings them to life as characters who have distinctive personalities and their own peculiarities, who interact unpredictably with one another.

Jessie begins as an attractive young woman, tall and shapely like her mother. The serious-minded Milton is a little too keen to dismiss her: "In outlook she was vacuous and small town; tennis, dances and young men were her only interests" (p. 58). But if she is not quite a rebel, she doesn't care too much for the Victorian outlook to which New Amsterdam society subscribes, particularly the rules that forbid young women of her class to be in the company of ordinary working people. She is much more intelligent and observant than the would-be avuncular Milton is at first willing to grant. Some readers might pick up that in some ways she is smarter than Milton: she has studied him, and has set her sights on him. She allows herself to be seen as vulnerable, no doubt knowing this will rouse Milton's protective instincts. As the novel progresses happenings press upon her, and she expresses fear (p. 154-156); she loses her sharpness and her vitality, and moves as if she is resigned to her fate and theirs. Mittelholzer uses her as the weak link through whom the group may be undermined. As suggested earlier, the give and take between her and Milton, and the subdued love story lighten and animate the novel.

Mrs Nevinson is portrayed differently and in more depth. She has a passionate love of company and a taste for the harmless pleasures of the world; has retained her good looks, has a gay roguish laugh, and can still stir the heart of Milton who had a crush on her when he was ten years old. She practices an amused acceptance of her husband's hobbies and bookish interests. She can change the key of her moods at will, and has a decidedly mechanical way of switching on and turning off her charming smile. Milton sums her up as a "one of those people who act, rather than live their lives, and whose gestures should never be taken literally" (p. 67). Her function in the novel is fully in keeping with her character. She is the voice of witty ridicule bringing Milton back to earth every time he talks like a book or like a lawyer or a great know-it-all – which for her is about every time he opens his mouth. She is the impatient voice of scepticism refusing to entertain solemn talk of the Dutchman's parchment, the flute and other apparitions. Her usual mode is exemplified by the exchanges on pages 98, 99 and 100.

Tired of all the "nonsense" about the manuscript, she steals off into Mr Nevinson's room and tries to burn it. The curse strikes back at once, and soon she is subjected to a recurrent dream in which, in daylight, she is being led along a path, but being stopped at intervals by a bony hand and a menacing voice (p. 168). Recounting her nightmare to the others becomes a morning ritual, her scepticism becoming weaker, until after one particular sighting she declares: " 'As long as I live I don't think I could ever forget it. The thing that was with him – my God! I never dreamt such evil beings could really exist.' Then she sniggered hysterically. 'Yes. I know I dreamt it – but I know it really exists. This wasn't an ordinary dream. It *happened* to me – to my astral body or whatever you call it. I really went through that jungle tonight – the spirit part of me" (p. 199). Thus was Saul struck down. Mittelholzer engineers the surrender of the unbelieving Mrs Nevinson in the interest of credibility.

Whilst Mittelholzer takes his time to bring Mrs Nevinson round to the point where she dramatically validates the happenings at Goed de Vries, his design needs Mr Nevinson's avowal quickly. **Mr Nevinson** is presented as a kind of father-figure to Milton, ascetic and self-contained, and they enjoy discussing "art and philosophy and human beings … the early history of British Guiana…" (p. 54). But the core of Mr Nevinson's character and role rests in his prestigious position in the Berbice Timber and Balata Company. We are ready for Milton's opinion of him as one of the most level-headed and upright men in the colony, a man immersed in the busy world and thus hardly likely to indulge in fantasy. Nevinson sees himself as a worldly unromantic person to whom ghostly flutes should not play, living in a place where ghosts are not expected to walk:

> "It's difficult to conceive of anything like this happening, Milton.
> I mean, in the midst of our cold, everyday existence, with traffic

in the streets and typewriters tapping in an office and everything
going on in the old, usual, reasoned commonplace way... And
happening to me of all people! A staid, unromantic old horse like
me! It seems absurd – grotesque" (p. 76-77).

Mittelholzer creates in Mr Nevinson the perfect foil for
Milton and together they grope towards a less fixed formula about
the composition of the world.

Mr Nevinson has the good sense and humility to turn to the
younger man in a matter that troubles him, and which could be
socially embarrassing. He explains why he has manoeuvred Milton
to come with him: "I need someone like you to help me find a way
out of this situation, Milton. You're the only fellow I could think
of who would be interested in this affair in a serious and sensible
spirit. Despite your reputation for being eccentric, I happen to
know you as you really are. The opinions I hear expressed about
you don't affect me one bit. I know I can depend upon you" (p. 78).
This assessment, coming from Mr Nevinson, strengthens Milton's
credentials as a trustworthy narrator and interpreter. Mr Nevinson's
main function is to make reasonable the questioning of established
attitudes to the paranormal. Because of his portrayal as a solid,
rational person, his admission that his values have been shaken has
a considerable impact both on the group in the cottage and on the
reader: "Tonight has completed the overthrow of my former
values, Milton. I've always been a thorough sceptic of the supernatural – but after tonight I would have to be insincere to myself if
I continued to take up a scoffing attitude" (p. 103).

There are many "resemblances" between **Milton** and his
author, but this novel cannot be described as one in which the
character exists to mouth opinions the author wants to try on or
give an airing to. Mittelholzer succeeds brilliantly in establishing
Milton as an interesting, intelligent, sensitive and intuitive person with an open mind. Milton confesses that at the age of
twenty-three, he is "hopelessly ignorant on matters pertaining to
demonology and the occult sciences" (p. 154) and he is not an
authority "on the mysteries of necromancy", but Mittelholzer
suggests his potential spiritual capacity by having him refer to "an
elementary knowledge of yoga and the fact of having perused and
minutely digested the Bhagavad Gita". He is presented early as a

well-read and culturally literate young man interested in life and in the making of his society. He has contempt for "the middle-class philistines of New Amsterdam", despises the worship of money, and moves freely among all classes and races.

As a character, Milton is subject to two related processes. One we can call a process of maturing. The other is a process of enlightenment. The first process depends upon the fact that the narration is being made in 1954 by a Milton who is at least twenty years older than the Milton who kept the diary and participated in the events of 1933. Again and again, the older Milton pokes fun at the pompous, bookish manner of his younger self, as does Mrs Nevinson who is always asking him to come to the point or get on with what he is trying to say and not sound like Gibbon's *Decline and Fall*. Jessie tells him he is in some ways a big ass for the way he expresses himself (p. 95) whilst even Mr Nevinson gives him a diplomatic put-down when he mouths some pretentious verbiage in their discussion of poltergeist phenomena. When Milton out-lines his grand theory, a smiling Mr Nevinson cannot help himself: "Milton, I can't blame you for doing your best to arrive at some plausible solution, my boy, but I'm afraid it won't help us very much if you let your imagination run riot" (p. 173).

Over the twenty years, Milton has matured in manner, has begun to understand himself, and has developed a sense of irony that applies even to himself. As a narrator seeking to make the story credible, the older Milton is not averse to letting us see Milton's impulsiveness, his excitability, his nearness to a nervous breakdown, his hysteria; and he quotes from the young man's diary to let us catch the spirit. A good illustration occurs on page 202 when Milton virtually breaks down and sounds like a Van Groegenwel from the Kaywana trilogy who never runs: "I don't surrender. I never surrender. I fight to the last bloody ditch." It takes the joint efforts of Rayburn and Mr Nevinson to calm him down. Another brilliantly strategic use of the older Milton on the younger Milton occurs when the excitable but thinking young man "deems it propitious to tell them of my Theory." Since this is his seventh such offer, nobody is impressed and Chapter 15 is a comedic *tour de force*. To the accompaniment of chuckles, neat little barbs, studied inattention and gestures of amusement from all the

Nevinsons, the young man proceeds with pride and earnestness, carried along by the urgency of his discovery and his self-consciously sonorous tone. It is only when he gets to the point of Jessie being invaded by "the shadow mass" that they begin to take him seriously. Then he starts to fidget and speak hesitantly.

It is more than obvious that the older Milton, though calm and collected, is essentially in tune with the ideas and feelings of young Milton. None of the fun poked at the young Milton is meant to make us distrust his intelligence, or doubt his sincere undertaking to do "a good job in recording every salient and relevant incident with as great a faithfulness as is humanly possible".

At the time of his visit to Mr Nevinson's study, Milton, ever anxious to make himself better-known to his readers, informs us that "I am a romantic, and extremely susceptible to my surroundings" and we recognize it in his fanciful picture of "benign jumbies" with their "umber gaze" and "companionable breath" in the study.

Again, halfway through the journey to Goed de Vries, when Jessie tells him about her father's jumpy behaviour since his last short, aborted visit to the interior, we see Milton's imagination going to work. I reproduce this passage because it is a clear example of Mittelholzer insinuating Milton's romantic susceptibilities long before the matter of flute or ghost has come up:

> The chair creaked as I altered my position slightly, and, somehow, it was as though the rasping screechiness of the sound at once became transposed into a wisp of uneasy mist that curled through my awareness so that I had the inclination to fidget and glance about me. I found myself frowning at the black water. Then my gaze strayed to the trees which hung low over the stream. I began to wonder what might not be lurking in the damp gloom that simmered among that glittering welter of greens. Who knows what odd creatures might not be eyeing us as we rushed by? Tiny, warped insects unknown to entomology. Or some monstrosity that was neither reptile nor bird nor mammal – like the hoatzins near the mouth of the river and on the Canje Creek. Amber orbs in a green flat head… (p. 61).

We pass over this passage without taking it as more than Milton being his susceptible self, but it sticks; and it becomes more and more "true" as the chapters progress (see para. 2, p. 183). We are especially struck by those amber orbs in a green flat head when ironically Milton (p. 196) and Mrs Nevinson (p. 199) describe in turn the apparition that has begun to take shape. Throughout the novel Mittelholzer drops time-release capsules into the text that come later to haunt the unsuspecting reader.

As a character, Milton is an unusual person. He takes pride in not belonging to any religion, responding with awe, nevertheless, to an animated Universe full of beauty and mystery. Although he enjoys living he can see death in a favourable light – "an adventure which should offer a pleasant solution to my earthly fumblings" (p. 105). He has the peculiarity of falling from time to time into trances or half-world states, such as when (p. 82) he becomes aware of a shadow voice that assures him that there is no substance in the scene he is beholding. Visitations like this, Milton says, "tended to upset the values I had painfully established between what is real and what is not" (p. 81). These moods depress him and make him question "the ultimate value of present action, a questioning of the worthwhileness of continued existence." In this particular instance, the mood is succeeded by a return of substance, beginning with feeling the weight of his own body, the breeze on his face, his beating heart, the crowing of a cock or some other banality; and he would view "the whole vitalizing flood of actuality rush through me again, and the forces which had entrammelled me only a moment before would melt away and leave me once more a rational, struggling human engaged in the everyday occupation of being alive" (p. 82). Milton falls into this kind of trance a few times in the novel. On page 118 he describes how the projection of his being through time causes him to "lose" an hour and a half. Thus does Milton invite the reader into a consideration of what is actual and what is not, and make the beginnings of his case for the existence of different kinds of realities surrounding us. Surely, Edgar, this makes *My Bones and My Flute* one of your "serious" novels?

Milton's intuition that the marvellous realism of the human condition is an alternation between substantial and insubstantial worlds, or participation in both at the same time, is validated by the experiences at Goed de Vries. The key phrases in his plaintive appeal to the reader on page 121 are repeated word for word on page 174: "We were aware of that not-too-sane, aerial feeling of being in the midst of occult events and yet still conscious of the commonplace routine of existence; sensible to the normal around us, yet within, intelligent of something beyond our control that had intruded upon the accepted pattern of our human actions" (p. 174).

Milton insists, at first, and often shows, that under his romanticism he is a strong rationalist; he does not for an instant believe that supernatural influences were responsible for Mr Nevinson and Jessie hearing the flute while he does not; he is sure that there must be some natural explanation (p. 65). Part of what makes him interesting is that over the course of the novel he achieves enlightenment. He becomes clearer about how he sees the world, clearer about the shape-shifting relationship between the material and the immaterial and even aggressive in his declaration about complacency and inflexibility in our measuring of the world and our experience of it:

> If these were times when the psychic was not looked upon as something surrounded with an unscientific aura – that is to say, a subject about which nothing rationally concrete can be stated and hence one to be treated with smiles and gentle waggings of the head – my task would be a much easier one. But the harshness of our materialistic age is such that I suppose we cannot be blamed for scoffing at that which does not conform with the physical laws that drive us on day after day in our blind, itching urge for survival. What can we *prove* about ghosts and ectoplasm and all the rest of it! (p. 201).

The older Milton reproduces the young Milton's enthusiasm. He shares in young Milton's disappointment with the way people keep their minds closed and their eyes open only to self-advantage, even as he reproduces with affectionate irony the anxiety in the ardent young man's tone. The older Milton is expressed when he describes the group's sense of danger (p. 201) with a distance and a conviction that only time could have brought.

In the Postscript, the older and younger Milton are one. He is secure and bold in the enlightenment that has come to him:

> So far as I am concerned, what happened to us at Goed de Vries

was of supernatural causes. There is no explanation that will satisfy conventional canons of reason – and I cannot help if I am called irrational or unscientific for saying so (p. 227).

15. The Diary of Jan Pieter Voorman

Two texts-within-texts inform *My Bones*. The first is Milton's diary, which he uses to write up the narrative in polished story form, and from which he sometimes reproduces daily jottings. The second is made up of the writings of Voorman represented by the two sheets of brown parchment, translations of which are inserted in the text of *My Bones* (pp. 74-75 and pp. 115-116); and jottings from his diary that appear in the Postscript.

The brown parchment contains the curse on whoever handles the manuscript in the canister and the directions for finding the harrowed Dutch planter's bones and flute. Mittelholzer helps the reader to understand the drama by allowing Milton to speculate on what might have happened to Voorman.

The insertions in the Postscript establish a connection between Milton and Voorman as diarists, and as artists who are not taken seriously. Milton has had his run-ins with philistine New Amsterdam. Voorman's wife Jannetje is annoyed by Voorman's flute-playing, by his tinkering with the notes like a panman. She places no value on his research and takes no pride in the possible fulfilment of his ambitions. Her uncle detests him as a Catholic and they object to his not joining the Dutch Reformed Church.

Thrown back upon himself, the lonely artist calls up sleeping forces. "If I have to sell my soul to Beelzebub I shall succeed (p. 228)". He succeeds and he gets scared. The seven diary entries from 20 August 1762 to 20 February 1763 only hint at the six months of lonely torment and haunting (not 16 days like the Nevinson group) that he has suffered. "They" call on him day and night. As a Roman Catholic he calls upon the Virgin Mary to pray for him. His candles burn. The statue of Mary stands. "I will fight them with fire, symbol of my faith, for though errant, I am still a Christian. My church is my rock, and they know this and they fear it, they of evil (p. 229)".

As we follow Voorman's jottings we realize that Mittelholzer's novel has another hidden dimension. In November 1762, Voorman says "the Dark is within me" (p. 229), but it is not till 22nd February that he gains insight: the evil emanations and influences that torment him come out of himself. His concentration upon "deeds of greed and ambition" has produced damnation: "It is evil from me that has taken unto itself shapes and odours of frightful nature. It is I myself who plague myself in several forms projected and created by my own errant will… There are no demons but the demons our own wills evoke (p. 230)".

We can read this as a kind of moral fable with Voorman being punished for his greed and overreaching ambition. After centuries of purgatory, the Roman Catholic Voorman is released when his bones and flute are buried.

But the truth this novel ultimately delivers to a warring world through Voorman's dark nights of suffering is a truth that invites meditation and self-reflection. The real battle between good and evil is within.

Notes

1:   Juanita Cox Westmaas to Kenneth Ramchand (March 12, 2014): "Mittelholzer was fond of 'onomastics' for want of a better word and sometimes gave personally significant characters names that related to that of his own. Mittelholzer – meaning something like middle wood – was transformed into names like Milton Copps (i.e., Copse) and Oakbent. I'm assuming the name Woodsley emerged out of the same impulse." I am grateful to Juanita Westmaas for responding so helpfully to my several inquiries in the course of preparing this introduction.

2.   See V.S. Naipaul, *Caribbean Voices*, a review of *My Bones and My Flute*. This script is numbered 1120 (13 Nov. 1955), but is placed after script 1221 in the files.

3.   This and all subsequent references are to the Peepal Tree Caribbean Modern Classics Edition (Leeds, 2015).

4.   Up to 1970, the British Guiana census used the category "Coloured" to distinguish the Mulatto minority from the much larger African/Black population, a distinction that was once important to the brown middle class. After 1970 the category "Coloured" was

replaced by "Mixed". It is also evident that after 1970, many "mixed" Guyanese began to identify themselves as "Black".

5. See *With a Carib Eye* (London: Secker & Warburg, 1958), Chapter 18, for Mittelholzer's account of New Amsterdam.

6. A.J. Seymour, *Kyk-over-Al*, vol. 6, no. 25 (December 1958).

7. See Therold Barnes, *Bim*, vol. 6, no. 23, Dec. 1955, p. 202. Though a positive review, Barnes did not approve of the apparatus of the Introductory Note or the description of the ghost story as being in "the old fashioned manner".

8. See V.S. Naipaul, BBC *Caribbean Voices*, a review of *My Bones and My Flute*. (See above note 2).

9. Mark McWatt, Introduction to the Longman Caribbean Writers edition of *My Bones and My Flute* (London: Longman, 1986).

10. Readers may find some of the sources that inspired Mittelholzer's view of what comprised a good old fashioned ghost story in M.R. James, *Collected Ghost Stories* in an Oxford World Classics edition; there are numerous modern editions of Poe – many of the short stories are included in the Penguin Classics, *The Fall of the House of Usher and Other Writings*; Sheridan Le Fanu's ghost stories are to be found in *In a Glass Darkly*, amongst several other collections; there are several cheap, modern editions.

11. *Ghost Stories of an Antiquary* (London: Edward Arnold, 1904).

12. Quoted in Westmaas, J. A. *Edgar Mittelholzer (1909-1965) and the Shaping of his Novels* (Ph.D. thesis, University of Birmingham, 2013). I am grateful to Dr Westmaas for sending me a copy of Chapter 2 of this dissertation.

13. Mittelholzer E., "The Intellectual Cissies" in *Books and Bookmen* August 1962. Cited by Westmaas in Chapter 2 of her doctoral dissertation (Ph.D. thesis, University of Birmingham, 2013).

14. The details of the books published before 1955 include: *Creole Chips* (Georgetown: Lutheran Press, 1937); *Corentyne Thunder* (London: Eyre and Spottiswoode, 1941); *A Morning at the Office* (London: Hogarth Press, 1950); *Shadows Move Among Them* (London, Nevill, 1951); *Children of Kaywana* (London: Nevil, 1952); *The Weather in Middenshot* (London: Secker & Warburg, 1952); *The Life and Death of Sylvia* (London: Secker & Warburg, 1953); *The Adding Machine* (Kingston: Pioneer Press, 1954); *The Harrowing of Hubertus* (London: Secker & Warburg, 1954). Apart from *A Morning at the Office*, which is set in Trinidad, and *The Weather in Middenshot*, which is set in England, all the other titles are set in Guyana.

15. *A Swarthy Boy* (London: Putnam, 1963)

16. *Corentyne Thunder* was first published by Eyre and Spottiswoode in 1941. Most copies were destroyed in an air raid. It was reprinted in the Heinemann Caribbean Writers series (London: Heinemann, 1970), and again in 2009 in the Peepal Tree Press Caribbean

Classics series, which is in print, and from which the page reference is taken (Leeds: Peepal Tree Press, 2009), pp. 240-241.

17. Stories in *Bim* are: "Of Casuarinas and Cliffs", no. 5, Feb. 1945; "Miss Clarke is Dying", no. 5, Feb. 1945; " Breakdown", no. 6, Dec. 1945; "Something Fishy", no. 6, Dec. 1945; " Samlal", no. 7, 1946; "The Cruel Fate of Karl and Pierre", no. 8, 1947; "Romantic Promenade", no. 8,1947; "Tacama", no. 9, Dec. 1948; "We know Not Whom to Mourn", no. 10, June 1949; "Mr. Jones of Port of Spain", no. 11, Dec. 1949; "Amiable Mr. Britten", no. 12, June 1950; "The Sibilant and Lost", no. 13, Dec. 1950; "Wedding Day", no. 14, June 1951; "Only a Ghost We'll Need", no. 17, Dec. 1952; "Portrait with a Background", no. 19, June 1953; "Van Batenburg of Berbice", no. 19, June 1953; "Hurricane Season", no. 20, July 1954; "Towards Martin's Bay", no. 21, Dec. 1955 and "Heat in the Jungle", no. 26, June 1958.

18. The stories published only in *Caribbean Voices* are: "Carnival Close-up" (Script no. 96, 23 Feb.1947); "The Paw-Paw Tree (Script no. 97, 9 Mar.1947); "The Burglar" (Script no. 202, 11 April 1948); "Sorrow Dam and Mr Millbank" (Script no. 372, 30 Jan. 1949) and "Plague of Kindness" (Script no. 567, 17 Feb.1950).

19. Along with the early out-of-print work such as *Creole Chips*, *The Adding Machine*, in 2016 Peepal Tree Press is publishing a compendium of Mittelholzer's uncollected work, including plays, poems, journalism and short stories, including those referenced here.

20. "Breakdown", *Bim* vol. 2 No. 6, 1945, pp. 9-10 and 66-71.

21. "The Paw-Paw Tree", *Caribbean Voices* Script 97, 9 March1947

22. In the short story "Sorrow Dam and Mr Millbank", *Caribbean Voices* (Script 204), Mr Millbank revolts quietly against the dead town and builds his house among country people.

23. "The Burglar", *Caribbean Voices* Script 202, 11 April 1948.

24. "The Sibilant and the Lost", *Bim* vol. 4 no. 13, 1949, pp. 2-6.

25. "Romantic Promenade", *Bim*, vol. 2 no. 8, 1945, pp. 12-13.

26. The novels published after *My Bones and My Flute* include: *Of Trees and the Sea* (London: Secker & Warburg, 1956) – set in Barbados; *A Tale of Three Places* (London: Secker & Warburg, 1957) – set in Trinidad, England and St Lucia; *Kaywana Blood* (London: Secker & Warburg, 1958) – set in Guyana; *The Weather Family* (London: Secker & Warburg, 1958) – set in Barbados; *A Tinkling in the Twilight* (London: Secker & Warburg, 1959) – set in England; *The Mad MacMullochs* (London: Owen, 1959) – set in Barbados; *Eltonsbrody* (London: Secker & Warburg, 1960) – set in Barbados; *Latticed Echoes* (London: Secker & Warburg, 1960) and *Thunder Returning* (London: Secker & Warburg, 1961)– set in Guyana. All of the following novels are set in England: *The Piling of Clouds* (London: Putnam, 1961); ; *The Wounded and the Worried* (London: Putnam, 1962); *Uncle Paul* (London: Macdonald, 1963); *The Aloneness of Mrs Chatham*

(London: Library 33, 1965) and *The Jilkington Drama* (London: Abelard-Schuman, 1965).

27. A.J. Seymour, *Edgar Mittelholzer: The Man and His Work,* 1967 Edgar Mittelholzer Memorial Lectures, 1st Series, (Georgetown, Guyana:1968), p.14.

28. *The Mad MacMulloch*s was published under the pseudonym of H. Austin Woodsley (London: Owen, 1959).

29. Mittelholzer records in *A Swarthy Boy* that in 1929 he wrote novel called "The Terrible Four". No copies of the rejected manuscript seem to exist but Mittelholzer's summary of it shows that the idea of creating a Utopia or commune came to him when he was 20 years old, long before he left British Guiana. Here is Mittelholzer's summary of the book: "The setting was a network of caves behind the great waterfall, Kaieteur, in the interior of the colony (caves do exist behind the fall), and four men, an Englishman, a German, a Frenchman and a Spaniard, each an eccentric who had become tired of civilization, had banded together and decided to cut themselves off from the world. They established their own community within the caves behind the fall, inviting others tired like themselves to join them in their troglodyte existence. Peculiar orgies and ceremonies took place, and all was going well until two people, a young man and his fiancée, arrived. They were not tired enough and objected to much of what they saw, so they were made prisoners. The rest of the story described their attempts to escape, and the eventual fate of the whole community. *Shadows Move Among Them* ends with the arranged death (murder) of Sigmund who had been acquitted because Mabel declined to testify against him. Is Mittelholzer remembering "The Terrible Four" and thinking of Mabel and Gregory as objecting to some of the things that can happen and are happening in Rev. Harmston's kingdom? There may be a searching dialectical quality, a little humour, and an ironic presence in *Shadows Move Among Them* that are ignored by those in a hurry to condemn the work as fascist or praise it as a description of an ideal commune.

30. There is a slight but significant misreading in the introduction to the Longman edition of *My Bones* where Voorman is described as being put to death by the rebel slaves of 1763 (Longman ed. p. XII) whilst his wife returns to Europe (Longman ed. p XV). According to Voorman's account (*My Bones*, p. 62), it is the wife and children who are murdered by the slaves, whilst he commits suicide. The suicide is important both structurally in the novel (it is in part because he is a suicide who has not had a Christian burial that Voorman has not found rest), and thematically in Mittelholzer's work as a whole (Voorman as the unappreciated artist who commits suicide).

31. "Tacama", *Bim*, vol. 3, no. 9, Dec. 1948, p. 6.

MY BONES AND MY FLUTE

INTRODUCTORY NOTE

THIS story should have been written about twenty years ago, but, for more than one reason, it got shelved. First, it's not the kind of thing one likes to go hurrying into print, and, secondly, I could never decide exactly what form it should take. I had intended to publish my diary notes as they stood and leave it at that, but Mr. Nevinson thought that this would be most unsatisfactory. My diary style, from a literary point of view, he considered too ragged and undignified for a published book, and, moreover, he was of the opinion that the narrative, as set forth in my diary entries, lacked proper form and shape.

Mrs. Nevinson and Jessie, too, objected to my publishing my diary notes – but on different grounds. According to them, why shouldn't I do it as a story? Let it be chronological, as in my diary, but "let it be a good thrilling sort of old-fashioned ghost story, with the mystery solved at the end", as Jessie put it. Her mother agreed with her, and thought that "it would be a shame to publish those scrappy notes in your diary. They're dull – and so un-romantic! Why not write them over and put a lot of atmosphere and excitement into them! You haven't got to insert anything that didn't happen, but at least make them readable or don't publish anything at all."

Well, I have tried to please all three of them. For Mr. Nevinson – the "dignified", sonorous prose style (at least, as much so as I could get it) and as much "form and shape" as I could manage; for Jessie "a good thrilling sort of old-fashioned ghost story, with the mystery solved at the end" (though whether the mystery can really be said to have been solved in the end is a matter for serious debate); and for Mrs. Nevinson "a lot of atmosphere and excite-ment".

So far as I myself am concerned, I am satisfied that I have made a true record, including nothing that might be attributed to my imagination. I have gone through this work repeatedly with a fine-toothed comb to make quite sure that the factual framework is intact, and while it is true that good taste has compelled me to give fictitious names to the characters involved, that does not make them any the less actual beings who are, even today, very much alive.

MILTON WOODSLEY,
NEW AMSTERDAM, BRITISH GUIANA,
July 1954.

[Publisher's note: References to the ethnicity of characters in this novel reflect colonial usage. Hence "Indian" signifies someone who is a Guyanese Amerindian rather than someone whose ancestors came as indentured labourers from India, where the then contemporary term would have been East Indian. "Buck" is the other (offensive) term for Amerindian that Mittelholzer uses realistically in dialogue.]

1

We must have been well over half-way to our destination when I received the first hint that there might be some other reason behind Mr. Nevinson's invitation to me to spend time with him and his family up the Berbice. When the steamer left New Amsterdam the ostensible understanding was that I had been commissioned by Mr. Nevinson's firm, the Berbice Timber and Balata Company, to paint some pictures depicting jungle scenes which, if satisfactory, would adorn the walls of their head office. That Mr. Nevinson could have had any other motive in wanting to have me accompany him and his wife and daughter into the interior had never for an instant occurred to me – nor, as I realized afterwards, to his wife. His daughter, Jessie, however, seemed to have suspected something; indeed, it is through her, as you will see, that I got this first inkling that things were not what they appeared to be.

At the time of these events – the early nineteen-thirties- the steamer made the trip up the Berbice River only once a week. It left New Amsterdam, the little town at the mouth of the river, every Wednesday morning, arrived at Paradise, the terminus, a hundred and ten miles up, any time between seven and half past seven in the evening, setting out on the return trip for New Amsterdam on the following morning. This meant that once you missed this Thursday morning opportunity you were committed irrevocably to jungle life for at least one full week. Knowing the Nevinsons as I did, however, I had no qualms about this fortnight we had planned to pass at Goed de Vries where the Berbice Timber and Balata Company have their up-river station. The cottage in which we were going to stay would be well-furnished and equipped – of this I had not the slightest doubt – and there would be no effort spared to make me comfortable.

Like myself, Mr. Nevinson comes of an old coloured family. We can both trace our ancestors back to the late eighteenth century, at which time the Nevinsons and the Woodsleys had not yet acquired the strain of negro slave blood that runs in them today. While I myself am of an olive tint, Mr. Nevinson is almost as fair in complexion as a pure white. His father, who was slightly darker, was the managing director of the Hardware Arcade in New Amsterdam, and had twice been Mayor of the town, and his grandfather was the Reverend Mr. Rawle Nevinson, an Anglican priest well known in Berbice for his good work among the lower river districts and for the church he erected at Huisten Rust on the Canje Creek.

Mr. Ralph Nevinson, like his father and grandfather before him, is a cultured man, and so is his wife who is a Groode, another well-known coloured family of Berbice. Mr. Nevinson's hobby is the collecting of anything relating to the early history of the colony, and as a boy I used to be fascinated with his private museum of relics, Indian and Dutch.

Normally, I think I should have expired from sheer astonishment had the Berbice Timber and Balata Company offered me a commission to paint some pictures for their office, but it was Mr. Nevinson, their managing director, who had put the proposition to me, and that made all the difference. For though he had spent all of his forty-seven years in New Amsterdam (forgetting the two years during the First Great War when he was with the West Indian Regiment in Egypt and Palestine), Mr. Nevinson was no small-town philistine who treated artists with a simpering patronage. In him I knew I had one who genuinely wished me well in my career as an artist. At the time of this narrative my own people had long since given up hope of seeing me "settled in a good, steady job" as an accountant or a Customs officer. After leaving school, I had been put to work as a sales assistant in the Hardware Arcade, Mr. Jack Nevinson, a brother of Mr. Ralph Nevinson, and my father having, between themselves, engineered this. After three months in the gloom of nail barrels and shelves of hinges and hasps and staples, I had been summoned upstairs by Mr. Jack Nevinson, and with much finger-tapping and avuncular smiling on the part of that gentleman, informed that "an opening" had been found for me in the office. I would begin as a junior clerk, and Mr. Jack Nevinson had no doubt that it would only be a matter of time before I rose to a high position in the firm.

Unfortunately, high positions, whether in well-established and illustrious firms or in colonial society, have never quickened my heartbeats. So I thanked Mr. Jack Nevinson and told him I was sorry but that I did not want an office job. I wanted to be a painter. I need not bother to describe the expression on his face as I left his screened-off sanctum and threaded my way between the desks of the outer office toward the stairway.

From that day I was regarded by the respectable people of New Amsterdam as an eccentric crank who would "get nowhere in life". I became renowned for the bad company I kept; I talked philosophy in barbers' shops with bus drivers and stevedores and porters – people far beneath me in class; I was a disgrace to my family.

The first one-man show I held was a depressing failure. But on the third day Mr. Ralph Nevinson dropped in and not only congratulated me but bought two pictures. He spoke to me not as the son of a family with which his own family had been friendly for decades, but as one man of the world to another. He made me feel that he and I were equals in a knowledge of humanity. He did not try to recall the days when I used to play with his children in his big Queenstown residence; the good-uncle-to-small-boy patronage in his manner had vanished; he seemed to consider me seriously as a grown-up person, and no fool, either. He invited me to come and see him any time I liked, and added that his bookshelves were always at my disposal.

That was how the friendship began between us – or perhaps I should say acquaintanceship, for no real intimacy ever developed between us. I have never been able to rid myself of a certain awe and respect for people appreciably older than myself, and the great disparity in our ages produced within me a rigid reserve which debarred that camaraderie I might have experienced with a person of my own years. Added to this, too, I was forever conscious that his wife and children considered me a ridiculous figure and something of a social outcast (I had never been very chummy with Jessie and Fred; Ronald, the eldest, used to be my play-companion, but he was in Georgetown now, having been manoeuvred a year before into the Civil Service as a clerk in the Treasury).

Despite my aggressive airs, and a decided pomposity of manner, and the contempt I was forever expressing for "the middle-class philistines" of New Amsterdam, as I called them, I was extremely sensitive, and so much dreaded the scorn and ridicule of Mrs. Nevinson and Jessie and Fred that my visits to their home were extremely infrequent.

Whenever I did call to see Mr. Nevinson, however, the occasion never failed to prove satisfying and enjoyable. Apart from art and philosophy and human beings, we discussed the early history of British Guiana, a subject of which Mr. Nevinson was passionately fond and on which he would readily have gone on talking all night until daybreak (with sundry delvings now and then into old books and letters and manuscripts) had I chosen not to take my departure at a discreet hour. He saw that the subject interested me intensely too, and this must have helped in great measure to strengthen his attachment to me, especially as in a town like New Amsterdam he would have had to do quite a lot of searching to discover another fellow-enthusiast in such matters as slave uprisings in the eighteenth century and the doings of the old Dutch settlers.

It was one morning, ten days before we set out for Goed de Vries, that he telephoned our home and asked me whether I could drop round that evening to see him. There was something important he wanted to discuss with me, he said. "Something I'm sure you'll be interested in, too," he added. "It's just in your line."

That was the evening on which he put the proposition to me. He sat in his favourite easy chair, behind him a glass case containing Dutch and Indian relics. He was a man of medium height, thickset and with the suggestion of a paunch. His close-cut, rather bristly dark hair was thinning on top and was touched with grey, though in this soft pink light the grey was not obvious. He had a long head, and features that betrayed no trace whatever of the negroid; it was a fine head and one that I had often wanted to do, though, up to now, I had not had the temerity to ask him to pose for me.

His grave grey-brown eyes regarded me with an affectionate humour as he said: "I can see you're curious, my boy. Well, I won't keep you waiting" His voice was deep and quiet, and went well, I thought, with the old-book scent of this study and the restful gloom that always lurked in the spaces between these dark mahogany bookcases with their rows of volumes and stacks of yellowed manuscripts and the relics that occupied some shelves – old Dutch jars and Indian goblets and pots and balata ornaments, chunks of masonry from ruined Dutch forts, daggers, and an eighteenth-century horse-pistol, the dented silver flagon reputed to have been the property of Laurens Storm van's Gravesande, the Directeur-General of Demerary and Essequibo in the middle eighteenth century.

In this study, with whose atmosphere I had been familiar since childhood days, I felt perfectly at ease – and not only at ease but filled with a deep serenity, for, of course, I am a romantic and extremely susceptible to my surroundings. There was a perfumed magic in the soft pink light, and benign jumbies seemed to crouch in the gloomed spaces between the bookcases, watching us as we chatted. I could feel their umber gaze on the side of my face, and their companionable breath was mingled with the cool February night breeze that came in at the open windows. Yes, there was no reason whatever for me to be sceptical of Mr. Nevinson's project nor for me to look for ulterior motives. The directors of his company, he said, had decided that the head office was in need of repairs and general renovations. The work would soon commence, and the idea had struck him that while they were about it why shouldn't they make a thorough job of it and acquire a few good pictures to decorate the walls?

"At first, I'd thought of your doing some murals – painting a few things of local interest – familiar scenes, birds, animals and so on – direct on to the walls, but after reflecting a bit I realized this wouldn't work. The boards we're going to use won't take artist's paints very well. That's why I thought of your doing a few canvases instead – and we're in the timber business, so what could be better than a few jungle scenes! You could come up with me on my next visit and see something of the timber-grant and sawmill. Good outing for you, if nothing else."

A tiny midge was fluttering around the pink-shaded reading-lamp on the desk at my right, and from the Canje Creek came the chug-chug of a motorboat, clear and deliberate on the night air. Already I thought I could sniff the watery vegetable rankness of the jungle, and a shiver of pleasant anticipation ran through me. Without hesitation I told him that I thought it an excellent scheme.

"Nothing would please me better," I said. "And perhaps we could hunt out some old Dutch ruins and do a bit of nosing around generally for anything interesting in that line," I added with all the enthusiasm of my twenty-three years.

"You'd like that, would you?"

At the time I attached no significance to it, but afterwards, on reflecting back, I realized that he had said this with a note of eagerness. He even clasped his hands together and leant forward a trifle, smiling at me and nodding.

"Well, certainly, sir! Anything to do with old ruins and relics and such things fascinates me terrifically. I've told you that before."

"Yes, I know. Ah, well. We shall see. When we get up there time enough."

The rest of the evening we spent in a discussion of practical details, and it was not until I was on my way home that it occurred to me that, for once, we had not plunged into our favourite topic – local history. But again, I thought nothing of this. Not for an instant had it occurred to me that my host might have purposely steered our conversation clear of the subject. I had detected nothing whatever in his manner to make me feel that there might be something troubling him, or that he could be withholding from me information relating to some secret aspect of our proposed trip.

On the Wednesday morning of the following week, the steamer cast off its moorings precisely at seven-thirty. It was a rather grubby little steamer called the *Arawana* (the name of a local fish). The lower deck, which was second-class, had a perpetual odour of cow-dung, tar and humanity; on this deck every conceivable type of cargo – from ground provisions and fruit to lumber and cattle – is dumped. The lot of second-class passengers is never a happy one on these river steamers. The upper deck, first-class, smells of tar only, and is tolerable, if far from being a sybarite's conception of paradise. We found a few shaky wicker chairs into which we sank to the accompaniment of loud creakings. And there was a dining-saloon intended evidently for dining and nothing but dining; there was no room in it for moving around. The deck-space was extremely limited, and had there been a large number of passengers – even as many as twenty – conditions would have been definitely uncomfortable, especially as the wicker chairs did not amount to more than ten.

Fortunately, very few people ever travel up the river first-class, and this occasion was no exception. Besides Mr. Nevinson, his wife, Jessie and myself, there were only three other first-class passengers – an Anglican priest and his wife, and a cattle-rancher on the first leg of his long journey to the Rupununi Savannah. The Nevinsons were acquainted with all three of them, but only the Reverend Mr. Lumsden and his wife were known to me; I had met them at the home of my own people whom they not infrequently visited. My people, of course, are staunch Anglicans – as I myself, indeed, used to be in the days before I began to think for myself.

Not being in a mood to participate in polite, trivial conversation, I secluded myself aft with a book from which I occasionally glanced up to observe the passing scenery – bush and more bush, with now and then a lonely homestead to relieve the monotony of green.

No one bothered me – and no one seemed surprised that I had cut myself off from the rest of the company, for, no doubt, it was taken for granted that I was an odd young man who despised respectable society.

At lunch – not at all a bad meal; the ship's cook evidently knew how to make a good coconut curry – Mr. Nevinson and I exchanged a few murmured commonplaces, and the Reverend Mr. Lumsden smiled at me once with a friendly facetiousness, wagged his head and made a purring comment on the habits of "you bookworms – tut, tut, tut!"

Mrs. Nevinson sat opposite me. At the time of this account, she looked much younger than her forty-four years. Pale olive and shapely, she had a gay, attractive laugh and a most intriguing mole just beneath her right eye. As a small boy I had always welcomed her presence in our home, and, in fact, at ten, I had found myself violently in love with her! She treated me now in the manner of a dutiful aunt and said that she had promised Kate (my mother) to see that I did not neglect my meals. She kept pressing me to help myself to more vegetables, to more rice, to more chicken… "What about some more gravy, Milton? Come, pass your plate…" I responded with pleasant, polite firmness, eating what I wanted and rejecting what I did not want.

After lunch I returned aft with my book, but this time I was not to be left undisturbed. I heard footsteps and glanced up to see Jessie approaching. She stopped near my chair, peered with mild curiosity at the book in my lap and said: "Poems, I suppose."

I nodded gravely in confirmation. "Yes, poems."

"I could have bet anything on it."

I did not rise to offer her my chair, but this in no way discouraged her. My chair stood near a locker in which, I believe, life-belts were stored. She gave me an amused look and seated herself on this locker.

At nineteen she was tall and shapely like her mother. But she had her father's wide brows, deep-set eyes, arched nose, dimpled chin. In outlook she was vacuous and small-town; tennis, dances and young men were her only interests. I have told her this to her face on so many occasions – to her great amusement – that I know she won't mind me saying it here. She has never taken me seriously.

"You never get tired of reading, Milton?"

"Never. Did your mother send you here to relieve my loneliness?"

She giggled. "No, I came of my own accord. I felt like taking a walk. This heat is getting more terrible every minute."

The heat had certainly increased in intensity. The low deck-awning, if anything, made it worse. And now that we were far from the coast, there was no wind. The jungle, glittering in the sunshine, reared up in two dense walls on either bank, shutting us in. It had a rigid, listening look as though held in a spell. The river, from a light muddy amber, had turned black and ominous. Already I could envisage myself amid the gloom of hanging vines and prickly-trunked palms, already I could sense in the air a mystery and isolation.

"It rather baffles me why you've come on this trip," I said. "I didn't think you would consider yourself capable of standing up to a fortnight of jungle life."

She laughed. "You have a very low opinion of me, I can see. I hear there are a lot of nice Indian boys up the river. I'm going to see if I can catch one. Buck men make good husbands."

"I see."

"And in any case, you forget it's Lent? No dances on. What's the use of remaining in town?"

"Quite so. I'd forgotten that. Lent. Very appropriate time, I should say, to go into the wilderness."

She giggled. "But no fasting for me, though, you can bet! I'm looking forward to my *labba* pepper-pot. But wait! What's this I'm hearing about your going up to paint pictures for Daddy's office? Is it true?"

"You're unusually well informed today."

"Oh, so that's how he managed to inveigle you into going up with us?"

"I'm afraid I don't quite follow."

"All right. Never mind."

I lit a cigarette, watching the smoke shape itself into grey-blue phantoms across the narrow strip of deck before it finally dissolved into the heat-quivering air. Jessie crossed her legs and began to whistle a popular dance tune, tapping her foot against my chair in rhythm.

Looking down past the rail, I could see the water rushing foamily along the side of the vessel. Swell-waves fanned out perpetually toward the bank. The deck throbbed to the monotonous thump of the engines.

"What are you getting at, Jessie?"

She stopped whistling and gave me a mysterious smile. Her flippancy was gone. There was, to my surprise, even a slightly worried frown on her face. I was not accustomed to seeing her look worried.

"I don't want to talk about it," she said slowly, "because it may be only a fancy of mine – but I believe something is on Daddy's mind."

"On his mind?"

She nodded. "I mean concerning this trip. For the past two or three weeks he hasn't been his usual self. Mother thinks he's overworked, but it isn't that."

"What else could it be, then?"

"I don't know, but I feel it's something to do with this trip."

"But isn't it the custom for him to visit the up-river station once every six months?"

"I know it is – and that's what set me thinking. He paid his first visit for the year last month. By all rights he shouldn't be going up there again until June or July."

"Did he go up to Goed de Vries last month? I didn't know that."

"He went up – but he came back to town by the same steamer the next morning. He said that Rayburn the caretaker was down with a bilious attack and the place was in a mess."

"That seems a pretty good reason to me."

"Yes, I know. Daddy is very fussy about his comforts, and he hates a dusty or untidy house. But that wasn't the only reason why he came back to town by the return steamer. Mother believes everything he tells her – but he can't fool me so easily. Since he came back from that trip last month he's been nervy and jumpy – and sort of excited inside, as if he has a secret he's afraid we might discover."

I smiled. "Are you sure you aren't allowing your imagination to be influenced by those magazine stories you and your mother devour?"

"It's no imagination! Why did he ask me to come up with him? It's true Mother has been up with him on one or two trips, but she's always had to invite herself. He's never asked her. But this time he invited both of us. And look at you! He's gone and asked you, too. If he isn't afraid of something up the river there why does he want so much company?"

"But afraid of something like what? Spooks?"

"I don't say that – though I've heard them say the sawmill is supposed to be haunted. The men say they've seen an old Dutchman walking on the greenheart logs near the winch."

"Always an old Dutchman, isn't it?"

"Or a headless slave. Remember those tales Milly, our nurse, used to tell us when we were small, in Daddy's study?"

"I've suffered too many nightmares on their account not to remember them."

On the lower deck one of the sailors – or it might have been a passenger – was strumming a ukelele and singing in a crude but melodious voice, *If you were the only girl in the world.*

Jessie began to whistle the tune softly and tap her foot on the deck.

"I've heard both your mother and father scolding you about that whistling, Jessie. Not ladylike."

"Do *you* think it not ladylike?"

"I didn't say *I* did."

"These are not Victorian times. I'm always telling Mother that."

"I agree with you in that if in nothing else."

We fell silent after that – at least I did. Jessie continued to whistle. I dabbed at my forehead and cheeks which were damp with perspiration. The chair creaked as I altered my position slightly, and, somehow, it was as though the rasping screechiness of the sound at once became transposed into a wisp of uneasy mist that curled through my awareness so that I had the inclination to fidget and glance about me. I found myself frowning at the black water. Then my gaze strayed to the trees which hung low over the stream. I began to wonder what might not be lurking in the damp gloom that simmered among that glittering welter of greens. Who knew what odd creatures might not be eyeing us as we rushed by? Tiny, warped insects unknown to entomology. Or some monstrosity that was neither reptile nor bird nor mammal – like the hoatzins near the mouth of the river and on the Canje Creek. Amber orbs in a green flat head…

It came upon me that Jessie had grown silent. She sat with her head tilted at a listening angle, a slight frown on her face. As she became aware of the curiosity in my stare she murmured: "Well, that's strange. I wonder if he's going up with us, too."

"Are you addressing me or speaking to yourself?"

"Don't you hear that flute? It's the same one I've been hearing for some days now in Queenstown. The fellow who plays it must be on his way up, too."

"What are you talking about? What flute is this? And who is the fellow that plays it?"

"I don't know him from Adam, but he must be on the steamer with us. I'm sure it's the same fellow. Somebody has been playing a flute in Queenstown near our house for the past week or two."

"And what of that?"

"Nothing – only I'm saying he seems to be travelling up with us. Don't you hear the flute on the lower deck?"

"I hear a ukelele, but definitely not a flute."

She laughed. "Don't be silly, Milton. You, such a keen enthusiast on highbrow music and can't even recognize a flute when you hear it!"

At this point I observed her father approaching along the deck. He did not come aft, however, but paused amidships at the top of the companionway. I noticed that there was a frown on his face. He was smoking a cigarette, his manner, on the whole, a trifle puzzled and intent; he might have been listening to some conversation taking place at the foot of the companionway, on the lower deck.

Jessie called to him: "Daddy, don't you hear a flute down there?"

He started and glanced up as though noticing us for the first time. "What did you say? What's that?" There seemed to be an unusually sharp note in his voice. He began to come towards us, his gaze on Jessie. "What did you ask, Jessie?"

Jessie evidently had not failed to note the tenseness in his manner. She said: "I thought you were going to snap off my head. I was only asking you about the flute down there. Milton swears he can't hear it."

He flicked his half-smoked cigarette over the rail, if anything tenser. "Yes, I do hear a flute. Are you hearing it, too?"

"Of course. I'm not deaf." She looked at me triumphantly. "You see! Dad can hear it too, Milton."

I sat forward, beginning to be puzzled in earnest now, because

I knew perfectly well that there was no such thing as the sound of any flute on the lower deck. Except for that ukelele and the voice singing, there was only the throbbing of the engines and the rushing hiss of the water as it foamed past the steamer, an occasional mumble of conversation: simply the sum of noises that our senses had come to take for granted.

"Mr. Nevinson, are you hearing a flute?"

"Yes, I'm afraid I am – but don't let it trouble you, my boy. I suppose your ears aren't attuned to it." He smiled at Jessie, but I knew that he was being casual with a purpose. I knew that beneath this outward show of nonchalance there was a layer of deep concern and nervousness. "When did you first hear it, Jessie?"

"The flute? A few days ago. A week or so – or perhaps longer. If it's the same one, of course – and it sounds so to me. Why do you ask?"

"I simply wondered. By the way, young lady, did you borrow a book from my study recently?"

"A book? I should think not. You know I never touch any of your books. I don't think I've even been in your study for months."

He tweaked her ear. "That's an exaggeration. Don't you filch stamps from my desk when you write Fred?"

"Oh, yes, I forgot. I did take a penny stamp from your desk drawer some time early last week. Or the week before. I'm not sure."

"Which drawer was that? The right-hand one? Can you remember?"

"I think it was the left-hand one. The one you keep a lot of old papers in – with Dutch writing. You generally keep it locked, but, somehow, it was open that day. I found two penny stamps in a little cardboard box."

"That's why I can never keep any stamps in the house. What are you reading now, young man? Something philosophical?"

After glancing at the book in my lap, he patted me affectionately on the shoulder and moved off.

Jessie looked at me. "You see what I told you! Are you satisfied now he isn't himself?"

"For that matter," I returned, "you aren't yourself, either. All this talk about an imaginary flute. Are you both dreaming?"

She stared at me. "But how do you mean? Didn't you hear it?"

"Oh, has it stopped now?"

"About a minute ago. But are you serious, Milton? You really didn't hear it?"

"I didn't."

"But – oh, this is silly. I wasn't dreaming. I heard it. And it isn't the first time. I heard it up to yesterday evening before I came downstairs to dinner. It sounded somewhere nearby in the neighbourhood. And Daddy heard it a few minutes ago. He said so. How is it you couldn't?" She laughed. "You're trying to pull my leg."

"Literally, such an occupation would in no way revolt me, but in the figurative sense – well, I'm afraid you're off the track, Jessie. Honestly, I'm not trying to spoof you. I never heard anything like a flute. That ukelele and the voice down there are all I've heard during the past few minutes. There's been no flute."

"Seriously? On your word of honour?"

"Seriously. On my word of honour."

2

It is true that, as I have mentioned, I am a romantic, but under my romanticism I am a strong rationalist, and I can state quite frankly that not for an instant did I believe that any supernatural influences were responsible for the incident I have just described. I was convinced that there must be some natural explanation for the fact that Jessie and her father could hear a flute while I could not, so without delay I told her to sit in my chair and wait until I returned.

"What are you going to do?" she asked.

"I'm going down to make inquiries on the lower deck."

"Let me come with you."

"I don't think your mother would like the idea of a respectable young lady like her daughter venturing among the rabble of the lower deck."

She told me to stop being sarcastic, and accompanied me below.

The second mate and I were already acquainted. He was one of my barber's shop companions in debate. In reply to my enquiry he said: "A ukelele and a mouth-organ de only instruments we got down here, so far as I know."

"But what about the passengers? You're sure none of them have been playing a flute during the past few minutes?"

"No, Mr. Woodsley, not down here. I been here all de time. I woulda hear it. Only Mitchell and his ukelele been playing."

"But I'm positive I heard a flute," said Jessie. "My father heard it, too. And it came from down here."

The second mate smiled and shook his head. "Not down here, Miss. I can swear to dat. Nobody didn't play no flute on dis deck today. Aubrey, one o' de deck-hands, got a mouth-organ, and

Mitchell dere got his ukelele – and dat's de only musical instruments I hear on dis boat. None o' de passengers didn't play no instrument since we left town dis morning."

As we returned to the upper deck Jessie said: "Well, that's the queerest thing I've ever known to happen. If it wasn't a human being who played that flute then it must have been a jumbie, because I did hear it – as plainly as I can hear you speak." She spoke lightly as though the whole thing were a joke.

"What was the tune?" I asked. "Did you recognize it?"

"It was no particular tune. It was as if the person was practising his notes or something – or it might have been something highbrow." She gave me a teasing glance. "Like one of those dry-as-dust pieces you like to listen to."

"I see."

"Remember there's a piece you used to play on that portable gramophone Ronald had – something about a faun."

"Debussy's *L'apres-midi d'un faune*?"

"That's the one. It was a tune like that. A kind of aimless, wandering thing."

"What about the previous occasions on which you heard it? Was it always the same tuneless, wandering thing?"

"Yes, always the same. I never really paid any attention to it. I heard it coming from somewhere in the neighbourhood, and didn't think anything of it."

"You never remarked on it to your mother or father?"

"No. Why should I have? Some violin or piano or saxophone is always making a noise. A flute was nothing so unusual to comment on."

"That sounds fairly reasonable. And don't you remember exactly on what day you began to hear it?"

She laughed. "What's this now? Am I in the witness-box?" But she shook her head. "No, I don't remember the exact day, but it wasn't more than two weeks ago, I'm sure."

"Our place isn't so far from yours in Queenstown – just around the corner – and I can assure you I've heard nothing like a flute during the past few weeks."

"Well, either you're deaf or I'm enchanted."

"No, but joking apart, I'm puzzled, Jessie. You're not renowned for your brain, it's true, but I'm sure even you wouldn't go imagining things like this. And as for your father, I don't think there's a more level-headed man in the colony – "

"Here's Mother! I wonder if she didn't hear it, too."

Mrs. Nevinson approached us, the slight smile on her face widening the nearer she came – the smile which, to myself, I called her drawing-room smile, for she had a way of switching it off and on that was decidedly mechanical. It was an attractive smile but so obviously studied! It was not until she had arrived at where we sat that I observed that there was a slightly troubled light in her eyes despite the smile.

"What mischief are you two up to here?" she said.

"Milton is trying to convert me into a highbrow. We're discussing flute music."

"Don't let her plague you, Milton. I wish you could get her really interested in music. Nowadays everything is this jazz. And Jessie simply laps it up." She sighed dramatically. Most of her gestures are dramatic. She is one of these people who act, rather than live, their lives, and whose gestures should never be taken literally.

"Jessie, have you said anything to your father to upset him?" she asked.

"To upset him? No. Why?"

"Well, he's certainly not himself. He wants to make out it's the heat and that he's tired, but it doesn't seem to me a good enough reason why he should settle down alone in the dining-saloon to smoke and look through old papers."

Jessie shrugged. "I don't know what it's all about, but Daddy hasn't been himself for weeks now – since he came back from Goed de Vries last month. I told you so but you would insist it was overwork."

"But what should he want to get down in the dumps for because he went up to Goed de Vries? He was only there for a night last month. What could have happened up there to upset him?"

"That's what I'd like to know myself. Oh, but wait! Have you heard about the latest mystery, Mother? There's a jumbie-flute on the steamer."

"A what?"

"Didn't you hear it? You don't mean you're one of the deaf ones!"

After the situation had been explained to her Mrs. Nevinson cried: "That's utterly impossible, child! You and your father are both dreaming. If there was a flute on the lower deck why didn't Milton and I and everybody else hear it? And I don't remember hearing anything like a flute in Queenstown during the past week or so. Old Mr. Culley used to play one, but he's dead now, and I know of nobody else who has one. What time did you hear it mostly – at night?"

"It wasn't a nightmare, if that's what you're trying to hint," Jessie said. "I've heard that flute at all times of the day and night – and I was very much awake. I've heard it in the middle of the morning, I've heard it in the afternoon when I was having a bath, and I've heard it in the evening. One night late when I was coming home from the Selkirks with Randolph Hart I heard it. We'd just got to the corner of Ferry Street."

"That would be near where Milton lives. Perhaps it was Milton himself. Milton has such surprising habits. It won't amaze me to learn he's a flute-player in secret."

"Just so," I murmured. I turned to Jessie as something occurred to me. "Jessie, can you remember if it was constant in pitch – or did it sort of vary – rise and fall with the wind? You know how sounds vary in Queenstown, depending upon the wind."

Her mother laughed – her gay, roguish laugh which had never failed to quicken my heartbeats (I believe I must still have been in love with her), for though she might have been artificial in her behaviour, Mrs. Nevinson could not be described as lacking in charm. Changing the key of her mood, so to speak, in her characteristic fashion, she gushed: "But, Milton! You don't mean to tell me you're taking her seriously about this flute!"

"And why not? Why shouldn't I? Personally I think it's a most mysterious incident. I'm sure both Mr. Nevinson and Jessie wouldn't have imagined hearing a flute on the lower deck."

"Oh, Lord! I suppose I should have known it without your mentioning it. In many ways you're exactly like Ralph. Always ready to make a mystery over something so as to give you an excuse to spend days and weeks puzzling over it and delving into old books and papers. Anyway," she went on, with another grand sigh, "I do hope Ralph won't keep up this mood for days as he sometimes does. As it is, it's most embarrassing for me his going into the dining-saloon with those old papers. Mr. Lumsden must feel quite slighted. And poor Mr. Herrick was so eager to talk over the cattle situation with him."

After she had left us I repeated my unanswered question of a few minutes before regarding the flute, and Jessie replied: "No, I won't say it varied in pitch with the wind. But now you mention it, something has struck me. During the last two or three days it seemed to have got nearer."

"Nearer?"

She nodded. "That's the best way I can describe it. When I began to hear it a week or two ago it seemed to come from a distance – a few streets off. But yesterday and the day before it was much nearer – in fact, it might have been in the next yard." She looked at me in sudden anxiety and alarm. "I say, Milt, you don't think there can be anything spooky in it, do you?"

I grunted noncommittally.

She shifted her feet about uneasily. "It's no joke. I didn't think anything of it before, but now that Mother and the rest of you say you didn't hear anything I'm beginning to wonder about it. You don't think it could be some sort of – some sort of manifestation – isn't that the word? Something only Daddy and I can sense?"

"I'm afraid I don't care to express an opinion yet," I told her, my voice heavy with pomposity, as it often could be in those days.

"But don't you think there can be some natural explanation?"

"I should hope there is," I replied. "I always prefer to find a natural explanation before plunging into speculations about the occult. The best thing will be to wait a day or two more and see what happens. Whenever you hear your flute again don't forget to let me know at once."

"Ugh. This means I'm always going to be listening for it now. I really hope we'll be able to explain it. I detest anything ghostly. I've never seen a ghost, and I don't ever want to."

We sat in silence for a long while, staring at the monotonous greens of the jungle. The heat swirled around us like invisible twining tendrils of silk, and the dull throbbing of the engines beneath the deck produced a drowsiness which I found myself fighting hard to resist. I felt myself possessed with an urge to remain awake and alert. It was as though I could sense something menacing in the still array of green foliage that loomed up on either side of us, and dared not shut my eyes lest I were overwhelmed by some stealthy horror only waiting for an opportunity to pounce.

Suddenly I rose. "I think I'll go and see what your father is doing in the dining-saloon," I said, and Jessie rose, too, but did not seem enthusiastic.

When Daddy is in a mood I never go near him," she said. "You can risk it if you like. I'll go and talk to Mrs. Lumsden."

"Your father is not half the ogre you think him," I told her. "I'm willing to bet he's in no mood at all. He's probably bored with the small talk your mother and the church folk have been pouring forth like characters in a Jane Austen novel, and he's discreetly decided to do a bolt into the dining-saloon. It's what I would have done myself."

A minute later I proved myself right, for when I entered the dining-saloon Mr. Nevinson greeted me with a smile, glancing up from a yellowed document spread out before him. "Well, young man! Looking for me?"

"Yes, I came to see what you were doing. Mrs. N. says you're in a mood, but I didn't believe it."

"Nell is generally suspicious of me when I retire to enjoy my own company for a spell. Sit down and let's talk."

He spoke as though he had been expecting me, and I felt a grain of curiosity itching its way through me as I drew out a chair and seated myself at the table opposite him. He held out a tin of cigarettes and I accepted one. And then, seeing that there was one already between his lips unlit, I produced my lighter, clicked it alight and pushed it across the table toward him.

To my surprise, he drew back his head with some haste, saying: "Oh, it's all right, my boy. Don't trouble. I'll get it lit in a moment." He spoke with evident embarrassment, and at the same time swept the manuscript towards him in a swift, protective manner. It fell into his lap, and he retrieved it, folded it in two and slipped it between the leaves of a thick volume lying on the table at his elbow. It was a Dutch-English dictionary that I knew well, for I had often seen it on the desk in his study.

"I've been doing a little translating," he murmured.

For a few minutes we spoke of trifling matters – the heat, the discomfort of travelling on these steamers, the quality of the food we had had at lunch, Mr. and Mrs. Lumsden's disembarkment in a few minutes' time at Brave Lands where the Anglican church stood. He seemed to take care not to refer to the manuscript, and I thought it discreet not to ask him a direct question concerning its contents or its origin.

Abruptly, however, he glanced down at the dictionary and said: "It's really too warm to be doing this sort of thing, but I couldn't resist the temptation." He looked across at me. "I'm going to tell you about it before long, and I'm sure you'll be interested."

After a pause, he went on: "About this flute, Milton, I know you're puzzled. I am myself, and, in fact, I meant to talk to you about it, but in the meantime tell me something. I heard you and Jessie went below to inquire after it. Nell mentioned it to me just before you came. Do I understand that Jessie thought it was being played on the lower deck?"

"That's right, sir. So she said. Wasn't it there you heard it, too? I saw you standing by the companionway looking down."

He nodded. "I simply wanted to know. As a matter of fact, I wasn't looking down the companionway because I thought the sound was coming from below. I was pacing the deck and happened to pause there for a moment."

"Then you mean you didn't hear it coming up from the lower deck?"

He shook his head slowly. " No, Milton. It was up here on the deck – right beside me."

3

NOW that I look back on it, I realize that his statement did not instil into me half as much dread and dismay as it ought to have done. I think, too, that it is because I had always held him in such deep respect and had so much confidence in him that I did not exclaim or show incredulity. I simply continued to stare at him, puzzled and waiting for him to go on, not doubting for an instant that a perfectly simple explanation was about to follow.

Even when he had come to the end of the astounding story he narrated to me, I somehow did not feel an urge to ridicule him or smile with scepticism. Had you known him as I did you would have agreed, I am sure, that he was the kind of man you would no more have attempted to associate with the fantastic or the occult than you would have thought of attending a play by Bernard Shaw with the expectation of witnessing a pretty little love drama featuring sentimental song-hits.

"Absurd as it may sound," he said, "I couldn't risk letting you touch this manuscript, my boy, because there is every likelihood that exactly what has happened to Jessie and me would happen to you. That's why I drew back so hastily and swept it into my lap when you stretched across to light my cigarette."

That was how he began. Then he went on to tell me about the manuscript. He had seen it for the first time at Goed de Vries one Wednesday evening in January – exactly three weeks before. It had belonged to an old buffianda (Indian-negro half-breed). "He had lived two miles higher up, at Horstenland, but had died recently. His name was Patoir, and he was a very likeable fellow. He used to trade an occasional raft of greenheart with us. He told me of this thing nearly two years ago, but he said he couldn't let me have it – or even see it – because there was a superstition attached to it. It was supposed to bring good fortune to its possessor, provided it was kept shut away in safety from daylight and fire. But it must never be handled at any time. What would happen if it were handled Patoir himself didn't seem to know. He was a fairly intelligent chap, I must admit, and he was quite frank with me. He said that so far as he could see, it had brought him no especial good luck, but, all the same, he wasn't going to run the risk of being harmed, so he always kept it shut up in the canister in which it had been kept since the moment it had come into his possession. He said that even he himself had only peeped at it once.

"As it happens, I've done him many a favour in the course of our transactions up here, and he took a liking to me. We were good friends, and he always promised that when he died he would leave the canister for me – though he warned me that it wouldn't be safe to tamper with it. He said that while he didn't believe himself in the stupid nonsense that most of the people up here believe in, he knew that there were certain things that men could not explain, and he preferred not 'to trouble evil lest evil trouble me'. It was his favourite saying.

"I never pressed him to let me see this manuscript, though, naturally, I was very interested in it, especially as he once hinted that the writing on it was Dutch and that he believed it came down from the early days of the colony. He said an Indian gave it to him in the canister in which it was kept. It was a present to him for having cured the Indian of a bad attack of malaria. This Indian fellow, it appears, had never heard of quinine in the form we know it in, and Patoir dosed him regularly and got him better within a few days.

"To my surprise, when I arrived at Goed de Vries three weeks ago, the first thing Rayburn, the caretaker, told me was that Patoir had died of an attack of jaundice the week before, and that before dying he had asked that his 'good-luck canister', as he called it, be given to me. He had no relatives. He wasn't married. The Buck woman he lived with was only a paramour. So there was evidently no fuss about the canister. Rayburn collected it the day after his death and brought it to my cottage at Goed de Vries. I found it on the dressing-table in my bedroom. It's a small thing, ten inches by seven, and three inches deep. Made of tin and rather rusty-looking.

"Well, Milton, as you know yourself, I'm the last person on earth who thinks twice about superstitions, and without hesitation I opened the canister. There was no lock on it. It was simply shut tight, and I just had to prise up the lid."

He paused here and opened the dictionary at the place where he had inserted the manuscript. From where I sat I saw what looked like two sheets of strong parchment folded over once. The writing on it was reddish-brown – evidently from age.

"This is what I found," he said. "There was nothing else in it but this. And just as you yourself might have done, I lifted it out and glanced through it. I could only translate it roughly because I hadn't thought of bringing up my dictionary, and my knowledge of Dutch is moderate.

"I should have mentioned that I found the house in a rather untidy condition when I arrived. Rayburn was down with some sort of diarrhoea, and he said he hadn't been able to do much cleaning up. He's a hard-working and trustworthy fellow, and I excused him. But if there's anything I can't tolerate it's an untidy house, so the following morning I took the return steamer and went back to town. Of course, between us, I could have remained and roughed things, but the truth is I was itching to translate this thing properly. I simply couldn't remain a whole fortnight up there without my dictionary.

"Before I go on I think the best thing would be to read you a translation of the first part of it. It's divided into two parts." He produced from between the leaves of the dictionary a slip of paper which, I saw, bore his own handwriting. "I'm afraid the fellow was certainly demented when he wrote it – but we'll discuss that aspect of the matter later on. It reads like this: 'He who touches this parchment seals himself in a pact with me, Jan Pieter Voorman, to listen to my music, and, later, when I beckon, to join me in death. They have robbed me and massacred my wife and children who should have departed for St. Eustatius on the *Standvastigheid*. I shall never rest till the day that my bones and my flute are found and interred with Christian rites. I place a curse and plague upon the person or persons who may touch this parchment. My roaming presence shall pester him or them unto death unless my wishes are carried out. Gnashing my teeth on this fourth day of March, I shall end my life on earth. I curse these black wretches, even as I curse the Blacker Ones. To him who seeks release from this pact and would put my soul at peace, let him heed what now follows and so be led to the discovery of my bones and my flute and my musket.'" Mr. Nevinson glanced up. "All this is on the first page and about two-thirds of the second. He wrote on both sides of the paper. The rest of the space is taken up with a long account of how to recover the writer's bones and so forth. It's fairly intelligible, but the only difficulty is that he seems to take it for granted that the finder of this document would know the whereabouts of his plantation. He evidently didn't foresee that the plantations up this river would eventually be abandoned and the jungle allowed to take charge again."

Mr. Nevinson spoke in a voice that was even and in no way upset. It was only his eyes that made me realize that he was inwardly perturbed. He folded up the manuscript again and placed it between the leaves of the dictionary, then clasped his hands lightly and looked across the table at me.

"That's one part of the story," he said. "I come now to the part that is going to sound like something out of Edgar Allan Poe – or that other writer, M. R. James. Anyway," he chuckled, "it's happened, and I can assure you that no one could wish more earnestly than myself that it could prove mere fiction. You've noted what the writer said in this document? Well, as you can understand, Milton, I never gave a thought to the threat contained in the thing. I was only interested in it as an antiquary. It's obvious that this fellow was some planter who was persecuted during the slave insurrection of 1763. The 'black wretches' he refers to can only have been rebel slaves who must have pillaged his plantation and murdered his family. All that seems plain – especially as he speaks of committing suicide 'on this fourth day of March'. The insurrection, as you know, started on the Canje Creek on the twenty-first of February, but the rebels didn't reach this river until the twenty-seventh, and everyone was taken by surprise. On the fourth of March the situation was chaotic. The Predicant's house at Peereboom was under siege and the planters were in flight or skulking in the bush in hiding. Well, that was my only interest in the thing. But you can imagine my consternation when one evening in my study it suddenly occurred to me that I was listening to a flute in the neighbourhood! I don't want to exaggerate or paint a melodramatic picture. You know me better than that. And, as a matter of fact, I may tell you that simply hearing this flute didn't cause me any alarm. There are all sorts of musical instruments in that town, as you know yourself. If somebody isn't plaguing the air with a saxophone it's a piano or a squeaky violin.

"But, naturally, hearing a flute, I remembered the manuscript, and I began to think back idly. It was absurd, of course, to attach any significance to a flute in the neighbourhood simply because I happened to have read this, as I thought, idle threat in the manuscript – but I'm human, and I couldn't help letting my thoughts dwell on the thing. Then it struck me that previous to this I'd been hearing this flute for two or three days past. This wasn't the first time. I felt distinctly uncomfortable now, and began to do some serious thinking, trying to remember exactly where and when I had heard the flute. And in a flash I recalled that in the early hours of the Thursday morning at Goed de Vries I had heard it, too. I'd awakened to the sound of it. It seemed to come from some way downstream, and I never gave a thought to it, because the men have their logies just beyond the sawmill and it might have been one of them amusing himself. They are early risers. But thinking back on it there in my study, I began to wonder other things. I began to connect it with this warning in the manuscript, and it was this that caused me consternation. I traced back carefully, and began to realize that it was from that Thursday morning I had begun to hear this flute, and, what was more, that every day since then I had heard it."

He paused, and I regarded him in silence as he rubbed his hand slowly down his cheek. His forehead was perspiring slightly.

"It's difficult to conceive of anything like this happening, Milton. I mean, in the midst of our cold, everyday existence, with traffic in the streets and typewriters tapping in an office and everything going on in the old, usual, reasoned, commonplace way… And happening to me of all people! A staid, unromantic old horse like me! It seems absurd – grotesque. And yet there it is. It happens once or twice a day. Once at the office, when I wasn't even thinking of it, I heard it. No definite melody. A sort of trail of notes, as if – as if someone were practising a Debussy scale but weren't quite getting it right."

He drummed with his fingers musingly on the table.

"I didn't say anything to Nell or Jessie, of course, because the last thing I wanted was to alarm them. And I kept hoping that it was some peculiar phenomenon that would cease eventually. But on the contrary, it has got worse and worse. It's getting closer. I mean it. Closer and closer."

After a silence, he said: "Yesterday at noon, when I was on my way home from the office, I heard it, and it seemed to come from the footboard of my car. Yet there was no one there. I stopped the car and made a thorough search within the car itself and around it. And there can be no question of ventriloquy. I've tested that possibility in a dozen different ways. Why, look at today. It sounded right at my elbow when I was sitting there with the others, chatting. I was so startled I had to rise and pace up and down the deck. But it followed me. Everywhere I moved it followed me. Really, it's incredible. It's like living a part in a tale you've read in some book. I can't describe the sensation, Milton. This is the very last thing I'd ever dreamt possible."

He shifted in his chair. "And you can imagine the shock I got when Jessie called to me and asked me if I was hearing it. You can't conceive the effort it took me to control myself. Because I knew in a flash she must have been fishing about in my desk drawers. I'd put the manuscript in the left-hand drawer because I always lock that drawer. But I've been taking the manuscript out to glance through it so often that I must have omitted to lock the drawer on one or two occasions."

He dabbed at his forehead. "It's like some – some unpleasant dream. I still can't believe it's happening." He looked at me and gave a short, uncomfortable laugh. "If this gets around, people won't hesitate to pronounce me out of my mind – and I couldn't blame them."

After another silence he smiled at me in that quiet, grave manner of his which goes a long way to contribute to the confidence he inspires in the people who know him. "I'm afraid I wasn't very honest with you, youngster. The firm does want you to do those pictures – the commission still holds good – but it was really I who manoeuvred it so that you could come up here with us. I need someone like you to help me find a way out of this situation, Milton. You're the only fellow I could think of who would be interested in this affair in a really serious and sensible spirit. Despite your reputation for being an eccentric, I happen to know you as you really are. The opinions I hear expressed about you don't affect me one bit. I know I can depend upon you. Nell and Jessie I've brought along to provide us both with company. In many respects, I'm far more chicken-hearted than you may imagine. Somehow I couldn't stand the thought of going up there without company while this mysterious ghost-play was happening around me."

Anyone but Mr. Nevinson might have been surprised at my rigid and unbroken silence all this while, but Mr. Nevinson was accustomed to me. We understood each other perfectly, and I knew from experience that once he set out to narrate any happening or any set of circumstances he was thorough about it and left out nothing that was vital, hence obviating the necessity for his listeners to interpose questions. I was aware, too, that he considered me a first-class listener, and I was in no way eager to damage my reputation. That was why I waited until I thought he had finished before uttering even as much as a grunt.

The first question I asked him concerned the second part of the manuscript, for I was curious to know what these "instructions" could be. He smiled and nodded, withdrawing the parchment from the dictionary again. "I intended to read you the translation I've made," he said, "but it's a dull, rather rambling affair – not particularly interesting – and I can't see that it's going to be of much help to us. I think we'd better leave it for another time. This evening perhaps, after dinner, we'll go through it carefully. But, Milton, tell me, what do you think of this thing? Can you suggest any explanation?"

"I'm afraid I'm just as baffled as you, sir. I've never heard of anything like it. I know there are such things as *Poltergeists*, but from what I can gather, such phenomena generally occur in a haphazard and unpredictable fashion. Bricks and vases sail around a room, furniture gets shifted about, live coals spring out of fireplaces, bells ring in churches – all without seeming rational cause. But this affair of a flute is something new – and it seems so deliberate and studied."

"Just what struck me," nodded Mr. Nevinson. "I've read of *Poltergeists* myself, but this thing doesn't seem to fit in with *Poltergeist* phenomena. And another thing, why should merely touching this parchment cause a manifestation of the kind Jessie and I are experiencing?"

"Well, as for that," I said, "I did read somewhere that physical objects can retain a sort of psychic effluvium. Not much is known about it, of course, and it's all guesswork, but there is a theory that buildings in which people have died under violent circumstances and under great emotional stress can retain certain psychic vibrations. A kind of etheric magnetic field, so to speak, exists around the locale, and when conditions are right manifestations occur which may be sensed by anyone who happens to be on the spot. In other words, let us suppose that this Dutchman had left some strongly psychic emanation of his personality – some etheric magnetic effluvium – within the fibres of this manuscript. Isn't it possible that touching it could bring you into tune with the psychic stuff and so produce this manifestation of flute music? When we think of it, an exposed wire with electric current in it looks a harmless thing, but touch it and the result can be sensational. We can't *see* the current in it, but it's there. Similarly, we can't *see* the psychic force in this manuscript, but that is not to say that it might not be only too real."

Mr. Nevinson smiled and wagged his head slightly. "Sounds a pretty hare-brained theory, my boy, but – well, I'm in a position now where I'm ready to believe anything. Just anything."

We were silent for a moment, and I was on the point of asking him a question when Mrs. Nevinson appeared at the door of the dining-saloon. She stood there, heaved a great theatrical sigh, clicked her tongue softly and regarded us with an expression of indulgent long-suffering.

Her husband glanced at her with a frown.

"Just look at the two of them! Just look at them!" She sighed again.

I could see that Mr. Nevinson resented her intrusion. Normally his attitude towards her is one of affectionate tolerance. I had long ago discovered that while he did not share her passionate love of company and her craving for the more harmless pleasures of the world – for he is of the ascetic, self-contained type – he never censured her for being what she was, but merely let her go her way while he went his own. This policy, I knew, did not always work successfully – there were sometimes long periods of coldness between them – but, on the whole, they were a sensible couple and seemed to have learnt how to avoid major disasters affecting their relationships. I had no fear about their ever separating or finding themselves in the divorce court.

"What is it, Nell? What is it?" asked Mr. Nevinson testily.

"Mr. Lumsden and Mrs. Lumsden are getting ready to go ashore, Ralph. Don't you think it would be polite to see them off?"

"Are we at Brave Lands already?"

"Look outside and you'll see for yourself. Haven't you noticed that the steamer has slowed down?"

"Ah, well, I suppose I must be courteous. Very well, I'll be along."

She uttered another of her magnificent sighs and went off, and Mr. Nevinson looked at me and smiled. "It looks as if we'll have to adjourn until another convenient occasion, Milton." He rose slowly – and then uttered a soft exclamation and stared at me, consternation and slight annoyance in his manner.

For, deliberately and before he could anticipate my intention, I had stretched out my hand and laid it on the manuscript.

4

No doubt it has happened to other people, too, and is, therefore, nothing new, but, nevertheless, it is an interesting fact that many a time I have known myself to sit and watch trees and buildings and traffic, and found myself, for no reason that I could explain, abruptly engulfed in a whirl of illusion: a kind of vacuum of ephemerality; an air-pocket in my consciousness which, while I knew it would not last more than a brief space, was, at the same time, disturbing. Disturbing because it tended to upset the values I have painfully established concerning what is real and what is not.

Call it a mystical experience if you will, but whatever it may be, the fact remains that in such moments I am aware – or, at least, tell myself that I am aware – of a shadow-voice which assures me that there is no substance in the scene I am beholding, that everything I discern is simply a grand imposture thrust upon me through the artifices of my functioning nervous system. The buildings I am looking at, I would be made to feel, are composed of matter subject to corrosion and, therefore, insecure, not to be trusted; at any instant they may disintegrate in a cloud of dust. The traffic is merely metal marshalled into form and order and set into motion; in an instant, perhaps, it will oxidize softly into fine brown rust and be washed away as so much silt. And the trees – the trees are shedding their leaves, and, like the humans hurrying by under them, are in a state of perpetual chemical flux; the cells of which they are composed in seething billions are breaking down with the passage of every second; complete extinction is a mere matter of accumulated seconds and minutes. In short, everything – all the mobility, all the aliveness, all the pregnant vigour, of this array of symbols that shimmers in my awareness – is, in reality, death.

Death in the guise of movement and sunshine, death in the guise of green leaves and a pattern of sounds, death in the guise of human figures loving and fearing and fretting over the making of money.

Such moods are always accompanied by a sense of depression and emptiness, a speculation as to the ultimate value of present action, a questioning of the worthwhileness of continued existence, and this stage would invariably be followed by one in which, as though imbued with a fumbling hope, I would begin to make an examination of the palpable stuff of life – that is, palpable inasmuch as my illusory condition permitted me to admit of the palpability of matter. I would ponder the evident solidity of my body – the feeling of weight in relation to the floor or the chair in which I was sitting, the tendency of an arm or a leg to droop when relaxed suddenly; pressure, stress and strain; and, finally, the persistent throbbing activity of the heart and pulses. This last factor would always prove most encouraging – the sound of a beating heart is, to me, something remarkably brave and inspiring – and with a little quiver of joy and relief I would let myself grow aware of the cool indifference of the breeze blowing past my cheeks. And perhaps the distant crowing of a cock or the barking of a dog would create a twinge of banality which would make me appear to myself a figure of some absurdity, and, with a brief, silent guffaw, I would view the whole vitalizing flood of actuality rush through me again, and the forces that had entrammelled me only a moment before would melt away and leave me once more a rational, struggling human engaged in the everyday occupation of being alive.

Often during the rest of that trip to Goed de Vries I found myself inclined to lapse into these what I can only describe as half-world states. But I would not allow myself to yield to them, because I was determined that when my turn came to hear this spectral flute – if it ever did come – I must be a harshly rational individual, sensible only to what my five known and accepted faculties were capable of discerning in the scene about us. There must be no ambiguity whatever. There must be no question of my being doubtful as to whether the phenomena were illusory or actual. I must be certain that my ears were behaving as they always behaved.

For my precipitate action in touching the manuscript Mr. Nevinson did not scold me. After his first annoyance and surprise had passed, he simply shrugged and murmured that it was my lookout. Then he smiled and added: "I suppose I should have anticipated it, knowing you as I do. After hearing such a fantastic tale, you couldn't very well be expected not to want to experience the 'magic' for yourself, eh? Well, I hope you won't live to regret it, my boy. You can't say I didn't warn you and do my best to avoid your coming into contact with this document."

"If I am to be of any help to you, sir," I rejoined, "don't you think the best way of getting myself into a serviceable condition is to inoculate myself without delay, as I've done?"

That word remained with me until we reached Goed de Vries, for that was how I felt – as though I had been inoculated with the bacteria of some strange but exciting disease and was waiting now for the symptoms to appear. I found myself possessed of that cheerfulness which anticipation of the unknown sometimes produces.

We reached Goed de Vries at twenty minutes to six. The sun was low over the jungle on the right-hand bank, and its soft reddish light gave to the cluster of wooden buildings that stood in a clearing on the left-hand bank an air of ingenuous peace and reflectiveness. There was the sawmill with its thin black chimney – the day's work seemed to be over, for it was still and dreamily idle – and in its vicinity along the bank the clustered rafts of crude timber which extended right down to the water's edge. A group of seven or eight logies with trash roofs, evidently the abode of the sawmill labourers, stood some distance to the left; that is to say, in a downstream direction. The residence, a one-storied cottage raised on tall pillars, was situated about a hundred yards above the sawmill, and had a detached, aloof, even snobbish, look.

I found myself smiling as I tried to imagine what Goed de Vries must have looked like two centuries ago when it was a flourishing sugar or coffee plantation under the Dutch. All that jungle that loomed beyond the clearing must have been cultivated terrain. Apart from the large plantation house, there must have been rows and rows of logies for the accommodation of the slaves, a sugar-mill or coffee-lodge, two or three cottages for the use, respectively, of the overseer and his assistant, the carpenter and a surgeon, as he was called in those days. Perhaps at this very hour a bell would be clanging stridently or a horn cooing to call in the gangs from the fields – or, if they had already come in, to summon them to evening repast under the soughing branches of a sandbox tree; or for the day's punishments which the overseer or his assistant had to superintend. This same reddish sunshine must have shone on many a naked black body secured in the stocks, and the casual overseer, puffing at his long, thin-stemmed pipe, must have stood and watched these bodies on many a day turn a richer red than even sunshine can distil...

I noticed a solitary figure standing on the pier, which was situated about fifty yards above the section of bank where the rafts lay. Jessie, who was standing at the rail with her mother and myself, exclaimed: "There's Rayburn! I wonder where's Timmykins."

On inquiry I discovered that Timmykins was the Indian cook. His name was Timothy, but Jessie said she always called him Timmykins because "he has such a chubby little face. He's the sweetest Buck boy I've ever seen!" Her mother confirmed this, adding that Timmy was a very good cook and that she had often thought of stealing him and keeping him when he and Rayburn went down to town as they sometimes did.

It was not long, however, before Timmykins and several others were on the pier to meet the steamer as it drew alongside, for the weekly steamer is, of course, an event in these parts. Parcels and crates and letters for the labourers had to be discharged before the vessel could resume its trip to Paradise.

Rayburn, a slim, alert-looking negro of about forty, smiled and raised his felt hat respectfully at us, and behind him, like a dwarfed sprite, Timmykins also automatically raised his.

Just as I had expected, the cottage proved to be a most well-fitted and comfortable place. The walls were painted a pale green in the sitting-room, and a pale blue in the dining-room, and the furniture was modern and well kept – Rayburn was evidently no slacker – and there was a mauve bedroom and a pink one and a buff one. The veranda went right round the house, and Jessie and I, with a kind of childish enthusiasm, went round "testing out the deck-chairs", as Jessie put it. She chose one, and said that if she found anybody in it he or she would be promptly hoofed out. "And I hope *you're* hearing me, Milton!" It appeared that this was her second visit to Goed de Vries; the first visit was in June three years before, when her father had nearly made Fred and herself faint with astonishment by asking them to come up with him.

I was glad to see that she seemed to have dismissed the incident on the steamer from her thoughts, and I purposely did my best to keep the conversation from straying back to it, for her father and I had agreed not to tell her anything about the manuscript nor of our suspicions concerning the spectral music of this flute which was proving so difficult to explain away.

The bedroom allotted to me was one of two which adjoined each other on the southern side of the house. It was a buff one. Mr. Nevinson – his wife informed me – could have the other, the pink one. "Jessie and I will have the big northern room," she went on. "Ralph likes that one, I know, but he'll have to do without it this time. Serve him right for asking Jessie and me as well as you to come up here with him!"

"I thought," I returned, "you would have preferred to discourage him from being too close to me. Aren't you afraid of our locking our doors and getting so immersed in old books and papers we might even forget our meals? There's a connecting door, you know."

She raised her arms and tilted her head, her gaze on the rafters. "Milton, I beseech you. *Please* don't encourage him to become engrossed in old books! Already as it is, I see he's brought up a whole suitcase of books." She sighed with the air of a martyr and went hurrying off toward the kitchen, exclaiming: "Oh, my God! That meat! I've just remembered! I wonder if Timmy has put it in the fridge!"

A low regular spluttering broke out downstream, and for an instant I thought it was an approaching motorboat, when I realized that it must be the Petter generating plant Mr. Nevinson had told me about, because I saw a bulb glow in the pantry. Somehow it had slipped me for the moment to wonder about light, and the sight of that bulb coming into life gave me a sense of comfort and reassurance, for there is nothing I detest more than a house lit only by lamps or candles. I dread spiders, and lamplight or candlelight has always seemed to me an ally of these repulsive creatures.

After Jessie and I had explored the house thoroughly, I left her and went out to join Mr. Nevinson and Rayburn. I saw them in the now deep twilight, standing at the foot of the front steps in casual conversation. Mr. Nevinson was smoking a pipe and there seemed no figure of greater contentment to be found anywhere. Not by the slightest gesture of a hand nor the lift of an eyebrow did he betray that something was troubling him. He smiled at me as I came up.

"Rayburn, this is the gentleman I was telling you about who paints pictures – Mr. Milton Woodsley."

"Very pleased to meet you, sir!" Rayburn exclaimed, with a wide, very deferential smile – and I fear I embarrassed him considerably by extending my hand. He took it, shook it briefly and released it as though it were a chunk of hot metal – and this despite the firmness of my own grip. Naturally, he could not know that I was accustomed to shaking the hands of such people as porters and stevedores and other 'low-class persons'; he must have expected from me just the cool, patronizing smile and nod of a middle-class young man.

After we had chatted casually for a few minutes, Mr. Nevinson knocked out his pipe against the heel of his shoe, and in the most nonchalant voice possible, said: "By the way, Rayburn, you remember that little canister you left in my room when I was here last month? Who was it that actually handed it to you to give to me? Was it Patoir's woman herself?"

"Yes, sir. Matilda – she give it to me herself. She hand it to me and say de old man promise it to you when he dead and Ah must take it and give you."

"Matilda, eh? I didn't know that was her name. Is she still at Horstenland in Patoir's cottage, or has she gone to live with her own relatives now?"

"Well, no, sir. Matter of fact, she dead. Day before yesterday, she get drowned in de river near de cottage where she and de old man used to live."

"Drowned? How did it happen? I thought all these Bucks were good swimmers."

"Sir, I don't know really how it happen meself. Ah been hearing some stupid story. Dese river-people too superstitious, sir. I glad I come from town. If you born and grow up on dis river you must get stupid and superstitious."

"You find superstitious people in town, too, Rayburn – don't fool yourself. But what was this stupid story you heard?"

Rayburn chuckled. "Sir, people saying Matilda dead because a spirit haunt her after Patoir dead. They say she didn't treat de old man good when he was alive, and as soon as his eyes close in death he begin to haunt her. They say his spirit haunt her till she dead."

"I see. And what form did this haunting take?"

Rayburn shifted about his feet in a self-conscious manner, as though he felt that he had made himself ridiculous enough as it was by repeating such a tale. He said: "Sir, it's just a lot of nonsense. I didn't worry to pay too much attention to it. Ah hear dem saying dat Matilda used to hear some kind of music near her cottage. She tell people she hear a flute playing but yet she couldn't see nobody playing it. She was out of her head, sir!" laughed Rayburn. " Every day she say de flute get closer and closer to her till just de day before she dead she cry out and say she see a white man dancing before her. And her sister who was staying wid her say Matilda tremble all over and swear de spirit call out to her in a soft voice and tell her to follow him and join him in de grave. Dat was how she get drowned, sir. She follow de spirit into de river and get drowned." Rayburn laughed again. "De woman was clean out of her mind, sir. Dat's what was wrong wid her!"

5

Candle-flies abound on the coast of Guiana. They are fragile, unhurried little creatures the size and weight of the old three-penny pieces, and will serenely crawl over your wrist or sleeve, glowing at brief intervals. On a dark night you can see them like soft sparks amid the foliage of shrubs and even very tall trees, for they fly high sometimes. Or you may be lying sleepless in bed, and at your window a green-white eye will suddenly glow into being and vanish in silent mystery. Sometimes among the rafters one of them will appear as a fluffy bleb darting swiftly from beam to beam or in a downward arc, green and deadly still, so that you have the inclination to bury your face in your pillow as though to avoid some intangible menace.

In the interior, however, there are no candle-flies. At least, I encountered none. But of fire-flies there are a plenty. These are about an inch in length, with bodies roughly cylindrical in shape. Candle-flies glow on their underbellies, but with fire-flies it is different. I know it will sound incredible to people who have never seen one at close quarters, but, nevertheless, it is a fact, and you can always verify it by taking a trip up the Berbice River. Fire-flies are equipped with two brilliant bluish-white headlights and a reddish tail-light. Yes, it is no joke; it is actually so. I have examined them too many times not to know.

Standing at my bedroom window on this first night at Goed de Vries, I caught one as it emerged out of the dark and alighted with ghostly silence on the windowsill. Holding it between thumb and forefinger, I observed it with fascination. The tail-light glowed only at intervals, but the twin lights in front never went out. They would be bright now, now dim, now bright again, evidently as the creature's mood varied. Once they did fool me that they were about to go out when, with alarming abruptness, they came alive – and came alive with such a shock of brilliance that instinctively I had the inclination to release the creature for fear of being burnt.

The two windows of my room looked out upon the southern or, if you will, upstream section of the clearing, which meant that only jungle and river met my gaze as I stood here staring out. The northern bedroom on the other side of the cottage, which Mrs. Nevinson and Jessie were occupying, commanded a view of the downstream section where the sawmill and the labourers' logies stood.

The air was heavy with water-vapour – and the scent of vegetation and river water: a musty, sweetish rankness that at one instant would seem very refreshing and make you want to breathe deeply, then would suddenly awaken your distrust, for there would seem to enter it an earthy dankness as of centuries of rotting leaves and the bones of long-buried corpses.

The insects whirred and hummed in a deep background chorus to which the senses very easily grew accustomed because it was such a monotonous bourdon. Occasionally a frog would chirp somewhere in the jet darkness and then grow still, never to be heard again, almost leaving the impression that some hand had deliberately stifled it.

But what held me most of all were the fire-flies. Against the unbroken black of the jungle and over the surface of the slug-gishly flowing river, in which the stars could be seen reflected, the fire-flies made a perpetual display. It was a dance, wavering, untiring, silent. Aimless flecks of glowing down, they hovered and dived and rose and crisscrossed, futile and unmeaning. Pigmy lanterns weaving pencils of light in the moist gloom. When I watched them too intently I found that their effect on me began to be mesmeric. I seemed to see them coming at me and then receding, coming and receding… And once in coming they seemed to multiply into thousands and millions of cool, intense points, and a feeling cloaked down upon me that there was a quality about them furry and wicked, frosty, as though they might be things from a region of polar lights, and might themselves be segments of an icy peril that would probe into the human frame with a numbing rigour. I just had to stand watching them, engrossed, until I smiled and shook off the spell. Though even when actuality invaded me again I had to shudder slightly and warn myself not to get too wrapped up in dreams and white specks of light.

The river made a soft sucking at the shrubs that bordered the bank – a secretive sibilance that, somehow, seemed even more remote and lost than the whirr and hum of the insects. When I did bring myself to an awareness of it, I felt startled, imagining it to be the hiss of a snake or a rustling of light garments. Almost at once I did feel certain I could hear someone moving in the darkness out there – someone arrayed in silk. Perhaps some ethereal gossamer. I stiffened and peered frowningly into the dense blackness.

Then there was a sound in the room behind me, and I started round and saw the dim pyjama-clad figure of Mr. Nevinson appear in the doorway that connected our two rooms. With a quake of relief I realized that it must have been the sounds of his limbs in contact with the silk of his pyjamas that I had heard. I told him about it and he grunted and said yes, he had just changed into his pyjamas. Why hadn't I got into mine yet?

"I was watching the fire-flies," I returned.

"Yes, I like looking at them myself," he said, and in the starlight that flooded in upon us through the window I saw him smile.

It was late – very near eleven. The whole house was in darkness, for the Petter plant had been stopped at ten o'clock, there being no necessity for it to go on to a later hour. The fresh meat we had brought up had been cooked and the refrigerator did not contain anything of a perishable nature.

After listening-in to radio music in the sitting-room for about an hour after dinner, Mrs. Nevinson and Jessie had retired, and soon after that Mr. Nevinson had called down to Rayburn – Rayburn's room was just beneath the sitting-room, being the only room built right down to the ground – and told him to have the Petter plant switched off for the night.

Leaning out of that window smoking cigarettes, Mr. Nevinson and I talked for a long while – perhaps until after midnight. We agreed that, from what Rayburn had told us earlier that evening, it appeared that Patoir's woman, Matilda, must also have fallen a victim to the spell of the manuscript.

"It's perfectly natural, of course," Mr. Nevinson said, "that she should have been curious to see what was inside this canister. Very likely she never believed the tale about there being a superstition attached to it. More likely she must have assumed it was a blind of Patoir's to discourage her from opening the canister. She must have thought he used to hoard money in it, and when he died the first thing she did was to satisfy herself on the point."

"Yes, I can see that, sir," I said, "but what I want to know is this. What plan of action have you got in mind? I mean, I take it you don't intend to let's sit idle and allow events to take their course?"

"Far from that, my boy. You can be sure I came up here with fighting intentions. I'm not going to resign myself to this mystery so tamely. I mean to settle it some way or the other. The obvious thing is to find these bones and the flute referred to in the manuscript and then see what happens. That's where the snag comes in, of course. I have no idea of the whereabouts of this plantation the writer speaks of. I searched eagerly at Colony House, but the records there proved blank. Couldn't find any name like Voorman as the proprietor of a plantation around the time of the Rebellion. Not surprising really, though. As you know, the records contain strange gaps. The Government Archivist once told me that the eighteenth century is his greatest despair so far as records go. Scanty, patchy. Many valuable documents have been lost – especially documents relating to the period around 1763, but then that Rebellion itself might have been responsible. Hoogenheim, the Dutch governor, burnt practically all the documents at Fort Nassau before spiking his guns and retreating down-river."

After a silence he said: "Anyway, tomorrow we'll visit Patoir's cottage and have a look around. Then we'll have a chat with Matilda's sister. She may be able to tell us something helpful. Another thing is to try to trace who this Indian fellow could be who made a present of that canister to Patoir. If we could find him he might be able to tell us where he, in turn, got it from. That is, if he's alive," he added with, I thought, a significant note of grimness.

From the river came a bubbling, as though a palm-berry had fallen into the water. Or it might have been a fish. When the sound died away the silence fanned down upon us once more, heavy and charged with that waiting quality characteristic of the jungle in these parts. There was no wind. The air seemed to hang like dissolved curtains in space. The river lurked like a sullen enemy which at any instant might send black, sluggish tentacles groping towards us through the dark. From upstream there came a low gruff barking, and I found myself stiffening, for I knew that no dog could utter such a sound; it was too powerful and harsh.

"Baboons," Mr. Nevinson murmured. "This is your first trip into the jungle, that's why they sound to you so impressive. Well, I think it's time for bed."

I agreed with him, though, for some reason, we neither of us made a move. We continued to lean out of the window.

There was real fascination in the night. A dense aliveness and intelligence – a watching calm. The jungle, silhouetted like a ragged lace-edge against the starry sky, held an indigo smile in its wet depths, and the occasional chirp of a frog concealed a chuckle that might mean anything. The river's soft sibilance now and then took on a derisive quality. From out of its secretive gloom it seemed deliberately to breathe up into our faces a humid vegetable miasma expressive of its deep antagonism towards us. The fire-flies, engaged all the while in their deadly silent dance, heightened the vigilant aspect of the dark, as though within the core of their cool incandescence they knew the meaning of this night – the hidden motive behind the jungle's smile, the message the frog kept chirping at intervals, the reason for the river's sly animosity.

The barking of the baboons ceased as abruptly as it had begun. The insect-chorus wove a net around us. Then the shrubs at the edge of the bank rustled sharply, and after the rustle had faded, the silence swooped back into place, swaying and moist once more, scented with the musty old-leaf scent of the centuries. I had the sensation of being able to see and hear and touch the essence of the scene – the night itself, the intimate spirit of trees and water. The insect-humming whirled, spiralled, made a purple spinning...

I jerked my head aside, aware that a tenseness had come into Mr. Nevinson's manner. I heard him utter a murmured exclamation.

"What's it, sir?"

He withdrew from the window and looked round slowly without replying.

In this instant my trance of introspection vanished. I knew it was actually happening. I stood and listened. There could be no doubt. It had nothing of the imaginary about it. It was a flute, clear, leisurely, distant. A tuneless, wandering trickle of treble notes coming from out of the trees that stood so still in the night.

6

I remember that my awareness became focused on the furniture in the room – the starlit outlines of the dressing-table, the bed and the washstand, the easy chair – and that the irrelevant, banal thought came into my mind that I had forgotten to unpack my shaving things. I remember, too, that a firefly strayed in at the other window, glowed on the wall near the dressing-table, then returned into the darkness outside like a blue-white neon arc. These things I noted in my diary because they constituted, so to speak, the symbol of the first occasion of my hearing the flute, but they are registered in my memory as well, so that without reference to my diary I would have been able to record them here.

What happened in the minutes that followed this instant I remember with less intensity. The aura of the sequential surrounds it, and, to me, in chronicling it, it holds no glamour save that of commonplace reportage.

I said: "It was no fairytale, sir. You were right. I can hear it."

Mr. Nevinson made no reply.

From the northern bedroom I heard a stirring, then Jessie called out: "Daddy! Are you awake? Are you hearing it?"

The bed creaked and her foot thumped on the floor. Her father did not make any response, and she called out again: "Daddy! Wake up! It's the flute again! Milton! Are you awake? The flute is playing in the sitting-room!"

Her mother made a mumbling sound of irritation and I heard her exclaim: "Jessie! What's the matter? Have you got out of bed?"

I felt Mr. Nevinson's hand on my arm. "Come into the sitting-room," he said in a low, urgent voice, and I followed him into the sitting-room.

Outside, the flute still sent its notes through the night. Somehow, it did not alarm me in the slightest. It had such a harmless, even idyllic, air about it. In no way did it seem to me phantasmal or weird.

Mr. Nevinson collided with a chair and murmured something about matches, and at this very instant the scrape of a match came from the northern room, and light gleamed ruddily at the latticework at the top of the wall. In usual tropical fashion, the rooms were not sealed in; the walls were more in the nature of tall screens.

Mrs. Nevinson's voice was evident all the while scolding Jessie.

"Have you had a nightmare, child? Where are you going to? What are you lighting the lamp for? Jessie, what's wrong?"

Jessie was protesting: "But can't you hear it, Mother? It's in the sitting-room – now, at this very minute. Don't be silly. Somebody is playing a flute in the sitting-room. I'm not imagining it."

"Oh, stop being absurd. What flute? There's no flute being played in this house. You ate too heartily at dinner. Get back into bed."

Jessie called again: "Daddy! Are you awake yet?"

"Yes, Jessie! I'm in the sitting-room. Come. Bring the lamp. Hurry."

Jessie appeared. The northern bedroom opened directly into the sitting-room. Her face looked scared. She had thrown on a dressing-gown over her pyjamas. The lamp in her hand lit up the room with a yellowish uncertainty, and the girl's shadow loomed large and grotesque on the door behind her, part of her tousled head merged in a fantastic pattern with the latticework along the top of the wall.

"Daddy, aren't you hearing it? It's there. Just over there – near the chesterfield. But it's funny. There's nothing. Not a soul. I don't see anybody."

"Very well, my girl. Don't get too excited. You're not the only one hearing it." Her father spoke with a calmness that surprised me. He looked very pale, and every now and then, I noticed, he would glance over his shoulder in an alert, searching manner.

His wife appeared, struggling into a dressing-gown.

"Ralph! What ridiculous nonsense is this? Do you know it's after midnight? What's gone wrong with all of you?"

"Mother, you really don't hear it?" Jessie spoke in a tone that was almost pleading. In this moment the weakness of her character showed up sharply. There was in her poise a fragility and a baffled helplessness that touched me and brought out the male protectiveness in me. She pointed. "Look! It's shifted over there now! It's coming from that corner there near the table!" She clutched her mother's arm. " But what's happening in this house tonight?"

"You're trembling," said Mrs. Nevinson. "But what on earth is this?" She glanced across at her husband, her consternation a little comical. She had recovered from the shock and irritation of being roused from her sleep, and her keen sense of humour was beginning to function. Some of the dramatic was returning to her manner. She looked from her husband to me with a half-smile. "Milton, are you hearing this mysterious flute, too? You all stand there like statues!"

"Yes, there is a flute," I told her, trying to smile. "But it sounds outside the house to me. Somewhere downstream now. At first it was upstream."

She wagged her head in a kind of patronizing exasperation. "Well, I don't know, but either I must be stone deaf or the three of you are quite, quite out of your minds. I can't hear a single note."

I felt my arm squeezed, and turning my head, I saw Mr. Nevinson's face. He stood close to me, and his grip on my arm was vicelike; it hurt. He was staring over his shoulder towards the door that opened on to the front veranda, and there was something unnatural in the way he focused his gaze. I seemed to have the impression that he was not actually staring at the door so much as he was observing something to the right of the door – something that was visible in the corner of his eye.

All at once I realized that the sound of the flute had stopped.

Jessie gasped: "It's gone now!" She kept peering round the room, her eyes frightened behind the lamp which she was still holding.

Her father, however, had not moved a muscle. He remained

silent, his head still turned, that fixed, watching glitter still in his eyes. His grip on my arm was now so tight that I had difficulty in repressing a groan.

His wife gave him an alarmed look and approached. "Ralph! What's the matter? What are you staring at like that? Is there something at the door?"

"Get away, Nell. Go back to your room." His voice came in a growl, and he spoke without altering his gaze. The tips of his fingers dug so hard into my arm that in my fancy I could see the blood frothing in anguish to circulate.

Mrs. Nevinson stood her ground, frowning puzzledly at him. "Really, this is most peculiar," she murmured.

Suddenly, and to my profound relief, her husband's grip on my arm relaxed. I could sense the deep breath that went through him. "Nell, I asked you to return to your room, didn't I?" He spoke irritably. "Please do so at once. Jessie, go back to bed, too."

"Ralph, what do you mean? Don't you think you owe me some explanation for this peculiar behaviour?" There was a hurt note in Mrs. Nevinson's voice.

At another time Mr. Nevinson would have been immediately repentant, but he was too deeply upset now to be himself. He returned: "Yes, I know. I admit that – but I'm still asking you to go to your room. Tomorrow we'll discuss everything. Allow me to judge the wisdom of postponing all explanations until tomorrow."

Firmly as he spoke, however, Mrs. Nevinson would not yield to this ruling. She is a lady of much fire and not to be easily put off. "But what's the mystery about?" she said. "Am I to understand that this cottage is haunted? Surely you can't expect me to go back to bed with the knowledge that there's something wrong in the place. It's unreasonable of you."

Jessie added with a rather wild note: "Yes, Daddy, you've got to tell us. I'm not remaining in this house another night if there's something queer in it. I'll pack my things and go back to town by the steamer in the morning."

Her father smiled. His calm amazed me. "You and your mother are such an excitable pair! Just try to think before you make wild suggestions, please. Is this the first time you've heard that flute? Didn't you hear it today on the steamer? And also for the past week or two at home in New Amsterdam? Then why should you want to run out of this cottage and go back to town? Do you think that will help the situation?"

"But what's causing it, then? Who's playing it? It woke me – and I'm sure it was in this very room – and yet I couldn't see anyone playing it. I'm frightened. I don't like this thing at all."

"Very well, very well. I myself am alarmed, but I'm trying to keep my wits about me. You do the same. Milton, too, has heard it, and I don't hear him raving."

He glanced at me. "You heard it, didn't you, Milton? Distantly, I suppose?"

"Yes, it came from upstream at first – then from downstream."

"But how can that be, Daddy? If it was the same flute playing, how could Milton have heard it far off while you and I heard it in here?"

Mrs. Nevinson, who had been glancing in complete perplexity from one to the other of us, broke out: "Really, this is getting beyond me! What *are* you talking about? What flute-playing is this? Jessie, do you seriously mean to say you heard a flute being played in this house a few minutes ago? In this sitting-room here?"

"Of course, Mother. As plainly as I can hear you speaking. It's the same flute I've been hearing at home for days now. And remember I told you I heard it today on the steamer?"

Her father held up his hand. "Very well. I can see it's no use. We'll have to thresh the matter out on the spot. Put that lamp on the table there, Jessie, and both you and your mother sit down."

"Ralph, you seem to be taking this affair very casually. If there's any truth in what you say about this flute, then the place must be haunted – or at least, the three of you must be haunted." She could not repress a splutter of mirth.

Her husband smiled. "If nothing else, we ought to be thankful for your sense of humour, Nell. Come along. Get seated. Milton, take this chair."

That was one of the oddest scenes in my experience. The lamp, standing where Jessie had placed it on the low, green-topped table with chromium legs, cast its yellow rays on our faces with a sickly uncertainty as we crouched forward in our chairs, seated in a circle like people round a campfire or a séance table. A stack of old magazines – *The Strand* and *Pearson's* and *The Connoisseur* – lay on the table beside the lamp, and their combined shadows made a frayed rhombus on the front of Mr. Nevinson's pyjama jacket.

While Mr. Nevinson explained to his wife and Jessie his theory about the manuscript and its connection with this spectral flute I kept glancing behind me often, noting our own shadows on the walls, huge and misshapen. I shuddered now and then, but not through fear of ghosts. It was of spiders I kept thinking. Several times I could have sworn I saw a swift scrawl of brown legs dart from one crooked shadow to another.

Once Jessie started and uttered a gasp, and I saw her looking intently towards the door that gave on to the western veranda. We all turned our heads to follow her gaze, but she giggled and said that it was only a fire-fly. "It flashed on so suddenly it made me jump." She drew her gown more closely about her, and at that instant we heard outside in the jungle the harsh, gruff bark of the baboons, and the scent of dark water and vegetation swirled into the room as though some unseen presence had breathed it in at the open windows.

Somehow, there was a silence, and we began to look about us, listening to the sucking murmur of the river. The very lamp on the table had an expectant air.

Mr. Nevinson laughed softly and said: "We're letting ourselves in for the jitters now," and resumed what he had been saying to his wife and daughter.

Mrs. Nevinson, as I had expected, was incredulous and inclined to be outright derisive. She pronounced the whole tale to be absolutely absurd. "It isn't feasible, Ralph! Who do you expect to believe a thing like that! How could a mere silly slip of paper cause you to hear a ghostly flute! It's childish. And where's this manuscript? Why don't you let me touch it, too, and see if I can hear it?"

Her husband shook his head. "I'm sorry. Not another mortal will lay his hand upon it, if I can help it."

His wife laughed, throwing her head far back and stamping on the floor like a small girl. "Oh, but, Ralph my dear! You speak so gravely. What's come over you? Since when have you turned as superstitious as this? And you, too, Milton? A learned philosopher like you believing in such nonsense! I'm ashamed of you!"

"But, Mrs. Nevvy, you seem to forget the evidence – "

"Oh, blow the evidence! I'm sure there must be some natural explanation, boy. Somebody is trying to hoax you, can't you see?"

Mr. Nevinson did not attempt to argue. He rose. "Very well, my dear. I'm sure you're at liberty to hold whatever views you wish. In fact, I don't blame – "

He broke off. There was a knock at the kitchen door. Jessie started.

"Who the devil can that be now?"

"It must be Rayburn. That scream of laughter Mother gave must have disturbed him. She stamped on the floor, too."

I hurried out into the pantry, Mr. Nevinson after me.

The kitchen was in utter darkness, but I managed to grope my way to the door. Jessie's conjecture proved correct. It was Rayburn. He wanted to know if we needed anything. He had heard a stamp on the floor and voices. "Ah think it must be a tarantula or a centipede, sir."

Mr. Nevinson smiled and told him: "No, Rayburn, nothing so bad, I'm glad to report. It was simply a little domestic matter we were discussing. Sorry we disturbed you."

"Oh, no, no, sir. It's awright, sir. Any time you need me just knock on de floor and call me up – any time of de night. I killed one or two tarantulas in de house here last week, sir. Dat's why I come up to ask."

"One or two!" I exclaimed. "Good Lord! You don't mean they appear in numbers every week?"

"Oh, well, sir, you got to watch out for dem. We up in de bush, you know. You can't stop dese insects from crawling in de house."

"Thank goodness we sleep under nets, anyway."

Mrs. Nevinson came swishing out and called: "Rayburn, did you hear this flute, too?"

"Flute, ma'am? What flute, ma'am?"

Light suddenly shone on his face, for Jessie had come, too, bringing the lamp.

Mr. Nevinson clicked his tongue and said: "Nell, is there any need to keep Rayburn from his bed? It must be nearly one o'clock."

Refusing, however, to take the hint and be tactfully silent, his wife insisted: "Rayburn, I asked you a question. Did you hear a flute since you got into bed tonight?"

"What kind of flute, ma'am?" asked Rayburn in surprise, smiling awkwardly.

"So you were one of those who didn't hear it?"

"No, ma'am. I didn't hear nothing like a flute."

"Has any of the men a flute, do you know, Rayburn?"

"No, ma'am. Charlie Barnes got a guitar, and Willy James does sometimes play a mouth-organ. But nobody ain' got a flute dat I know of, ma'am."

"Very well, Rayburn. Thank you. It's just a little argument we were having. Mr. Woodsley here thought he heard a flute being played in the darkness outside. He's a very imaginative gentleman, so we're not really surprised. Being an artist, you know." I felt her crushing my foot. "Well, good night, Rayburn. And don't forget to get that *cassareep* for me in the morning."

"Oh, no, ma'am! Ah won't forget dat, ma'am. Good night! Good night, sirs! Good night, Miss Jessie!"

As we returned into the sitting-room Mrs. Nevinson said: "Frankly, I don't know what to think. I admit it doesn't seem fair to call the three of you liars, but for the life of me I can't believe that just laying your hands on a musty old manuscript can produce a spooky flute-player. It sounds too much like the *Arabian Nights* for my liking." She glanced at her husband. "And, Ralph, you mean you won't let me try the experiment, too?"

"No."

"I suppose I can't force you. Jessie, let's go back to bed. Come on. And I do hope old Mynheer Voorman will have the consideration not to put on any more concerts before morning." She went off into gurgles, and Jessie frowned at her.

"Mother, you're still taking it as a joke. You don't seem to realize it's serious."

"You sound almost as solemn – and pompous – as your father and Milton."

Jessie suddenly started and looked at her father. "But wait!

Daddy, there's something you haven't told us. Why did you stand staring at the door after the flute had stopped? Was it anything you were seeing?"

Her father, occupied in filling his pipe, frowned. I could see that the question had taken him by surprise. He hesitated, and then replied: "I didn't consider it necessary to explain that. Naturally I was waiting to see if the thing would start playing again – the flute, I mean."

Mrs. Nevinson laughed and said: "You ought to have known that your father is a keen musician. He was probably looking forward to the second movement. Ralph, I'd suggest that the next time you hear it you jot down the score. I'm sure Sir Thomas Beecham would be interested."

Both Mr. Nevinson and I chuckled at this. Even Jessie giggled.

A few minutes later Mr. Nevinson accompanied me into my room. He asked me to light the lamp on the table beside my bed, and I complied at once. There was an air of suppressed excitement about him, and I sensed that he had something serious to tell me. I did not press matters, however, but tried to be as nonchalant as possible, for I was eager for him to continue in his opinion of me as a fellow who could keep his nerve in trying situations. Nothing would have desolated me more than his losing confidence in me.

I said casually: "By the way, sir, I didn't expect to hear anything tonight. It took me by complete surprise. Didn't you say it only makes itself heard once every day?"

"Approximately, but there's no set rule, my boy. Once I did hear it as we've done today – about noon and then again late at night."

"I see. And – eh – was it right beside you again tonight?"

He inclined his head, lighting his pipe.

I moved over to the window and drummed lightly with my fingers on the sill, frowning out at the fire-flies. From the northern room came mumbles – and a brief, shrill laugh. I smiled affectionately at the thought of Mrs. Nevinson's light-hearted scepticism; it was so like her.

A wisp of smoke from Mr. Nevinson's pipe curled past my cheek and drifted out into the night. My host joined me at the window, and after a brief silence of staring out at the darkness, said quietly: "Tonight has completed the overthrow of my former values, Milton. I've always been a thorough sceptic of the supernatural – but after tonight I would have to be insincere to myself if I continued to take up a scoffing attitude."

I made no comment, and he continued: "Jessie asked me why I was staring at the door after the flute stopped. She's a rather excitable girl, so I had to prevaricate. But you can take it from me, Milton, that I actually saw him."

"Saw him? Saw whom?"

" I have no idea 'who' it was, but I know without the slightest doubt that I saw a hazy human figure hovering near the veranda door – the front door. Just inside the room. I tried to look at it directly, but every time I did so it shifted into the corner of my eye. There was something indescribably evil about it."

He grunted and continued: "I'm no alarmist, Milton, but I have a strong feeling we're up against something horrible. In fact, I think I can understand how that Buck woman Matilda met her death."

"What do you mean, sir?"

He took his pipe from his mouth and said: "When I gripped your arm I did so because I had the most overpowering desire to follow that spectral figure outside into the darkness. I *had* to grip you. After a while it began to move. I saw it gradually shifting outside, and I wanted to follow it. Within those few seconds it became an obsession. It took all my will to resist. And it may sound a sensational thing to say, but I knew without doubt that it was calling me to my death."

7

In a final analysis it will be discovered that I am a person possessed of an innately morbid disposition, and I have no doubt that it is because of this, coupled with the circumstance that at the age of nineteen I succeeded in ridding my scheme of thought of all my former religious fears relating to the perils of the Hereafter, that the prospect of my own death does not terrify or even dismay me.

My grandmother has had a bit to do with my outlook on death. In her lifetime I was very fond of her in my own undemonstrative fashion. She was a lady with a generous heart and a rich imagination, though, unfortunately, this imagination had been misdirected; it had been given a fanatical religious bias, with the result that she had developed the ability to produce terror in small boys like myself with her vivid and convincing word-picture of what would happen to mankind on the Day of Judgment. This Day, she would assure me, could come, literally, at any moment – yes, even this very night when I was asleep. We would all be lying in our beds, she might tell me, wrapped in slumber and not suspecting the slightest unusual event, when of a sudden the Trumpet would sound Above, and, on awakening, we would behold the Blinding Glory of Heaven shining out of the sky. Night would become day, and angels would flock down upon the earth. And then – here she would bend toward me, her blue-grey eyes wide with a frenzied drama – of a sudden again, a mother, or a brother, or a sister, would vanish from our midst, and in that instant we would know that the Lord had lifted them into Heaven as His Chosen because, in this life, they had obeyed His Laws. Those of us who remained behind would look around us in fear and wonder. "Why", we would ask ourselves, "have we not gone with the others?" And then the Voice of an Angel would thunder forth, saying: "Ye that remain are the Unrighteous who will now be called upon to answer for your sins before being cast into Eternal Flames with Satan and his Black Angels!"

To a small boy, this was an awesome prospect to envisage, but, somehow, it failed to instil into me all the terror it was intended to, and this is because – I am fairly certain of it – the very fervour of my grandmother's religious sallies had, paradoxically, made me into an extremely priggish youngster who believed without the slightest doubt that when that Day arrived, he would, if only through his grandmother's saintly tutelage, be numbered among those of the Righteous who would vanish from the earthly scene to be herded comfortably in That Place of Milk and Honey High Above.

The psychological effect on me of these childhood influences has possibly contributed somewhat to my attitude towards annihilation in a general sense, and, taken together with much more powerful inherited tendencies, has resulted in my viewing death in a distinctly favourable light. There is a strong vein of cynicism in me which developed from an early age, and the longer I live and witness the foulness of mankind and the ineffectual blundering that smudges with defeat every human endeavour, the more I come to look upon death as an adventure which should offer a pleasant solution to my earthly fumblings.

With death in relation to other people, however, it is not the same. As though in compensation for this suicidal tendency, I contemplate the death of others with incredulity and horror and an unreasoning compassion. In the netherland of my ego-consciousness I simply cannot conceive of anyone whom I can sense as an active, vociferous human creature being reduced to a condition of silence and clammy rigidity. To reflect for even a minute on such an occurrence not only makes me shudder with horror and wag my head with perplexity, but depresses me and brings tears of compassion to my eyes.

This is the mood I had to resist when Mr. Nevinson and Jessie and I set out for Horstenland at half-past eight the following morning. From what had happened the night before and from what Rayburn had told us concerning the fate of the Indian woman, Matilda, I told, myself that I could not disregard the possibility of imminent death. But instead of letting my mood become extraverted, I willed my thoughts to concentrate on the idea of death in relation to myself only. Accordingly, here in the boat now, I felt in no way tense and awed. If anything, the very intangibility of the threat heightened my sense of pleasurable anticipation. For, at the best, I had never been able to visualize myself dying in any but a conventional fashion – perhaps in bed from some dull illness concomitant with senility, or from a street accident. In heroic moments, it is true, I have seen myself falling in battle with a bullet in my chest, but the glamour of this would invariably fade when I reflected upon the depressing fact that millions of men have died like this, hence where was the distinction in my being added to their number? Where the unique poetry in the event?

Jessie had asked to be allowed to accompany us, and her father had agreed without argument. I could see that she was eager to be in our company, and later in the day, as it happened, she did admit that she had no desire to find herself alone when the flute made itself heard again. "Mother only pokes fun at it – just because she can't hear it herself. If anything serious happened she wouldn't be of the slightest help to me." (Incidentally, Jessie was still in ignorance of Matilda's fate and of the possibility of our experiences ending fatally.)

Watching her now sitting beside me in the little craft as the outboard motor spluttered harshly and sent a trail of foam through the black water in our wake, I felt a distinct tenderness towards her. She looked so furtive and frightened despite the air of light-hearted indifference she tried to assume. Somehow, I could not despise her because of the ineffectual traits of character she revealed. And in any case, provided she is not a complete moron, a woman who is ineffectual rather appeals to me; something elemental in my make-up prefers that, in moments of crisis, the female should show signs of irresponsibility and be dependent on the male. Nothing annoys and repulses me more than a too capable and self-possessed woman.

The morning was pleasant as only a February morning in the interior of British Guiana can be. The dawn mists which had hovered in wreathing spills and tufts over the surface of the river had dispersed, leaving the air fresh and tingling with the aroma of jungle-blossoms and the vague musky dankness of water and rotted leaves. Seeds of the aeta palm drifted in the water, bobbing up and down, three-parts submerged, shiny and dark purple in the bright sunshine and looking like ornaments fit to be worn round a woman's neck. Close along the bank, under the mysterious shadows cast by the overhanging jungle, fallen mora blossoms, like yellow dust, floated on the tide, seeming not to move yet moving.

Horstenland, like Goed de Vries, the site of another long-abandoned Dutch plantation, consists of jungle interspersed with occasional homesteads – small *troolie*-thatched logies or *benabs* (the *troolie* is a palm whose dried fronds are used for thatching roofs), each standing lonely and isolated in a clearing cultivated with plantains and bananas, cassavas and eddoes and other food crops.

Like Jessie, Rayburn, who had come with us to handle the motor, was in ignorance of the real object of this excursion, for Mr. Nevinson was still reluctant to have the tale of our experiences spread around, and had cautioned both Jessie and myself not to discuss the affair within the hearing of anyone.

Patoir's cottage did not differ greatly in appearance from the others dotted at intervals along the bank at Horstenland. As Rayburn pointed the bow of the boat towards it, we saw a grey, unpainted wooden structure with the usual *troolie*-palm-leaf roof. It stood in a clearing that seemed larger than those of the other homesteads, and there were one or two coconut palms and a mango tree as well as provision patches. An Indian *corial* (pronounced kree-all) was drawn up against the bank, and a woman was shooing off chickens near the cottage. She was short and squat and attired in what looked like a cotton dress of faded blue. Her coffee complexion, high cheekbones and long black hair removed any doubt as to her race.

"Dat's de other Buck woman I tell you about, sir," said Rayburn. "She's Matilda's sister. She name' Adina, and Ah hear she bring her two children and living in de cottage here. Her husband gone higher up de river to bring down a raft of crabwood."

107

"He has, has he? He's in the timber business, too, then?"

"Oh, yes, sir! He sell us one or two rafts of mora only last week, but he don't go in for it too regular. He lil' lazy – and Ah hear he very fond of de bottle. Always on de spree."

The woman approached the edge of the bank as we drew alongside, her face sheepishly smiling and curious. We could hear the voices of her two children but could not see them. They seemed to be playing in the rear of the cottage.

I had brought my sketching book and pencil, for the reason we had given Rayburn for our coming was that I wanted to make a few sketches preliminary to painting my pictures for the company. Mr. Nevinson had added, too, as a secondary pretext, that he wanted "to have a look over old Patoir's cottage and sympathize with the sister of the dead woman."

No sooner had we jumped ashore when Mr. Nevinson began to angle to get Jessie and Rayburn out of the way.

The woman greeted us shyly, showing teeth that were far decayed, and after Mr. Nevinson had introduced himself and the rest of us, he asked her whether she would let Rayburn pick a few young coconuts. "The Missy at home asked me to get some for her, Adina."

She agreed readily, of course, and Mr. Nevinson smiled at her and said: "Thank you, Adina. Rayburn, will you just see if you can get them for me while the rest of us potter around the cottage here?"

Then Jessie saved her father any further essays in guile by exclaiming: "I'll go and watch Rayburn pick them, Daddy. I can do with a water-coconut."

She and Rayburn went off, and Mr. Nevinson said to Adina: "I hear you're the sister of Matilda who used to live with Patoir, eh, Adina?"

"Yes, sir."

"Matilda died a few days ago, didn't she?"

"She dead – yes, sir."

"What happened ? How did she die?"

"She get drowned, sir."

By further questioning we discovered from her that Matilda had heard the flute since the day after Patoir's death, and had begun to

108

see a white man beckoning at her the day before she herself died. She just walked one afternoon straight into the river and drowned herself, said Adina, in her low, barely audible voice. And yes, she replied to more questioning, Matilda had opened the canister after Patoir died and taken out the piece of paper in it, but seeing that it was not money, she had put it back and given the canister to Rayburn to give to Mr. Nevinson as the dead man had requested.

At this point I asked: "You yourself didn't touch the paper, did you?"

"Me, sir? No, sir. Me na trouble it."

"You don't know who it was that gave the canister to Patoir, do you?" asked Mr. Nevinson, and Adina shook her head and replied: "No, sir. Me na know nothing about it. First time me see de canister was when Matilda take it from under de bed when Patoir dead."

"And look here, about Matilda's getting drowned, tell us something more. You say you didn't actually see her walk into the water?"

"No, sir, but I know she walk in, because de af'noon before she say de white man' spirit call from de water at her. It call her to come in de water and get drowned – and she say she had to turn away her face and hold on tight to de doorpost or she woulda go."

"How did you know she had drowned herself, Adina?" frowned Mr. Nevinson. "I mean, did you hear her cry out?"

"Yes, sir, me was planting in de cassava fields when me hear she call out. She call: 'Adina Adina! De spirit call me in de river! I going!' And I hear a splash, and by de time I run to de bank and look I na see she nowhere. But de water circle, circle, all de time like somebody just get drown."

"I see. And up to now the body hasn't been found, eh?"

"Not yet, sir. Me cousin and his brother been out all yesterday and dis morning in a *corial* searching, but they not find it yet."

"It's now three days since she's been missing, eh?"

"Yes, sir. Today Thursday. It was Monday when it happen."

We heard Jessie calling, and turned our heads.

"Daddy! Milton!" She appeared, beckoning at us. "Rayburn wants to show you something."

"What the devil could Rayburn want to show us?" muttered

Mr. Nevinson. "We'd better go, Milton. Adina, you'll excuse us a moment, will you?"

We moved toward where the coconut palms stood. A pile of nuts lay on the ground, and Jessie had evidently disposed of two already, for their shells gaped wide near the base of one tree.

Rayburn had moved away from the spot, and we saw him standing about fifty yards to the west, near a bed of eddoes. He was shading his eyes with his hands and peering at something in the sky.

"Rayburn, what's the matter?" I called.

He came toward us at once, his manner puzzled. "Sir, I see some carrion-crows circling just over yonder dere. Look and you'll see for yourself. I wonder if some dead thing not in de bush by the lil' creek what run past not far from here."

"And what of it? Probably the carcase of some animal."

"Yes, sir, but it would be worth looking about. It could be Matilda's body de tide wash up into de creek."

"You think so?" said Mr. Nevinson. "Perhaps we'd better investigate."

"How far is the creek from here?" I asked.

"About half a mile, sir. A track over dere we could take."

"Very good. Let's go. Jessie, I think you'd better remain with Adina until we return."

She seemed uncertain, then nodded. "All right. I'll wait here. I don't like seeing dead bodies. I didn't know a woman got drowned. When did it happen?"

"On Monday. Adina's sister, Matilda."

We left her and began to make our way along a rough track that wound its way through the jungle to the south of the clearing. It evidently ran parallel with the river, for every now and then, through a break in the dense foliage and the trunks of palms, I would catch a glimpse of black water.

We must have covered half the distance when the sound of voices became audible ahead of us. Then there came into view the dwarfed figures of two Indians in shirt and shorts. Between them they bore something bulky.

A few seconds later we found ourselves gazing upon the body of Matilda.

Mr. Nevinson, upon an instant's examination, exclaimed: "But this woman didn't die from drowning! Look. She isn't in any way bloated."

"Yes, sir. Same thing me and John say," agreed one of the two Indians who, we had discovered, were the dead woman's cousins.

Horrified and wincing, I noted that they were right. The corpse showed no signs of having been immersed at all, though the pinkish cotton frock did have a crinkly appearance of having dried after a drenching.

"We find her lying high on de bank of de creek, sir," said the Indian called John. He was a bright, alert fellow, and not like the usual run of Bucks. "She was flat on her stomach. Her face was bury in de leaves. De crows was just beginning to trouble her, but they only manage to peck at her foot and her hand. They couldn't get at her face. We just reach in time."

They had been searching along the river bank during the past few days, John explained, because they had thought she had been drowned. It was only this morning it had occurred to them to try hunting about in the bush in the vicinity of the creek. And the circling carrion-crows (the local term for vultures, I ought to explain) had made them suspicious.

Suddenly something on the corpse arrested my attention. "What's that mark on her leg?" I asked, pointing.

John pushed aside the skirt a trifle, exposing more of the right thigh than had already been exposed. Bending over the gruesome thing, we saw that there was some kind of weal on the fleshy part just above the knee.

In silence we kept peering at it. It was about eight or ten inches in length by about an inch in width, and spaced along it, at regular intervals, dark, round spots were apparent, these within the greyish-blueness of the weal itself.

Rayburn exclaimed: "Eh-eh! But, sir, dat's a funny mark! It look just like if somebody brand her with a flute!"

8

Later that day when the Government Dispenser arrived from a place called Ida Sabina, downstream – there is no medical officer stationed in these parts – we learnt that the cause of death was snakebite. The dispenser discovered two punctures on the left ankle which showed signs of puffiness, and said that it looked to him like the bite of a *labaria*. There was no water in the lungs, from what he could judge, and there were no marks of violence. The strange weal on her thigh puzzled him as much as it puzzled the rest of us. We questioned Adina, but Adina said that she was certain it had not been there on the day when Matilda vanished, because that same day she had seen her naked when she was having her morning wash, and she would have noticed it.

The dispenser, a medium-sized black gentleman, who though not a qualified medical man seemed to know quite a lot about medicine, said to Mr. Nevinson and myself: "That weal couldn't have been caused by a blow. It's more like a tattoo-mark – a fresh tattoo-mark, too. I couldn't describe it as a mark of violence."

We agreed with him, and he seemed glad of this, for later, as we knew, we would have to give evidence at the coroner's inquest, and it would he important that we should be able to concur on this particular point.

Mr. Nevinson still refrained from divulging anything concerning the manuscript and the spectral flute. In the course of a quiet conversation with me he said: "What I can't understand is how she happened to be high and dry on land in the vicinity of that creek. If she plunged into the river here through receiving a fright why should she have swum into that creek and climbed ashore?"

"Couldn't she have landed a short way along the bank here and then wandered through the bush towards the creek?"

"That's possible – even probable. But why should she have gone towards the creek instead of returning to the cottage here? I'm sure she couldn't have lost her way. Adina and her two cousins say she was very familiar with the country around here."

"But," I countered, "if we're going to take into consideration what you told me last night, don't you think it might have been that she was lured on through the bush by that figure you say you saw? You said it was only by exerting your will that you didn't go out after it into the night."

He nodded slowly. "Yes, my boy that has occurred to me, of course. It's simply that I'm reluctant to admit it. In the back of my mind there is still the hope that we may be able to find a natural explanation."

For a while we stood there in silence, staring out upon the dark, slow-flowing river. On the opposite bank the jungle glittered in the sunshine, a symphony of greens of all shades, and in the unruffled water every leaf was reflected with faithful detail. Now and then a berry would cause ripples to disturb the pattern, but the disturbance would be slight and fleeting.

Occasionally a sound, soft and flimsy, like the distant crash of waves on a beach, would come to the hearing, would swell gradually on the air, and then fade. It was only a breeze rustling through the jungle, but it was so far away that it never reached us here. It had a strange, phantom quality about it.

I did one or two rough sketches before we left, shortly after one, not waiting to witness the burial of the corpse. This could not be delayed, for decomposition was already fairly advanced.

Jessie refused to eat any of the sandwiches and bananas we had brought for lunch. She murmured to me: "Milton, do you think that thing we saw tattooed on her leg could have had any connection with this flute we've been hearing?"

She sat close to me in the boat, and looked so pale and frightened that I was tempted to put my arm around her to console her. I shook my head, assuming a casualness I was far from feeling. "My dear girl, why on earth should you come to such a conclusion?" I said, trying to make my voice as convincing as I could, for I felt it was my business to do everything in my power to keep her morale high.

She gave me a keen look and returned: "You must think you and Daddy can throw dust in my eyes so easily, eh? I know something is up that you haven't told me about. When we went ashore this morning Daddy purposely sent Rayburn to pick those coconuts because he wanted to get him out of the way so as to speak confidentially to that Buck woman. I knew it at once, and I knew I wasn't meant to hear, too, that's why I went off with Rayburn."

"So that's your theory concerning the matter, is it?"

"Look here, Milton, what caused that queer mark on that dead woman's leg? It was shaped exactly like a flute. You could even make out the finger-holes. It was just as if somebody had purposely drawn it on her leg with a bluish kind of ink."

"I'm just as much puzzled about it as you are," I said cautiously.

She gave me an intense look and gripped my knee. "Milton, did she hear it?"

"Hear what?"

"Oh, don't pretend. The flute. Did she hear it before she met her death?"

"I suppose you may as well know it. Yes, we've been told that she did. Adina said Matilda had been hearing the flute two or three weeks before her death. But that may mean nothing, so don't let it worry you."

When we arrived at Goed de Vries we found work at the sawmill in full swing. The chug-a-chug, chug-a-chug of the engines vibrated through the stillness of the mid-afternoon, and seemed almost tangible, as though had you put your hand before your face you would have been able to feel the waves of sound tingling in your palms.

Mrs. Nevinson was in a hammock on the northern veranda, asleep, the *Pearson's Magazine* she had been reading perched like a V-shaped roof on her stomach. We did not disturb her, and Mr. Nevinson said that he thought he would follow her example as he was rather tired from the activities of the past few hours. Jessie said that she did not feel sleepy but decided to get into bed and read. As for myself, I asked my host if he would let me have Mynheer Voorman's manuscript for a while, as I would like to make a copy of its contents in my diary.

So for the next hour or so I occupied myself in recording in my diary the events of the past two days. I had kept a diary from the age of seventeen, and, until 1937, when I began to grow rather lax in this respect; I never missed a day, no matter how uneventful. In those days of the early thirties, especially, I was particularly keen on my diary, and even if it was only to record the state of the weather and a few dull thoughts, I never omitted to write something in the space allotted to each day.

In writing this narrative it is upon my diary that I have depended chiefly, and while I am about it I think this would be an opportune moment to quote the second part of the manuscript – the part dealing with the instructions relating to the finding of Mynheer Voorman's bones and flute.

According to Mr. Nevinson's translation, this is how it goes, and I am quoting it faithfully, word for word:

"Starting from the bank of the river you walk along the track that leads to the sugar-mill which is now a ruin. This runs east along the drainage canal, but should the day have advanced beyond the fourth hour after noon, observe care to avoid the left side of this track, for at this time of day the first undesirable presences begin to roam. Continue past the old sugar-mill and cross the dam (*paal*) that separates Fields 17 and 18 from the main cultivation of the eastern section where coffee is grown. Pass through Field 4 and look for the bridge that spans the canal to the south-west. Cross this bridge and move towards the large barn (here it is that my wife and children concealed themselves when the rioting broke out, but alas! they were soon discovered and murdered). Skirt the large barn until you come to the smaller barn beside the canal (here is where I hid and was successful in evading the black rascals). Beyond this barn there is a track that runs parallel to another length of the canal. You proceed along this as far as the sluice (*koker*), and here will be found a large round granite stone (often used as an instrument of punishment for those of the slaves who stole or committed crimes of a serious nature). Roll away this stone and dig for a short way down, upon which there will be encountered a jar with my flute and a few papers relating to my life's work. Have no fear of these, as I shall impose no evil essence upon them as I shall upon this parchment on which I write. Directly north of this stone there is a shallow water-hole built of brick and in an abandoned state. It is down in this I shall descend with my musket and end my days, and it is in here that my bones will be found.

"I am leaving this manuscript in this canister in a niche in the brickwork at the brink of this water-hole, and God help him who may find it and lay his hand upon this parchment. He shall either join me in my wandering trouble (*zorg*) through these shadows where here on earth I am, and in death also shall be, a prisoner of unnameable presences, or shall release both himself and me by finding my bones and my flute and giving them a Christian burial."

For a long while after I had copied it into my diary I sat contemplating this strange document of Mynheer Voorman's. There seemed little doubt that be was either mad or a man who practised witchcraft or demonology. How else could one construe such phrases as "a prisoner of unnameable presences" and "undesirable presences begin to roam"? Could it be that he used to attempt to attract to himself evil entities? Whatever it was, he must certainly have been a superstitious fellow, for his instructions said clearly that the seeker after his bones and flute must take care not to walk on "the left side of this track" after four in the afternoon. For a plantation owner he must have been unusual. And what part could the flute have played in his activities? It seemed certain that he must have placed some great importance upon it, or why should he request that it be buried along with his bones? Could his hobby have been music? Did he specialize in the flute? But even so, why go so far as to curse anyone who should touch the parchment? And why the insistence on the burial of his bones and this flute with Christian rites? Could it be that he had repented at the last moment of dabbling in devilry, but with death facing him knew that it was too late to be freed of the evil influences which had made him a prisoner? (For it goes without saying that had he been captured and murdered by the negro slaves, he definitely could not have hoped to have been given a Christian burial; the slaves were heathens.) Was this why he had made it a condition that the finder of the manuscript should not be left in peace until he had unearthed bones and flute and had them reburied according to the rites of the Church?

I was still toying with this interpretation when I heard soft footsteps behind me – I was on the eastern veranda – and Jessie came up and asked me what I was doing.

"Writing up my diary," I told her, deftly slipping the manuscript between the leaves of the diary which happened to be one of these large foolscap-size Charles Letts', and lent itself admirably to the concealment of sheets of paper. "And what of yourself? What did you read?"

"Oh, nothing much," she replied, drawing herself up on the rail of the veranda. Poised there in a half-sitting, half-standing attitude, she looked across at the sawmill and remarked: "They've finished work for the day at the mill. It's after four, isn't it?"

"Yes. To tell the truth, I'd hardly noticed that the sawmill had stopped working."

We heard slow footsteps on the southern veranda, and saw her father appear. He was smoking his pipe, and had a thoughtful air. He gave us a glance, and then paused and began to stare idly across at the sawmill.

Jessie tapped her foot lightly against the balusters.

I could not help smiling to myself as I reflected upon the oddness of civilized human conduct. Without saying a word to each other we all three knew well what was the burden of each other's thoughts; we were aware of the expectancy that dwelt behind our outward semblance of calm. But as though by some silently mutual pact, we refrained from uttering the thought that hovered so tremulously within our ken. Our civilized inhibitions were such that we simply had to remain silent and pretend an equanimity we were far from feeling.

Yes, the day had advanced. The sun was low in the west. In another hour or so it would be shimmering reddish at the ragged-edged top of the jungle on the opposite bank, and then, within a few more minutes, would be gone, leaving behind it, for a while, a cluster of pink and mauve fans of light that would gently melt into the clear blue of the sky as the leafy-chill threads of night began to weave their funereal pattern over the scene.

So vividly did I envisage it that it might already have been happening. I seemed to have the notion that I had projected my being through time and was sitting now on the front stairs, watching the river and the sunset. On the silent air came the voice of one of the labourers in a snatch of song, and the sound, to me, seemed to become one with my reflection on the illusion of having travelled ahead an hour or two in time. I had the sensation that I was hearing that voice at six o'clock and not at half-past four, that I had succeeded in skipping the gap between now and then… Had anything unusual happened during the gap? Anything nerve-shaking?

I had to jerk myself to dispel the illusion, and Jessie glanced at me and giggled. "What's going wrong with you?" she asked. "What are you shivering like that for?"

"Shivering? I never shivered." I yawned elaborately, self-conscious, and leaning back, began to whistle.

Jessie laughed. "What's the sudden whistling for?"

"Can't I even whistle? Any objection?"

She gave a grunt that was half a sigh, stretched in a way that betrayed that she, too, was feeling somewhat self-conscious, and said casually: "I think I'll go and have a shower and dress for the evening. Not that there's any need to dress specially in the bush, of course," she added, and went off, humming softly to herself.

In spite of our tenterhooks, however, six o'clock came and the silence remained unbroken.

At about seven, just before dinner, it happened.

9

Jessie heard it within a few feet of her. She was in the dining-room helping Timmykins to lay the table. Her father was in the sitting-room trying to read a copy of *Life and Letters* I had lent him about half an hour before.

I was smoking in a deck-chair on the western veranda when I heard Jessie's scream. I sat up at once, tilting my head – and I heard it, as on the night before, coming from a distance on the river.

Mrs. Nevinson, who had been in the pantry engaged in making a mayonnaise sauce, rushed into the dining-room to see what was the matter with Jessie, but, in the meantime, Jessie had dashed into the sitting-room to her father. I found her, when I arrived in there, clutching his arm and staring distractedly about the room.

Mr. Nevinson, I noticed, did not glance about him in this uncontrolled fashion, but kept gazing towards where I stood at the western door which, as I might have made clear before, was the door that gave on to the front veranda. To go down the front steps you had to pass through this door.

Then Mrs. Nevinson appeared from the dining-room, Timmykins behind her. "What's happened, Jessie? Are you all hearing the flute again?"

Jessie nodded. "Yes, Mother, it's in here."

"Milton, are you hearing it, too?"

I told her yes in a murmur.

Abruptly I saw Mr. Nevinson shake off Jessie's hand and rise. There was deliberation rather than impatience in the action, and something trancelike and automatic in his demeanour impressed itself upon me.

Jessie uttered a whimpering sound and murmured: "It's over there now. Near the radio." She began to cringe off, moving towards her mother.

Her father came straight towards me, but I could see that he was not looking at me, but past me at the doorway. "Where are you going to, sir?"

"Out of my way, Milton."

I gripped his arm. "You can't go out there now, sir. It's nearly time for dinner."

He tried to shake my hand off, breathing in a rasp and muttering a few words fiercely – but I held firm. And abruptly his efforts to resist ceased, and he stood gripping my arm and staring past my shoulder into the deep dusk outside. I could see perspiration in minute blebs on his forehead.

The sound of the flute had ceased. I heard Jessie's gasped: "It's stopped! It's gone!" She approached, and I felt her cold fingers close around my wrist.

"What's Daddy looking at out there, Milton?" she asked.

I did not reply, and just at that instant her father's manner relaxed. I sensed that deep breeze of relief rush through him.

For a long moment there was silence among us.

Mr. Nevinson began to fumble in his pocket for his pipe, and Jessie stared at him, her face very pale.

Mrs. Nevinson stood near the chair in which her husband had recently sat. Even as I write I can see her aproned form and the fork in her hand – a dinner fork with the creamy traces of mayonnaise still adhering to it. There was no jesting in her manner this time. Her face was puzzled and anxious – and feminine, by which I mean she had that ineffectual, dependent look which, as I have remarked before, a female, in my way of viewing things, ought to have. It was so obvious that the situation was completely beyond her, and, like her daughter, she did not attempt to make a show of being able to cope with it.

At the door that gave into the dining-room, Timmykins stared at us with his naïve Indian eyes, blankly curious and wondering. There were three dinner plates and a napkin in his hands. I recall that for a brief second the fear that he might drop the plates darted through me.

Later, at dinner, we hardly spoke. We none of us ate heartily, and Jessie was very nervous. She kept glancing out of the window at the fireflies. More than once we heard the ominous bark of the baboons.

Shortly before we rose, I drew the glances of the others to myself when I uttered a gasp. I had happened to lift my gaze and look through the window to my right. Above the black ragged top of the jungle a bank of dense clouds had split to reveal part of a ruddy moon crescent. The sight startled me. I had not expected it, and I had never before seen the moon look so sinister and so lovely.

Jessie craned her head past my shoulder to look at it, and in doing so her knuckles touched my bare arm. They were cold. She said in a soft voice that yes, it was lovely but terrible. And just before we got up she asked her father about the lights, whether he were going to have Rayburn switch off the Petter engine at ten o'clock as on the night before. Her father said no, he had instructed Rayburn to let the Petter plant go on all night. He added in a murmur that he thought it would be a good idea to let us keep together in the sitting-room that evening until bedtime. He wanted to discuss one or two little things with us.

So when the meal was over we went into the sitting-room.

Mr. Nevinson took the Morris chair near the table with the magazines, and Jessie and her mother seated themselves nearby on the chesterfield. I was about to draw up a chair when Mrs. Nevinson said: "Come and sit with us here, Milton. There's plenty of room." And so I sat between the two of them on the chesterfield.

At any other time the solemnity of our behaviour would have seemed absurd, but on this night there was too much tenseness in the air, too much that was urgent and weighty on our minds.

Only we who have been through it can know the unique strangeness of those days and evenings – the not-too-sane, aerial feeling of being in the midst of occult events and yet still conscious of the commonplace routine of existence; seeing the furniture and the walls around us in that cottage and, outside, the trees and the river and the sawmill and the labourers, normal, ordinary, feasible symbols of the physical world, and yet, within ourselves, knowing that something beyond our control had intruded upon the accepted pattern of our human actions.

Throughout the evening Mr. Nevinson was awkward and out of his element. I could see that discussions like this were entirely foreign to him, especially where his family was concerned. Like myself, he is of the undemonstrative type and fears any situation in which there might be the possibility of a display of sentiment or emotion.

Most of the time he kept toying with his pipe and staring at the magazines on the table beside him. Now and then he would take up a magazine and flick through the leaves aimlessly and self-consciously.

He began by saying that we had seen for ourselves what we were up against, and that though it might seem a stupid thing for intelligent people to have to admit, well, there it was: the fact remained that we were being subjected to a series of hauntings. It was not pleasant to know that at any hour during the day or night this strange phenomenon might make itself obvious.

What he had to say, he continued, was this: there was danger – immediate danger for Jessie and himself. In two or three weeks' time there would be danger for Milton, too.

After lighting his pipe he went on. Some uncanny force, he said, had begun to draw him impellingly outside the house whenever the flute made itself audible. He uttered an awkward, self-conscious chuckle, his eyes lowered. "Sounds nonsensical to say a thing like that, I know, but I can assure you it's the honest truth. And there's another thing. On the last two occasions I saw a distinct spectral figure."

"A spectral figure?" said Mrs. Nevinson.

Her husband nodded. "Yes, Nell. A spectral figure. A ghost, in vulgar terms, if you prefer it. It kept beckoning at me to follow it. You can smile over that, but that was exactly the impression that was left on me."

None of us made any comment, and there were no smiles. We waited for him to go on, and after a silence he said that from what he could calculate, on the next occasion we heard the flute Jessie would begin to be aware of this ghost figure, and would probably feel the urge to follow it outside. It would require an immense effort of will to resist the inclination. He spoke from experience. In fact, the impulse was such an overpowering one that he had no doubt that he himself would have yielded to it that evening had not Milton stopped him at the door. Until the danger we were up against had passed we would have to take strict precautions to ensure that neither himself nor Jessie were allowed to give in to this urge. He had no doubt now that the woman at Horstenland, Matilda, had met her death because she had yielded to the impulse and followed this apparition when it beckoned. It was true that she had been bitten by a snake, but the fact remained that she had been lured to her fate by this sinister spectre (afterwards I told him he had sounded like a prosecuting counsel addressing the jury).

What he was going to suggest, he went on, was that a guard be placed over Jessie and himself, because, from what he could note, force might be necessary to restrain the two of them when the phenomenon occurred. We would have to take Rayburn into our confidence and elect him a guard over one of the two – himself for preference. It would be rather distasteful, but there was no help for it. As Jessie's guard he would suggest Milton, and perhaps Nell could stand by in the event of Milton's needing any assistance. What had we to say to the proposal?

Instantly Mrs. Nevinson said: "I don't like it at all, Ralph. Surely the situation isn't so desperate that we must have that black man hanging round us in the house here every moment of the day."

"You needn't adopt such a tone, Nell," frowned her husband. "It's only a suggestion. If you can think of a better let us hear it."

"Why couldn't Milton take care of you? I could see after Jessie if the need arose. I simply can't understand why it should be necessary to have Rayburn in constant attendance."

"Mother doesn't realize how serious this thing is!" Jessie broke out, her voice high-pitched and hysterical. "It's because it doesn't affect her that she can speak like this – "

"Very well, Jessie! Very well! Control yourself, please," said her father.

For the next half an hour or so Mr. Nevinson argued with his wife, but she stubbornly refused to hear of Rayburn sleeping upstairs with us. Such a thing was unheard of, and she could see no need for it. She held out that she would be adequate protection for Jessie if anything happened, and that I could see after her husband. She had never in her life hobnobbed with niggers, and she saw no reason now why she should do so – and what was more, she felt certain Ralph was making more fuss than was really necessary. How could any silly ghost have the power to lure him and Jessie out of the house to their deaths! The idea was absurd and fantastic.

Jessie interrupted several times – nervously, hysterically.

Eventually Mr. Nevinson, who throughout this harangue had shown remarkable patience, sat forward and uttered a sound of disgust. "You can have it your way, then, Nell," he said curtly. "We'll let things remain as they are. You see after Jessie and Milton will see after me – and I trust you won't live to regret it."

His wife laughed. "Really, Ralph, you surprise me. You're speaking like a sensational novelette."

"Mother, you're too dull – that's what's wrong with you!" Jessie flared. "You can't see further than your nose –"

"Look here, child, I think the best thing you can do is to go to bed. Your nerves are in a state. Take ten drops of Phospherine –"

"I don't want to hear anything from you. You're impossible. And I'm not going to bed. I'm staying in here with Daddy and Milton."

"Oh, certainly – as you please! You can all do whatever you like," said her mother, and, rising, went into her room, her manner decidedly frosty.

"She doesn't care a jot," Jessie mumbled. "Just because she's not going through it herself. It's selfishness. She's a selfish pig. I always knew it."

"That will do, Jessie. Be silent."

I smiled and patted her arm, and told her not to be upset, speaking in an awkward, self-conscious voice. "I don't think we'll be bothered again until tomorrow. It won't happen tonight – at least, the chances are that it won't. It seems to come at longish intervals."

Her father said: "Let's go and sit on the veranda until bedtime, Milton. It's a bit stuffy in here. Jessie, come with us."

Jessie and I hunted out the two deck-chairs which, on our

arrival the evening before, we had carefully selected and solemnly dedicated to our own exclusive use. We placed them side by side on the southern veranda while Mr. Nevinson settled himself into the hammock that was slung up nearby.

For well over an hour we remained out there, my host silent and puffing continuously at his pipe, Jessie and I exchanging a remark at intervals. She grew much calmer as the evening progressed, and her voice lost its shrill note. Even the baboons did not trouble her after a while, though once when a rather loud gurgling splash came from the river she put out her hand and touched my wrist, with a mumbled exclamation, adding at once: "It must have been a fish. A *perai* or something."

The fire-flies kept up their intricate dance in the darkness, silent arcs and spangles of radiance.

The beat of the Petter plant downstream had become an indigo blanket of sound, almost unheard – a background against which the occasional chirp of a frog would stand out like a pink wet petal.

More than once I was aware of movement inside the cottage – the footsteps of my hostess. The windows of the two rooms Mr. Nevinson and I occupied looked out on to the section of the veranda on which we were, and I felt certain it must have been my imagination when I heard a slight sound from Mr. Nevinson's room.

I glanced at Jessie in the chair beside me to see if she, too, might have noticed it. In the starlit gloom she seemed unusually still, and it came upon me that she had fallen into a doze, so I did not disturb her.

I heard the hammock creak. I glanced aside and made out the dim shape of my host's head. It was twisted round as though he were staring towards one of the bedroom windows, and in that instant I realized that it might not have been simply a fancy of mine that I had heard that sound in his room.

"Did you hear something, sir?"

"Pretty certain I did." He sounded puzzled. "Did you?"

"Well, I thought I heard a sort of footstep or something. It seemed to be in your room."

Jessie stirred and sat forward, our voices evidently having roused her. "What's the matter, Milton?"

"Nothing, nothing," I said hastily, not wanting to alarm her. "I was just asking your father something. You seemed to have been having a doze."

Mr. Nevinson had got out of the hammock and I could see that it was his intention to go into his room to investigate. Jessie was just asking him if he was going to bed when we heard a thump and a half-stifled shriek from the direction of the dining-room.

It was Mrs. Nevinson. We heard her cry: "Oh, my God! Oh, my God! Ralph! Milton! Come quickly!"

10

It was on the following day that I recorded in my diary the events of that evening. Reading through what I wrote, I find myself compelled to smile with an air of indulgence – that affectionate indulgence one sometimes experiences when reflecting on the impetuosities and immature posturings of one's extreme youth. I was more than two decades younger then, and I fear that, in writing, I had a weakness for the dramatic phrase and also an obsession for detail that, to me now, seems not only immature but almost vulgar.

Describing the happenings of that evening, I wrote: 'Then came the evening – fantasy! Horrible, inconceivably grotesque fantasy!'

The space allotted by Messrs Charles Letts' for the day's entries had not been sufficient for what I had to record, and there is a sheet of ruled notepaper pasted in on which my jottings are extended. Both sides of this sheet are covered with my writing, and there is one passage, in particular, that occurs near the middle of the unruled side of the paper which, for some reason, tickles me immensely. It goes: 'Mrs. N's face chalky-white, but the blood glowed pink at throat. Startling, unusual picture. Increased air fantasy.'

Yet, thinking back on it, I realize that this impression is among the most striking of those that still remain in my memory. Even without referring to my diary I would have recalled that picture of Mrs. Nevinson at the moment when we rushed into the dining-room. Her face was chalky-white, but through some freak of circulation, the blood still hovered in a pink patch around her throat.

We found her standing by the sideboard. There was a box of matches in her hand and she was staring with a scared fixity at something on the floor. I followed her gaze and saw Mynheer Voorman's manuscript.

The memory of that moment comes back with uncanny clarity. I even recall that I clutched my thigh hard and that a tiny white midge floated past irresolutely between Mr. Nevinson and myself, moving toward the light that dangled over the dining-table.

Jessie was the first to speak. She asked her mother why she had screamed, and Mrs. Nevinson pointed at the manuscript, and replied in an agitated murmur: "It must have been that – I don't know. Something – something frightened me." I could barely make out what she said. She glanced slowly round the room.

"Were you in my room a moment ago, Nell?" her husband asked.

"Yes, I went in there. I didn't want you to know. I tried not to make any noise." She spoke like a schoolgirl caught in some shameful act. I had never before seen her so thoroughly cowed and scared.

"I found the manuscript in the dictionary on the dressing-table," she mumbled as though hardly aware of what she was saying.

Some insect was making a soft ticking sound just outside one of the windows, and the scent of the river came in, warm and dank.

There was wonder as well as curiosity mingled with the annoyance on Mr. Nevinson's face. He stared at her with a heavy frown, as though he, too, found it difficult to articulate.

Jessie said: "But, Mother, what made you do it? You knew you shouldn't have done it. We've told you about the manuscript. It – it – you should never have touched it."

I picked up the manuscript and examined it. Then I looked at Mrs. Nevinson and said: "What were you trying to do with it, Mrs. N.? Burn it?"

"Yes, I struck a match and held it to it. I wanted to see if burning it wouldn't have got rid of all your mysterious flute sounds."

"But how did you know it was in the dictionary?" I asked.

"I heard you mention to Ralph this afternoon that you'd put it in there after you'd finished writing up your diary."

"But what happened?" her husband asked impatiently. "You haven't yet told us why you screamed. What frightened you? Why don't you explain?"

She hesitated, and again glanced round the room, then murmured: "I don't know. I can't understand it, Ralph. It doesn't seem – it's quite absurd – and yet it did happen. I know it did. I saw it plainly."

"Saw what? What happened, Nell? What *happened*?"

"As soon as I struck the match and held it to the manuscript I saw a kind of hand."

"A what?"

"I know. It – it seems ridiculous, but it's true. I saw it, Ralph. A sort of hand. It appeared from behind me – as if some creature had been standing behind me, waiting – watching me."

We simply stood there looking at her, waiting for her to go on.

"It knocked the parchment out of my hand – and the match. The lighted match. And I heard a shriek – a whistling kind of shriek – but it sounded like – well, not like a voice but some instrument. A police whistle – or perhaps a flute. Yes, it was more like a flute. Right in my ear it sounded – an angry sound. It was horrible. I've never had anything so horrible happen to me before."

"But what do you mean by a hand?" Mr. Nevinson asked her. "I don't understand this. Look here, you're trembling." His voice was distracted. "What possessed you, in the first place, to go looking for that manuscript in my room!"

Jessie cut in with a hysterical exasperation: "Oh, don't nag at her like that, Daddy! Hasn't she told you? She wanted to burn the thing – that's why she went in and got it."

"I don't want you to tell me how to behave, Jessie!" her father snapped.

"Sir, I think Jessie's right this time," I intervened. "We're all getting too excited. Let's calm down a bit and let Mrs. N. tell us exactly what happened." I turned to Mrs. Nevinson and asked: "Can you describe this hand you saw, Mrs. Nevvy?"

She gave me a grateful look and said: "I don't know how to

begin, really, Milton, because –" She broke off, hesitated, then went on: "It was nothing human. I've never seen anything like it in my life. It was greyish and sort of covered with fur – oh, it's no use. I can't describe it – but it wasn't human, I know. It looked devilish. And that whistling note that went through my head. It was almost like a cry of rage."

Jessie was gripping my elbow, and I could sense the rigidity of her body as she stared at her mother. Mr. Nevinson had paced off towards a window, and stood frowning out at the fireflies in the gloom.

Battling to keep calm, I said: "Go carefully, Mrs. N. Remember you said at first you heard an angry sound. Now you say it was like a cry of rage. Which would you say it was exactly? A cry or a whistling or an angry exclamation?"

"What does it matter?" she snapped. "I'm not in the witness box. You and Ralph always treat people as though you think yourselves barristers in a courtroom or something. It was a horrible sound – that's all I can tell you for certainty. And it was shrill as if some instrument like a flute or a whistle had produced it. I can't tell you any more than that."

"I see your point," I said patiently (and though I didn't feel so at the time, I can well appreciate now that I must, indeed, have sounded like a barrister). "But I have a good reason for asking, Mrs. Nevvy. It may be important. What I mean is this: so far none of us has heard anything like what you describe. It's always been this leisurely, aimless tune played on a flute. Why should *you* have heard a shrill whistling – an angry sound? For all we know, you may have succeeded in scaring off Mynheer Voorman." I laughed. "If it was really a cry of rage you heard it might have been the old chap's last despairing expression of fear and surrender. No, I'm not trying to be funny. I'm sure such things have happened in occult manifestations before. Perhaps by applying that match to the manuscript you may have broken the spell, and this could well be the end of the whole affair. What I want to know is whether you think it was a defiant *whistling* sound you heard or a sort of despairing *wail*."

She shook her head, bewildered. "I really can't be certain, boy. If anything, I should say it sounded defiant and angry. I just know it was horrible. I never dreamt that anything like this could happen in actuality. And that hand! But it's incredible. I can hardly believe I'm not asleep and dreaming this." She began to glance round the room nervously again.

The baboons were growling ominously up-river, and Jessie's grip on my elbow tightened. I glanced at Mr. Nevinson and said: "Sir, would you have any objections to my trying out the experiment Mrs. Nevvy attempted – just to see what happens?"

Mr. Nevinson, who had seated himself at the dining-table, turned sharply. "No, Milton. Nothing of the sort. We're trying no more experiments in this house. By the way let me have that manuscript if you please."

As I crossed the room and gave the manuscript to him I noticed the harrowed light in his eyes, and felt rather sorry for him.

Jessie, however, was not so sympathetic. She said: "Daddy, I don't see why you should speak like that. I think Milton is right. It may help if we try burning the manuscript. It might break the spell. Why can't we try it?"

Her father merely made a nervous gesture of dismissal with the stem of his pipe, and Mrs. Nevinson said: "Your father is right, Jessie. It mightn't be safe to try. There's something really uncanny about the thing." She spoke in a subdued tone, and her voice contained a humility that, for her, was most unusual. I was seeing a facet of her character with which I was entirely unfamiliar.

Jessie was not to be suppressed so easily. "But we have to do something, Mother," she insisted. "We can't resign ourselves to this horror."

I patted her shoulder in an avuncular manner and murmured: "My dear girl, don't get excited. Let's take things calmly." (Often I have to smile when I recall my behaviour on that occasion.)

She turned eagerly to me and said: "But, Milton, how are we going to go on like this? My nerves are in a state. Don't you think we ought to try burning the manuscript? It might get rid of these – these manifestations or whatever you call them. Don't you think so?" She asked the question not rhetorically but with a naïve sincerity, as a child might have done. She kept looking at me as though awaiting my answer with anxiety. That she could put so much confidence in me naturally flattered me immensely. I turned my pompous savant smile on her and replied: "It might and it might not – we never know. I didn't guarantee that it would be successful. Don't misunderstand me."

I lit a cigarette and, pacing off to a window, began to stare out at the darkness. With the help of my diary I can recall fairly accurately my thoughts as I stood at that window on that evening. I thought many things, no doubt, but the leading theme was my attempt to probe the nature of actuality in its relation to fantasy.

It may sound very trite, but at the time it meant a lot to me. It was no vain philosophical sally. To the four of us in that cottage, during those few weeks, the important thing above all others was to be able to assure ourselves that we were really sane and capable of sensing the scene around us in a rational spirit. I am sure that many times we came near to insanity, and it was only by doing what we could to keep our perspective true that we did succeed in preventing ourselves from going raving mad.

Jessie's voice interrupted my reflections. I heard her say: "Anyway, Mother, you'll have to agree now to let Rayburn sleep upstairs here with us. We never can tell what might happen when we hear that flute again – and you're in the soup yourself now. You won't be of any help to us in an emergency."

That reopened the argument of earlier that evening – and reopened it with fresh animosity and hysteria on the part of Jessie and her mother.

Mrs. Nevinson, however, despite the shock she had suffered as a result of her experience with the manuscript, held to her former decision. She refused, she said, to tolerate Rayburn's presence in the cottage with us. The position, she went on, had not become so desperate that we had to sacrifice our dignity to the extent of having a black man rubbing shoulders with us as though he were an equal.

She infuriated me, but I succeeded in keeping my temper. I said nothing.

Nor did her husband have much to say. He sat at the dining-table puffing at his pipe, a pensive, rather exasperated look on his face. I could detect a certain amount of contempt in the glances he kept throwing at his wife, and I could not blame him, for that was the emotion Mrs. Nevinson evoked in me, too. Had I not been a guest in this cottage I should have let my self-control go to the devil and blazed away at her in by no means polite language. (Only a week ago I reminded her of her behaviour on that evening, but she merely laughed; her views have not changed, and she is quite unrepentant.)

Jessie paced up and down and gesticulated feverishly as she argued, but her mother stood in one spot to do combat. She stood near a corner of the dining-table, one hand resting on the highly polished surface while the other she employed to emphasize her pronouncements.

People with nasty minds will probably explain it differently, but so far as I know, it was by sheer accident that my gaze happened to pause on Mrs. Nevinson's unstockinged legs.

The shadow of the dining-table cast the lower part of her person in gloom, but the light was a bright one, and even in their present state of eclipse her legs could be made out clearly and in detail. She is of a very pale olive complexion, and that made it all the easier to observe her legs in the twilight of the table's shadow. They were visible from just below the knees, her dress being on the short side, and watching them, I noticed how they kept up a continuous shifting motion – a slight, almost imperceptible sway: a reflex action, no doubt, set up by her present emotional state as she argued with Jessie.

Abruptly my observation ceased to be idle.

Craning my head forward, I focused my gaze on her left ankle. I was sure I could see a little bruise that I could not recall having noticed earlier that day.

Mr. Nevinson observed that there was something unusual in my manner and asked me what was wrong.

Jessie paused in the middle of a sentence and looked at me, too. "What's it, Milton?"

Mrs. Nevinson turned.

"How did you get that mark on your ankle, Mrs. Nevvy?"

She gave me a cold look and snapped: "What mark?"

I pointed. "There. On your left ankle."

Her husband rose and came round, and Jessie approached curiously.

The dank smell of the river and the jungle seemed to coil round us like a grey tendril thrust into the room from out of the darkness. A frog chirruped a lonely note amid the shrubs at the river's edge, and in the background the Petter generating plant beat dully in the night silence.

"What are you making a fuss over?" said Mrs. Nevinson impatiently, in no mood to co-operate with any of us. "I suppose I must have grazed my ankle accidentally somewhere." She began to stride away, but I rose quickly and grasped her arm.

"Just a minute, Mrs. Nevvy. Don't run off like that. We've got to examine this thing, if you don't mind." I tried to switch on as much charm as I could, and as Mrs. Nevinson has always been susceptible to this kind of thing, she hesitated, grunted and returned: "Oh, all right. Go ahead. Bring iodine and two or three lotions and make a thorough job of it. I believe it's nothing but an excuse to hold my ankle. I've warned Kate about you."

"Just so," I smiled. "It's not such a bad ankle to hold, anyway. Now, let's see."

She was standing now in the bright light, and as we bent to examine her ankle, our breaths made almost simultaneous rasping sounds.

"But – " Jessie broke off.

"What's the matter now?" asked Mrs. Nevinson.

"But it was the same mark we saw on that woman at Horstenland," said Jessie, finishing her sentence this time. "The dead Buck woman. Matilda."

Yes, it was the same mark – except that in this instance the mark was incomplete. It was about three inches long, and at one end it was blurred, fading gradually into the whiteness of the skin.

Mrs. Nevinson mumbled that it did look odd, didn't it? It was the first time she was seeing it, she went on. She was sure that up to dinner-time it had not been there because she had changed her shoes just before dinner and would have noticed it.

She looked at me.

We heard the frog chirrup outside.

11

Were I to attempt to give a detailed day-to-day account of everything that happened to us and of the sensations we experienced during those two weeks we spent at Goed de Vries, this record would probably begin to assume the proportions of *The Golden Bough*. I shall have to limit myself, therefore, to narrating only those incidents I consider to be of outstanding significance and interest. This does not mean, however, that I shall fail in my duty as a chronicler and omit mention of vital details.

For instance, I may say at once that after the discovery of that mark on Mrs. Nevinson's ankle nothing more of an unusual or alarming nature took place on the night described in the foregoing pages. We went to bed soon after and slept as well as might have been expected under the circumstances, and it was not until the following morning that Mrs. Nevinson complained of having had a strange nightmare. A nightmare, she declared, that was "different".

"I was in a small *corial*, and I was paddling it either up-or down-river – but I think it was up-river. And then for some reason I decided to land, so I steered the boat toward the left-hand bank – I'm sure it was the left-hand bank – and I got out at a place where there was a kind of opening in the bush. When I went ashore I found myself on a narrow track – and then something told me I wasn't alone. Ugh! I got a most shivery feeling. I sort of knew for certain I'd been brought to this spot for a definite purpose. I began to look around – and then I saw some creature – a greyish, furry thing with claws. It scurried past me, and I felt terribly frightened. I wanted to scream out. I began to run along the track into the jungle, not knowing where I was going, and as I ran I heard a grunting, scratching sound behind me, and I was certain something horrible was following me. Then what do you think? I heard a flute playing ahead of me, and I had a terribly strong inclination to follow the music. I just felt I *had* to find out who was playing the flute. I ran on along the path. And then the most horrible thing of all happened. I felt a bony hand grip my arm from behind, and a voice whispered in my ear. I can remember the words distinctly. 'No farther today.' I felt I was going to faint – and then I woke up."

None of us attempted to interpret this dream, though it seemed to disturb Jessie a great deal. When I was alone with her for a moment on the northern veranda, during the morning, she asked me in her naïve manner if I thought there might be any meaning in the dream, and, somehow, on this occasion, I could not bring myself to play the pompous savant. The expression on her face fanned alive in me one of those strong impulses I had been having of late to hold her and pet her. It was so strong on this particular instance that I had to ask myself whether it could be that I was falling in love.

I squeezed her arm and told her that personally I thought the dream nothing to bother about. "After her experiences in the dining-room last night, is it any surprise that she had a night-mare?"

The mark on her mother's ankle had faded considerably overnight. When we examined it at breakfast it was a mere bluish-pinkish smudge, and by noon it had vanished entirely.

Naturally, its disappearance caused us to wonder greatly, but we did not discuss the matter at length. We had already reached the stage where wonders had begun to be accepted as mere features of the day's routine.

Lunch passed without incident, and after we had risen from the table we went out on to the northern veranda to laze until teatime. We were four very tense people who tried to cover up our tenseness in desultory bursts of carefree conversation.

Outside, the day seemed so peaceful and greenly ingenuous. The river, like a black magic-mirror, reflected the bush on the opposite bank with such a faithful clarity that it almost appeared to have a quiet, smiling intelligence of its own which induced it to reproduce objects in its vicinity on pain of suffering some secret punishment if it failed. The sawmill chugged away in unvaried monotony. Now and then there would be a clatter of boards or the clank of chains as logs were hauled up from the bank to be cut. Now and then the strident cackle of human laughter or a shout of merriment exploded on the hot air.

It was shortly after three o'clock that the new manifestation occurred. I had finished writing up my diary and was doing some work at my easel when Jessie sprang up from her deck-chair, and her father stiffened in the Morris chair in which he was sitting. The book he had been making a pretence of reading dropped to the floor with a fluttering clop.

I got up at once, putting down my brush and palette on the stool.

I heard it coming from the river.

Jessie was hugging herself. She stood with her back to the veranda rail – leaning hard against the rail and biting her lower lip, staring before her, her face very pale.

In the hammock, Mrs. Nevinson sat up and looked around. "What's wrong? Is it happening again?"

I flashed her a glance. "What do you mean? Can't you hear it?"

She cocked her head and wrinkled her brows. "No, I can't. I really can't say I hear anything like a flute."

"Distantly. Listen again! Listen!"

She tilted her head again, but again she said: "No. Not even distantly. The sawmill is the only sound I can hear."

I could give her no more attention, for I noticed that her husband was preparing to rise. His hands were gripped tightly over the arms of the chair, and there was perspiration on his forehead. He kept his gaze on the door that opened into the dining-room, that trancelike look about him.

It was a repetition of the evening before. He tried to get out of the house, but I succeeded in stopping him. Both he and Jessie seemed exhausted after the ordeal. They sank down into chairs, breathing hard and with strained expressions.

Contrary to what her father had expected, Jessie did not see the apparition, but Mr. Nevinson told us "It's clear now. It's shifted from the corner of my eye and has come almost directly into my line of vision."

After a silence Mrs. Nevinson asked: "What is it like? Can't you describe it?"

He seemed reluctant to say anything, then, after a moment, shook his head and murmured: "There's nothing human in this, Nell. The figure I saw was misshapen – more beast than man. It was upright and bore a slight resemblance to a human – but it had no features I could make out. It seemed to keep its head – if it can be called a head – slightly averted." He shuddered and added: "And its limbs were cloaked in a strange grey fur – though at one instant I was inclined to think it might have been soiled rags instead of fur. It was definitely nothing of this earth. Of that I haven't the faintest doubt."

Listening to him, I could not help reflecting how utterly absurd his words would have sounded under different circumstances – what pitying scepticism would have stirred in me. Had I not had the events of the past few days as evidence that we were actually participants in a series of uncanny happenings, I should have wanted to laugh at him outright and tell him he had been reading too many of the ghost stories of M. R. James. The apparition he described could so easily have been one of the demon creatures of the late Professor James… "Misshapen – more beast than man… cloaked in a strange grey fur… " Even his way of describing it had a touch of James about it. Why "cloaked"? Why not "covered with"? (It was not until later that afternoon, when having a quiet chat with him that I discovered that his mode of expressing himself had, indeed, been subconsciously influenced by M. R. James. The book he had been reading at the moment when the manifestation occurred was *Ghost Stories of an Antiquary*! He had brought up with him, he admitted, several volumes, fictional and otherwise, that treated of supernatural matters. "In view of what had been happening before I got aboard the steamer, don't you think it's natural I should be intensely interested in every phase of the subject?" He smiled at me, though not without some discomfiture.)

Jessie said that the flute had sounded this time right beside her – almost at her shoulder.

"The next time we hear it I'm sure I'm going to see this demon-thing Daddy is seeing. Heavens! But can't we do something to stop it!"

"Something like what?" her father asked her.

"Burn the manuscript – or, at least, try to burn it. It might drive away this old Dutchman and stop him from bothering us. I can't stand this much longer. I feel as if I'm going off my head. Something terrible will happen to me if I see that thing you say you've seen. I don't want to see it!" She began to sob, and her mother and I had to do what we could to calm her. She was trembling uncontrollably.

Despite our excitement over Mr. Nevinson's description of the apparition and this outburst of Jessie's, I had by no means forgotten the new development which had attracted my notice when the manifestation began. As soon as Jessie had been calmed I tackled Mrs. Nevinson, doing my best not to sound like a police inspector, though I fear that this is exactly what I must have sounded like.

"Look here, Mrs. Nevvy," I said, "there's a little point we've got to get straightened out. It's about this flute-playing. Are you sure you didn't hear the flute when we were hearing it a little while ago?"

She shook her head with emphasis. "I never heard a single note. I purposely listened, but there was nothing at all. The only sounds I heard were the voices of the men over at the sawmill and the engines of the sawmill itself."

Her husband leant forward in his chair and gave her a perplexed look. "You didn't hear it, you say, Nell? But how can that be? You handled the manuscript last night, didn't you?"

"Of course I did. Don't ask me to explain it. I'm simply telling you I heard no flute-playing today. Since that awful shrieking business in my ear last night I've heard nothing. In the dream I've told you about I did hear a flute – but I certainly haven't heard anything remotely like a flute during my waking hours today."

"It's most puzzling," said Mr. Nevinson, though I could detect some relief in his manner. "At least, I had assumed there would be some consistency in the trend of events." He added this with such naïve dismay that I had to smile. Mrs. Nevinson gave a cackle of laughter and said: "You sound as though you want to scold Mynheer Voorman, Ralph."

Jessie, however, could see no humour in any of this. She said:

"I know what it is. It's because Mother tried to burn the manuscript. She's hit on the right thing, and she's driven off this demon or whatever it is that's plaguing us. And yet you won't try it, Daddy! I can't understand why you should be so stubborn. Where's the harm in trying?"

Her father fidgeted uncomfortably and told her: "You appear to forget the unpleasant experience your mother underwent for attempting what she did. Would you care to chance the same thing?"

"And why not? It would be one nasty horror – and the whole thing would be over."

Mrs. Nevinson shuddered and said: "Well, to be honest, Jessie, I don't think you'd like it – even that once. Ugh! That awful furry-looking hand!"

Mr. Nevinson smiled. Much of his former composure had returned, and though there were still several harrowed lines on his face, I thought I could observe the setting in of a tolerance (to employ a medical term) to the present situation. It was as though the shock of this last manifestation had produced a reaction more favourable than unfavourable and his nervous system were attempting to adapt itself to the general strain of events.

"Are you so sure," he said to Jessie, "that if you tried this experiment it would result in bringing the whole thing to an end?"

"But nothing has happened to Mother today, has it?" she parried. "She says she couldn't hear the flute. Doesn't that prove that she must have succeeded in frightening off whatever it is that's troubling us – or at any rate creating some kind of protection or immunity against it!"

"It proves nothing, my dear girl. We can't go jumping to conclusions in such a reckless fashion. We must wait and see. For all we know, your mother may be in as great danger as we are, due to her rash act – even greater."

Mrs. Nevinson paled a trifle. "What do you mean by that, Ralph?"

"According to what you've told us, that dream of yours last night was pretty vivid, wasn't it? And it wasn't a very pleasant thing that happened to you."

"But it was only a nightmare."

"I know it was only a nightmare, Nell – but you yourself had to admit that it was 'different'. You said you could have sworn that the events in your dream had actually happened to you. How do we know that what you dreamt may not carry some sinister significance?"

This, of course, started us off on a new phase of speculation.

For my part, I was inclined to treat it lightly. Dreams, I argued, were just dreams. It was true that Freud attached a great deal of importance to them – but Freud only explained them as being symbolic of the functionings of the subconscious mind; he never tried to suggest that a dream might be connected with a supernatural event.

Mr. Nevinson, however, pointed out that what was happening to us could not be explained scientifically, hence why should we not be justified in entertaining the belief that this dream of his wife's might be connected in some way with the events of actuality? Especially, too, he went on, as the dream in question seemed to resemble so closely, in general characteristics, the incidents with which we were so familiar. She had heard a flute in her dream, and it had seemed to compel her to follow it. And there was this glimpse of something greyish and furry scurrying past her. It all seemed to fit together perfectly, didn't it?

But, as might have been expected, this discussion soon fizzled out and left us where we were at the beginning. It was futile continuing it, we all agreed, for we could prove nothing; we could state nothing with certainty. There was no precedent that we could use as a basis for our deductions.

That very night, though, an incident occurred that made us wonder. At about half-past eleven Mrs. Nevinson awoke with a scream, and when her husband and I rushed in to see what was the matter she told us that the identical dream of the night before had recurred.

The room was in darkness when Mr. Nevinson and I went in, and it was I who switched on the light, using the electric torch I had brought to find the switch which was near the dressing-table.

As the sixty-watt bulb flared alive I assured myself that it must have been my imagination – but I could have sworn that just at the instant the light flooded the room I had a glimpse of some shapeless mass vanishing over the window sill. Automatically I ran to the window and flashed the beam of the torch on the veranda – but there was nothing to be seen, so I had to conclude that it must have been some optical illusion induced by the abrupt change from darkness to brilliant light.

In the meantime, Jessie was sitting up in bed blinking around with alarmed sleepy eyes and asking what was wrong, while her mother, on the other bed close alongside of hers, lay flat on her stomach, her face buried in her pillow, like a frightened child. Neither of them used mosquito nets, spiders holding no dread for them – and there are no mosquitoes at this season.

When, eventually, we succeeded in making Mrs. Nevinson realize that there was nothing to fear, she sat up and told us about the dream. She was perspiring, and her face looked pale. She breathed in a slightly laboured manner, as though from recent exertions, and her hair had a straggly, untidy appearance.

"It was exactly like last night," she said, "except that I seemed to advance a little farther along that jungle track. It was really peculiar. I felt far more frightened than last night. I felt as if I'd got nearer to some horrible place. And then just suddenly that bony hand clutched my arm and something whispered in my ear. It said: 'No farther today'. And then I woke up."

Her husband listened with a grave face – so grave a face that Jessie, who was very sensitive to his moods, kept watching him with anxiety as though impatient to hear what his verdict would be.

After a silence, Mr. Nevinson said: "There was one new feature in tonight's dream, it would appear. The fact that you progressed farther along the track." He glanced at me. "Milton, what do you think?"

I shook my head.

Jessie exclaimed: "I believe it's a kind of warning."

"A warning?" Her father gave her a frown.

"That's what I think it is," Jessie nodded. "Mother is going to be led to some horrible place, and then – and then anything might happen."

"Anything like what?" I asked.

"She might be killed."

"Killed in her dream?"

"How can we be sure she can't be killed in a dream? Perhaps she might just not wake up, or something like that. I think it's that manuscript – it's because she tried to burn it. She's roused up some terrible evil against her."

12

Jessie, in her fright, might have spoken rashly that night when her mother had the second nightmare, but her words turned out to be only too prophetic. That dream recurred without fail, and Mrs. Nevinson's terror increased from night to night. With every dream, she said, she advanced a little farther along the jungle track; with every dream the sound of the flute became louder and the horror that was waiting for her grew nearer. And every night the Thing that clutched her arm just before she woke whispered its warning into her ear. "No farther today".

She was quite sure about it now. It was the manuscript. By trying to burn it she had attracted some terribly evil presence to herself, and she was doomed – at least, it looked so, didn't it? She was being taken farther and farther along that track. Eventually she would reach the end of it and be confronted with some unspeakable horror – and that would spell the end of her.

She tried to say all this in a quiet voice, but could not keep out the hysteria that lurked behind her calm.

With the approach of darkness she grew restless and nervous, and kept glancing about her, and it was always with reluctance that she went to bed. She began to cultivate the habit of reading in bed until a late hour – "a thing I've never done in my life before," she said.

Meanwhile, the situation for Mr. Nevinson and Jessie continued to grow more acute. On the first occasion that the apparition became visible to Jessie she shrieked and rushed to one of the dining-room windows. We were at breakfast when the manifestation occurred, and it was the morning after Mrs. Nevinson's second nightmare. Before she could be stopped she had climbed through. She ran across the veranda and was in the act of climbing over the rail when I caught her.

She struggled, imploring me to let her go, and pointing out into the morning at something I could not see. She said that she must go out. It was calling to her. She did not seem so terrified as excited and eager to rush off towards whatever it was that was visible to her. She kept moving her head about as we struggled, seeming determined not to be robbed of the slightest glimpse of the apparition.

Eventually I succeeded in getting her back into the dining-room, though I had to lift her struggling form clear off the floor to do it. But even then she kept jerking her head about and peering past my shoulder in an effort to see outside.

So anxious had I been over Jessie's safety that I had completely forgotten her father. On entering the dining-room, I found Mrs. Nevinson fighting to prevent her husband from going out through the pantry door. She had succeeded in wedging him somehow in the space between the sideboard and the wall, but he was proving too strong for her, and it seemed only a matter of seconds before he won out and edged past her.

Just at that instant, as luck would have it, the flute stopped, and Jessie went limp in my arms. I let her down into the one easy-chair the dining-room possessed, and hurried to Mrs. Nevinson's aid, for even the cessation of the flute-playing did not bring to an immediate end the overpowering obsession that always gripped Mr. Nevinson to follow the apparition outside.

From what had happened on that first night of our stay in the cottage I should have realized this and should have known better than to have left Jessie in that chair, despite her relaxation. I had hardly sprung to Mrs. Nevinson's help and succeeded in holding back her husband (who, a moment later, relaxed and said quietly that it was all right), when my ear caught a stumbling thud, and turning, I saw Jessie move into the sitting-room.

I ran after her and caught her as she had reached the front door. She did not struggle this time, but simply stood rigid, her head strained forward toward the open doorway. There was a trance-like look about her face, and she mumbled in a flat voice so unlike her own that it chilled me. "Leave me. I'm going," she kept saying.

"I must go. I want to go. It's beckoning to me. Leave me and let me go. Let me go. Let me go." There was no intensity whatever in her manner or voice. She spoke in a droning monotone as though being prompted by some invisible presence.

Suddenly she gave a sigh and relaxed. She was trembling, and seemed on the point of collapse. But in a moment she was in control of herself. She looked at me and muttered: "It's gone. I saw it in the corner of my eye. Every time I shifted my head it moved. It's beastly, Milton. A horrible thing."

The events of that morning brought matters to a head concerning Mrs. Nevinson's foolish prejudices. She agreed, when we tackled her, that things had got to a point where we would have to "forget our dignity and call in the help of Rayburn".

Immediately after breakfast, therefore (yes, we did finish our breakfast. My diary notes: "Despite matutinal excitements and alarms, our appetites still intact – odd but true"), Mr. Nevinson and I went downstairs and explained the situation to Rayburn.

The man was incredulous. He kept frowning at us, and it was evident that had he not held Mr. Nevinson in great respect he would have laughed at us and perhaps seriously questioned our sanity.

He had suspected, he told us, that everything had not been right with us upstairs. He had heard his mistress scream out on one occasion, and had heard our voices afterwards. He had wanted to come up and inquire, but after he had "studied the matter over", he decided not to, because it might have looked like interfering in what didn't concern him, and that was one thing he never liked doing. Yesterday Timmykins had told him that something was wrong in the house, but that he didn't know what it was. Well! But imagine such things happening! And in broad daylight! Anyway, he would be only too glad to do whatever he could to help us – oh, yes, we could depend upon that. He would bring up his camp-cot at nights and sleep in the sitting-room if we wanted him to do that. And, of course, he would keep always ready in the kitchen so as to be within call at any minute.

Mr. Nevinson asked him: "You don't happen to know of anyone who might be able to put us on the track of this Indian fellow who gave the canister with the manuscript to Patoir, do you, Rayburn?"

"No, sir, I can't really say I know of anyone." He fell silent for an interval, looking thoughtful, but had to shake his head, at length, and admit: "No, sir. Ah really ain' know nobody, but Ah could make enquiries."

"Of course, we don't want the affair to get talked about too much, Rayburn. It's pretty fantastic, and it may not reflect very well on us if it gets around. People would probably want to think I'd gone off my head – or was practising black arts or something."

Rayburn promised to be discreet. He remarked that he knew very well what the people up the river here were like. They were always seeing some jumbie or hearing a *kanaima* whistling in the jungle. (According to Indian folklore, a *kanaima* is an evil spirit of the jungle which sometimes lodges itself in the body of a human being, turning the individual so possessed into a homicidal fiend whose sole occupation is to roam about the jungle in search of victims. It lured unsuspecting humans into its clutches by uttering a peculiar whistle.) Rayburn said that he knew better than to discuss any matter with the superstitious people in these parts.

As events fell out, without Rayburn's help we should have been in a bad way indeed. He kept to the kitchen during the day, but was always on the spot within a few seconds of being summoned. The cottage was small, it is true, with many windows and doors and a most convenient veranda, but had Rayburn been of a listless or dilatory temperament there were many occasions on which he would have arrived too late to stop Mr. Nevinson from leaving the house.

I learnt several lessons concerning human conduct during those weeks. For instance, not only did Mrs. Nevinson's prejudices vanish, but she could not do enough to make Rayburn at ease in the house, and, at nights, was fussy about seeing that he was comfortable on his cot in the sitting-room. She and Jessie drank Ovaltine before retiring, and she insisted that Rayburn should have a cup.

Another aspect of our behaviour that made me marvel within myself was the ease with which we began to adapt ourselves to the nerve-racking conditions; the deliberation with which we planned our "defence". Rayburn was assigned exclusively to Mr. Nevinson, and myself to Jessie, and the danger-call was "Come, Rayburn!", the non-emergency call being simply "Rayburn!". This distinction was, of course, necessary, for there were quite a few instances when Rayburn's presence was needed in the usual course of the day's routine. Mr. Nevinson might want some information concerning the work at the sawmill, or might want to give Rayburn instructions to pass on to the foreman, and, naturally, we had to do all we could to avoid "wolf! wolf!" alarms.

Our meals and our toilet, too, we soon arranged to suit the situation. If a manifestation occurred, say, at mid-morning, then we knew that we could safely have our lunch and tea in peace, but dinner would be "unsafe", so we would prepare sandwiches for this meal, because we could eat these in the sitting-room or on the veranda and could discard them at a moment's notice if the need arose.

Similarly, we took care not to be locked in the bathroom or the toilet for any length of time if we knew that a manifestation might be in the offing. And, except at nights, we kept together all the time, reclining, as a rule, on the eastern or northern veranda. In the late afternoon – between five and six – we took walks around the precincts, accompanied by Rayburn, "like prisoners taking exercise under the surveillance of the warder", as my diary puts it. And in the morning, after breakfast, if manifestation-conditions permitted (this was Mrs. Nevinson's quip), we indulged in boating excursions on the river.

After a particularly upsetting manifestation shortly after a sandwich lunch on Wednesday – our sixth day at Goed de Vries – Mrs. Nevinson announced that she could not stand this kind of life any longer, and intended to return to New Amsterdam by the steamer on the following morning. She was in earnest about it, too, and it took Mr. Nevinson and I nearly an hour to convince her that it was imperative for us all to be up here.

"Returning to New Amsterdam won't help matters, Nell," her husband told her. "I don't believe if we went to Japan it would make any difference. Those dreams would plague you just the same at night – and if it is decreed that anything horrible should befall you, your being in New Amsterdam wouldn't make you any safer than being here. We're not dealing with anything physical, or even rational, you know. I used to hear that flute in the office in New Amsterdam with traffic thick in the street outside and typewriters going within a few feet of where I sat. Distance wouldn't avail. Our wisest course is to remain up here and do what we can to find the remains of this Dutchman, and have them buried as he requests in his manuscript."

"But that's just the point, Ralph," she rebutted. "What chance have we got of finding his remains – and this flute of his? You say Rayburn has made enquiries and no one in the neighbourhood can supply any information about this Indian who was supposed to have given the canister with the manuscript to Patoir. Well, what's the good of remaining in this wilderness to be plagued by this uncanny business if we haven't the faintest clue as to the whereabouts of Mynheer Voorman's bones and flute? So far as I can see, we may as well give up hope of ever finding these remains. We don't even know the site of this old plantation where Mynheer Voorman died. We can't just go searching blindly over hundreds of square miles of jungle, so why not let's get back to our civilized comforts in town? At least, in New Amsterdam, we'll be away from this dismal jungle and river. We'd feel more confident in our ability to resist this horror."

This was a reasonable argument, but my host and I would not admit it, for we were both determined that a solution must be found to our problems before we returned to New Amsterdam. To leave Goed de Vries and go back to our homes in town would signify defeat, and, added to this ignominy, we would still have this uncanny curse attached to us.

I intervened and told Mrs. Nevinson: "I can see what you're driving at, Mrs. Nevvy, but do you think you'd be happy if you returned alone to New Amsterdam? Anything could happen to you in the house there. Up here you're with us, and we can protect you if any physical danger arises."

"What about the psychic dangers? Can you protect me from those? So far as I can see, the only dangers we know of are psychic ones."

"Another thing, too," I said hurriedly, ignoring her sarcastic sally, "is that your presence here may prove of help to us in ridding ourselves of this nuisance."

"In what way, pray?"

"Well, for one thing, your own experiences are a little different from ours, aren't they? They represent an unusual aspect of the phenomenon, and we never can tell what we might not be able to learn as a result of studying your case."

"Christ! Milton, you do speak like one of these heavy leather-bound tomes. You should have been a politician, boy. Not an artist!"

From her tone and the twinkle in her eyes I knew that her husband and I had won the debate, so I rose, deciding that this was the propitious moment to withdraw from the scene of conflict. To linger longer would have been tactically unsafe. One incautious word or gesture, and her defiance might have returned.

I lit a cigarette casually and said: "I think I'd better go and see what Jessie is doing. She's been out on the veranda there for some time."

"Try and see if you can persuade her to have some Bovril. She only ate one sandwich at lunchtime."

"I'll do my best," I said, and made my way on to the northern veranda where Jessie was lying in the hammock slung up permanently out there. (It may be as well to mention that during the four or five hours following a manifestation we generally relaxed our precaution of herding together, and gave ourselves a little more freedom of action. We had discovered that the minimum interval between manifestations was six hours.)

In me, as I tiptoed my way towards the hammock, there was no suspicion of the new development in our weird experiences that I was about to discover. I tiptoed because I did not wish to disturb Jessie if she proved to be asleep. But I need not have bothered; for I saw her protruding legs move slightly as I got near. She was awake but yawning, and her eyes were red as though she might not long since have awakened.

She confirmed this when I enquired, yawning again and adding: "I even did a little dreaming."

"Ah! Dreams. Not nightmares like your mother's, I trust?"

"No, I can't very well describe it as a nightmare exactly," she said hesitantly. "But I did feel a little queerish, all the same, as if it might have turned out to be a nightmare if I'd slept longer. What time is it?"

"About half-past two," I told her – and saw her sag with relief. "Nothing to fear until this evening."

"How much you want to bet it'll happen about eleven o'clock tonight when we're all trying to get our beauty sleep?"

"Such is life – in Spookland."

"Where are Mother and Daddy?"

"In the sitting-room. Your father and I have been having a strenuous time of it trying to persuade her against returning to town by tomorrow morning's steamer."

"She wanted to go back to town?"

"I'm afraid so. Anyway, the danger seems past. I think we succeeded in getting her to see reason."

She laughed. "Milton, in some ways, you're a big ass!"

"What do you mean?"

She half-stifled another yawn. "Nothing. It's just the way you express yourself."

"Oh. Just so. Anyway, let's hear about these dreams of yours. Have you forgotten them or do you think you can describe them in detail?"

"Why do you want me to describe them? You think they may mean something?"

"We never know, do we? Can't afford to ignore the slightest circumstance that may help to throw light on the mystery."

"It was nothing really startling," she said. "I've been having all sorts of queer dreams since things went funny with us up here."

"Still," I said, "I'd be glad to hear what it was like."

"It's getting hazy now, but from what I can remember, I was out on the veranda here in this very hammock, but it was at night and there was lovely moonlight outside. I was looking at the trees and the sawmill and saying to myself what a wonderful night it was – and then it just occurred to me it was late and I shouldn't be out here alone. I glanced at the window there" – the windows of the bedroom she and her mother occupied opened on to this section of the veranda – "and I saw Mother in bed. She seemed to be tossing about restlessly in her sleep – not tossing about in the usual way, but as if – well, as if she might have been fighting with something lying in bed with her. I don't remember much after that."

I stroked my chin and grunted. "Interesting, all the same. Especially the last part of it."

"Oh, wait," she said suddenly, frowning as though trying to remember, "I can remember something else." She hesitated, then nodded. "Yes, I remember now! Just before waking up it seemed as if the moon went under a cloud and everything grew darker around me. The last thing I knew was that I seemed to see a kind of shadow pass out of the window there and settle on my chest – but before I could get scared I must have awakened."

I exhaled a cloud of smoke, remarking: "I admit it could have been far more terrifying, but, nevertheless, it does sound a trifle out of the ordinary, doesn't it?"

"You mean the shadow part of it, I suppose?"

"Exactly – and the fact that your mother seemed to be fighting with something lying in bed with her. But don't go getting alarmed now," I went on hastily. "It could easily be a sort of postprandial semi-nightmare. That sandwich you ate might have done the trick."

"What's postprandial?" she laughed. "You and your big words!" She altered her position a trifle as another yawn attacked her. She was wearing a dress with an unusually low neck, and at the sink where her breasts divided I saw something that nearly caused me to drop my cigarette.

I opened my mouth to speak, then checked myself. Fortunately the watering of her eyes consequent on the yawn prevented her from noting my reactions.

Trying to control myself, I said as casually as I could: "By the way, your mother said I was to try to persuade you to take some Bovril."

"Couldn't stomach such a thing now," she replied. "I'll probably take an egg-flip before the afternoon is out. I'm not hungry."

"I say, Jessie, didn't you have a bath just before you came to lie in the hammock here?"

As might have been expected, she gave me a look of surprise. "What a question! Of course I did. I was afraid to have one this morning because we were on the lookout for the flute, but as soon as everything was over – just a while ago – I had a bath. Why do you ask? Don't I look as if I'd bathed?" She tried to smile, but she must have noted the tenseness in my manner. "What's wrong, Milton?"

"There's a mirror in the bathroom. I suppose you sometimes look into it when you're drying yourself, don't you?"

She went a little pink. "Naturally. Why shouldn't I?"

"Did you notice anything on your chest today?"

She bent her head and looked down at her bosom. "Oh, heavens!" She pressed the neck of the dress lower. "But I don't understand. How did this get here? It wasn't here before I got into the hammock. I'm sure of it. Oh, my God!"

"It's much fainter than the one that appeared on your mother's ankle last Thursday night."

Her face had gone greyish with fear. "What can it mean, Milton? Why should it appear on me, too? I haven't tried to burn the manuscript as Mother did. I haven't done a thing."

I shook my head, leaning against the rail and gazing out at the still wall of green that loomed up on the edge of the clearing. The sawmill chugged away in even, lulling cacophony – a jagged but hypnotic noise in the daytime silence. Then I became aware of a soft, soughing sound, so that I had to tilt my head.

It was a distant wind travelling through the jungle. It seemed to approach us, getting louder and louder as though it might be a shower of rain. Then it faded away and was no more.

Behind me, I heard Jessie mutter: "That shadow in my dream. Milton, remember what I told you? Just before I woke I thought I saw it pass out of the window there and settle on my chest."

13

As you must, in all likelihood, have realized already, I have suffered, in making this record, from the great disadvantage of being hopelessly ignorant on matters pertaining to demonology and the occult sciences. It is true that, at twenty-three, I was fairly well-informed and widely read, but an elementary knowledge of Yoga and the fact of having perused and minutely digested the Bhagavad Gita do not make one an authority on the mysteries of necromancy.

At the time of these occurrences at Goed de Vries, I was as much a blundering ignoramus as any of the others in that cottage, despite my airs and pompous pose at being a man of inexhaustible knowledge.

Being human, we each of us formulated theories in an attempt to explain the manifestations or arrive at some conclusion as to how things would develop in the long run, but as none of us happened to be in a position to refute or confirm the other's conjectures, we never took each other seriously.

That is why nobody seemed particularly impressed, or even politely interested, when on Monday of the following week I propounded my Great Theory, as my diary pretentiously designated it.

Before I set it forth here, however, I must first narrate what happened on Thursday, our seventh day at Goed de Vries, and on the Sunday night following, for it was the events on these days that formed, if not the foundation, at least the main superstructure of my theory.

The mark of the flute on Jessie's chest, as had been the case with Mrs. Nevinson, did not last. Within twelve hours it had faded completely, and, somehow, its appearance, though perplexing, did not create as great a sensation as it would have done a few days earlier. I think I have remarked before about the callousness we were acquiring towards what was unusual. Even Jessie herself soon grew resigned to the mark and stopped tilting her head down to examine it.

That night no manifestation occurred, and this, of course, came as no surprise to us, for we had already known the interval of quiescence to last as long as twenty-eight hours. We spent a bad night, all the same. Sleep was almost impossible. We tossed restlessly, expecting at any instant to be roused into alertness and activity. Shortly before midnight Mrs. Nevinson evidently dozed off, for we heard her cry – the cry we looked out for every night – and knew that she had just awakened from her usual nightmare. Mr. Nevinson and I did not go into her room nowadays; we just called out to ask her if everything were all right, and she would reply: "Yes. The same old thing."

Shortly before dawn, however, Jessie gave a shriek, and when we went in she told us that she had had a nightmare, too – a nightmare very similar to the one that was plaguing her mother.

She related it to us and we saw that the chief differences consisted in that, first, it was not as vividly realistic as her mother's, and, second, that instead of setting out from the cottage here in a *corial*, she had found herself abruptly on the jungle track. As with her mother, she had heard the flute playing ahead of her up the track, and there had been that strong feeling of something horrible in her wake and of advancing irresistibly towards an even more awful horror than that which pursued her. But, again, there was this difference: instead of the adventure taking place by the light of day, as it did in her mother's version of the dream, it happened at night in moonlight. She spoke of seeing patches of moonlight on the ground as she hurried along, and it was moonlight that filtered down through the foliage overhead and which made the path visible to her.

The closing phases of the dream, too, did not coincide exactly with those in her mother's. No bony hand on her arm had brought her to a halt. What had compelled her to stop was the cessation of the flute-playing. The instant the flute had fallen silent she had felt as though some invisible cloud had pressed against her body and checked her. No voice had whispered a warning into her ear, but she had an idea – she was not too clear on this point – that the moon must have gone under a cloud, for everything seemed to go densely black around her, and a dreadful musky odour entered her nostrils. She had heard a rustling, pattering sound of footsteps – not human footsteps, she was sure – in her vicinity, as though a goat or some such creature of that size and nature of feet were scurrying past her. She thought she heard it utter a hollow grunt – but this was not an animal sound; at least, it had seemed part human and part animal. She began to stagger about helplessly in the darkness, and once she knew that the Thing brushed past her bare legs. She had felt its furry body, and it was a damp, clammy kind of fur that sent a shudder through her. She had shrieked and then awakened – and she was certain that when she sat up in bed she could still smell that musky odour.

I am describing this dream incident of Wednesday night – or early Thursday morning, to be precise – merely as a prelude to relating what happened during daylight on Thursday.

On that day we had a light breakfast, taken in standing postures around the table. We did not want to risk sitting at table, and at the same time, we were determined that, come what might in the way of spectral phenomena, we were not going to be cheated of our coffee and boiled eggs. Sandwiches for breakfast, we decided, would have been intolerable.

The meal over, we went out on to the northern veranda to await events.

The early morning mists had not yet dispersed entirely. Shadowed spaces amid the tree-foliage had a bluish, smoky look, and grass and shrubs glistened in the mild, slanting sunshine. The sawmill engines were silent – milling operations did not begin until eight o'clock – but we could hear the usual jabber of voices and the laughter of the men, the clatter of a board or a low thud from a heavy log. The air was laden with the leafy, water-vapour scent of the jungle and the musky dankness of the river. A bird, far downstream, kept sending harsh cries on the wet air – a metallic, bleak sound well in sympathy with the general moistness that pervaded the scene.

Soon, however, the sun began to take effect. It shone from a sky remotely daubed and speckled with cirrus and cirro-stratus which dissolved as the morning progressed, giving way to large, puffy white clumps of cumulus. The dense water-vapour decreased, and heat began to rise in trembling silken veils from the grassy clearing around the cottage.

Though we could not see the river from where we were, we could hear it gurgling secretively at intervals or swishing amongst the shrubs that grew along the edge of the bank, and now and then, too, the splash of a *corial* going past would disrupt the silence.

Presently the engines at the sawmill began to splutter and growl – and then they were off. The day's chug-a-chug, chug-a-chug commenced, and smoke from Mr. Nevinson's pipe curled in abrupt blue wisps out into the morning, as though there might have been a little engine working in him, too, I thought fatuously. He adjusted himself more comfortably in the easy-chair.

He was reading an anthology of the world's best weird stories.

His wife, in the hammock, was knitting crochet doyleys, and Jessie kept turning the leaves of a copy of the *Strand Magazine*. For myself, I was entering in my diary an account of the events of the previous day and of the night just past. My easel stood ready at the other end of the veranda, a half-finished canvas displayed on it. Despite the strain of events I had already managed to complete two canvases so far.

I was still at work on my diary when the clear, leisurely flute-notes reached my ears. From habit, I glanced at my watch and saw that the time was nine twenty-six. The spectral flute-player had come much closer to me now. He seemed somewhere in the vicinity of the sawmill this morning.

Dropping diary and pen at once I shouted: "Come, Rayburn!" and took two swift paces towards where Jessie reclined in her deck-chair with the *Strand Magazine*. In the background of my awareness I could hear the quick thumping of Rayburn's foot-treads in the pantry.

This morning I was in for a surprise. I found myself standing foolishly by Jessie's chair, hands half-outstretched to grasp her.

But there was no need to grasp her. Instead of the expected

burst of activity from her, nothing happened. She stared up at me in a wondering, questioning manner. She murmured: "What's it? There's nothing wrong yet. I haven't seen anything of it – or heard the flute."

"But it's happening now. It's the flute."

She rose and looked about her. "But I don't hear a note. I don't see that awful thing, Milton. It – it should have been down there – in the clearing." She glanced towards where Rayburn had her father firmly in control. "Daddy's seeing it as usual, isn't he?"

"Of course he is. And I'm hearing the flute, too."

She gave a puzzled grunt – and then as I looked at her I noticed something. Her features were twitching slightly, as though she were about to grimace. I could not remember her ever having showed her nervousness in this way.

I looked down, and another thing struck me. Her fingers were curling in slowly, as though her hands were making an attempt to clench but for some reason never completed the action.

Then the flute stopped, and she seemed to sigh and look about her in new wonder – almost as though she had just been roused from a fit of deep reflection or had had her attention called off abruptly from a book in which she had been engrossed.

"Has it stopped now?" she asked.

"Yes, it has – but how did you guess?"

She shook her head, mumbling confusedly: "I don't know. I just seemed to guess. But why didn't I hear it, too, as usual, Milton? What's gone wrong now? You think I'm going to be left in peace now – or is this something new that's going to happen to me that I don't know about yet!"

What could I reply? I was as much mystified as she. I shook my head and told her that I was beaten. "Completely floored, believe me."

"I don't like it," she frowned. "It makes me feel as if – well, sort of uneasy. Oh, I hate all this mystery and horror!"

"Look here," I said, squeezing her arm, "better not say anything to the others about this. I mean, about not hearing the flute. It will only worry them more than they're already worried. We'll keep it to ourselves, and I'll keep a strict eye on you to watch developments."

She nodded, and said it would be all right. She wouldn't say anything.

For the rest of that day I kept remembering that grimace and the slowly curling fingers. My Theory had stirred into life, and it was so horrible a theory that I felt breathless at the mere thought of expressing it aloud to anyone. I could do no work at my easel that day.

When the flute sounded again at about seven that evening, Jessie reacted in the same way as she had done in the morning. I watched her face with an avid fascination – and again I saw it: that grimace. And I looked down and saw her fingers curling inward. It was as though, for those few moments, she had cast off her old personality and was having a new and unspeakably evil one thrust into her. And she put up no fight! She was allowing herself to be swamped by this ugly presence from outside, whatever it was and wherever it came from!

Once I noticed her glance across at her mother who stood by the pantry door watching Rayburn restrain Mr. Nevinson, and I knew that it was no fancy on my part. In Jessie's eyes there was a threatening, malevolent glitter. As she watched her mother, her fingers grew more restless in their curling, clutching motions. A tremor of horror and alarm rushed through me.

Afterwards I asked her what had been her sensations, and she gave a start as though surprised. Her expression became one of genuine blankness and innocence – I knew without doubt that she was not staging an act. She was unaware of the transformation that had taken place in her only a few seconds before. She said: "How do you mean what were my sensations? I tell you, I heard or saw nothing. It's stopped completely – and I hope it doesn't start up again, either." There was genuine relief in her voice.

I made a bantering remark and let the matter go at that, for I knew that it might do her more harm than good if I acquainted her with what I considered to be the true state of things. I said nothing to her parents, either, about what I suspected, for I had a sudden fear of their suffering from a nervous breakdown. We were none of us very far from this condition, and there was no predicting what effect the shock of my intimation might have on them. (As events fell out, however, it became imperative for me to tell them of my suspicions only a few days after my coming to this decision.)

That night Jessie was again inflicted with the moonlight dream, as we came to call it, and, like the previous night's, it occurred some hours after the one from which her mother suffered.

It was decided on the following morning that the two of them should, in future, sleep with a light. The suggestion came from me. I told them that it would give them both more reassurance. Mrs. Nevinson said that she never slept well with a light, but I told her that it need only be a ten-watt lamp, and it could be shaded to keep the rays from falling directly on the beds.

She agreed that this would be in order, and Rayburn, who kept a stock of bulbs over at the sawmill, brought the required one which we substituted for the sixty-watt normally in use.

At twelve minutes past three on Friday afternoon (the exact time, to the minute, of every manifestation, except perhaps two, is recorded in my diary) came the next alarm. This time, however, I divided my attention between studying the reactions of Jessie and taking down the notes of the flute. This was something I had wanted to do ever since these manifestations had started, but I had not had the opportunity. What with taking care of Mr. Nevinson, and then Jessie, I had been too fully occupied.

As I have already hinted, music has always been one of my leading obsessions (up to the time of these events I had even tried my hand at composing), therefore it was no difficult matter for me to jot down that simple, formless little tune with which, by now, I had become only too familiar. (Later I shall insert it somewhere between paragraphs).

Over the weekend Jessie's behaviour grew increasingly alarming. On Saturday afternoon when the flute sounded her face grew distorted in a most revolting manner – and I heard her utter a sound that seemed neither bestial nor human. It was indescribably terrible.

It was on Sunday night, however, that I had confirmation of the horrible thing I suspected. At the top of the page allotted to that Sunday in my diary I wrote: *Day of the Black Night*.

14

When we retired on that Sunday night we did so with compara-
tively easy minds (at least, the others did – I did not). We had been
looking out for another manifestation since dusk, and when nine
o'clock came and nothing had happened, we had begun to
become pessimistic, fearing that we would be roused during the
night. But at nine fifty-two the flute made itself heard, and when
the crisis had passed we went to bed, feeling that we could count
upon at least six hours of peace.

Jessie and her mother would be roused, in any case, when their
respective nightmares occurred, but this feature of our troubles,
upsetting as it was, somehow seemed to unnerve them far less
than did the flute manifestations. In a way, I suppose, it was
natural. A dream, when all was said and done, was a dream, and
no matter how vivid, could not hope to outdo for sheer dread and
terror a tangible event experienced when one was fully awake.

Jessie, though deaf to the flute and unable to see the apparition,
still anticipated the occurrence of the manifestations with nervous dread – a fact that did not fail to register on me. Her mother's
tenterhooks resulted from her anxiety on her husband's behalf.
Whenever a manifestation occurred it was always upon her
husband that Mrs. Nevinson's attention became focused. It was
because of this obsession with her husband, in fact, that she had
not, even up to this Sunday night, observed what had been
happening to Jessie. I had been the only witness to the girl's
strange antics. I was the only one on this Sunday night, therefore,
who knew of the horror threatening the girl, and that was why, as
I got into my pyjamas, I was far from easy in mind. Indeed, I was
in a particularly morbid mood.

I knew that sleep would be impossible for me, so instead of getting into bed I climbed out of my bedroom window and began to pace about on the veranda with a cigarette for company, little guessing the greater horror in store for me that night... Up and down the veranda I paced.

The moon crescent Jessie and I had seen with such startling abruptness ten nights before at the dining-table was now nearly full, and the grassy clearing around the cottage and the billowing walls of jungle that encircled the clearing glimmered with a soft loveliness that, to my poisoned senses, was completely out of keeping with the atmosphere in this cottage. It seemed wrong. The night out there, I told myself, had no right to look innocent and dreamingly beautiful when events in the lives of us four people were so ugly and troubled.

I heard a stirring in Mr. Nevinson's room, and my host appeared at the window. "What's the matter, young man? Is tonight to be another of your sleepless nights?"

"It's beginning to look so, sir," I replied. "Nothing like sleep in my eyes, I'm afraid."

"Try one of the hammocks. It proved successful with me two nights ago. It's a trifle warmer than usual tonight."

"Yes, that's so. I'll just potter around a bit and see how I feel after a while." For an instant I was tempted to break my resolve and divulge what I knew about the horror I had been witnessing during the past few days. But I restrained myself. Apart from my desire not to cause him more worry than he already had to bear, I felt that it would be embarrassing for both of us. Imagine having to tell someone, an old and respected friend whom you had known since boyhood, that you had seen his daughter becoming changed into a loathsome fiend, that the sight had made you shudder not only with terror but with nausea as well. Apart from the fear of hurting him, I dreaded being ridiculed. Spectral flutes and furry demons were absurd enough, but to talk now about Jessie's being possessed of an evil fiend! The thing sounded like the limit in medieval superstition!

Mr. Nevinson turned off from the window, and a moment later I heard him get into bed. This was by no means the first night I had paced the veranda through not being able to sleep, so he must have thought nothing of my presence out here. He himself had done it. Mrs. Nevinson, too, and Jessie.

An hour must have elapsed, and the cottage had fallen into absolute silence, when the sudden desire to move around on to the northern section of the veranda took hold of me.

I heard the river gurgle secretly as though something in its depth had divined my thoughts.

Putting out the cigarette I had just lit, I went round on to the northern section to find rhombuses of dim light on the floor – light from the ten-watt bulb in the room occupied by Jessie and her mother.

Walking silently I paused near the hammock and looked into the room.

Outside, a frog had begun to chirrup.

They were both asleep – Mrs. Nevinson on her stomach, Jessie on her right side, her face towards the window. As usual, they had not let down the nets.

I could detect nothing strange about them – nothing grotesque or unreal. They were simply two women asleep – one a middle-aged one with a young-looking face, and the other a girl of nineteen. Had a stranger stood at this window and gazed in at them lying there he would have had no reason to associate with them such things as demons and spectral manifestations, stigmata and recurrent nightmares.

I began to ask myself what on earth could have possessed me to want to come round to this side of the cottage to peer in at them. What had I expected to see?

I looked about the room, but everything was as I had known it before. It was true that the white-enamelled dressing-table, in this dim, shaded light, had a ghostly air, looming up in the north-western corner with a waiting intelligence, the toilet articles on it sparkling dully like sly eyes on the watch for unknown presences. But this impression I knew how to treat: it was the result of my over-sharpened imagination. I could ignore this. Sniff at it.

I turned off and got into the hammock, and for the next hour or so tried to induce sleep by staring with wide-open eyes at the roof, this being a trick of mine which sometimes works. The eyes get tired, and, after a while, the lids have the inclination to sag heavily; immediately this happens you force them open again in a wide stare, and go on doing this until, at length, from sheer fatigue, you find that you have no more will left to open your eyes again, and soothing blackness descends – or should descend, for it is not always that it proves successful.

This was one of the nights when it did not. Too many thoughts kept plaguing me. Too many thoughts and fears. And the hammock rope creaked every time I shifted my position. Often, too, I would gaze hard at the dimly visible roof of the veranda, and my whole body would freeze in terror as I thought I could discern a dark moving blob with sprawling legs. It seemed just about to drop on me when I would realize that it was only a flaw in the paintwork – not a spider.

Once or twice I heard Jessie or her mother turn over and breathe heavily. Once a fire-fly darted over the veranda rail in a silent green-white arc and alighted on the hammock rope near my outstretched feet, and instinctively my feet recoiled, and I could hear the toes cracking faintly.

Another time a sharp rustling came from the shrubs that grew near the sawmill, and I sat up stiffly in a jerk and stared out towards the spot – but I heard nothing of it again.

The steady, high-pitched churr of insects was the only sound in the moonlit night that seemed entirely free of innuendo, for the steady beat of the Petter engine held a metallic threat, as though at any instant it would turn into a fiendish stutter or a cold, dry cackle of laughter, or a death-gargle.

The fire-flies danced their perpetual dance against the background of silent jungle.

The scene of sawmill and trees stared back at me with a knowing and abstruse smile, shifty amid its glimmering loveliness, and I could hear the river. The dankness of rotting leaves and the vegetable reek of black water came to my senses. A midnight chilliness tingled in the air.

I lay back once more, and after a while a soothing restfulness came over me so that I was in no doubt that, at last, sleep was near. I tried to resign myself to the feeling, relaxing physically and mentally.

But to no avail. I would imagine I was asleep, but would know that it was only a belief into which I had wishfully lulled myself. Thoughts would continue to weave unending patterns in my head. Now and then Jessie's distorted features drifted fearfully in the blackness behind my closed eyes, and I would sigh and fidget about.

Presently, the horror began.

I became aware of a musky smell. It was not the river or the jungle. At first, I thought it might be a residue of some perfume on a garment in the women's room – but the next instant I knew it could not be so. There was a rankness in it, and this rankness grew stronger.

I lay still, frowning up at the roof. I tried to convince myself that it must be my imagination again playing a trick on me. But the conviction refused to take root. The smell persisted. Could it be some kind of incense that one of the men in the logies was burning? No, I felt sure it was not incense. There was an animal quality about it. That goatish reek could not be associated with incense. It baffled me completely. I could not identify the thing no matter how I tried.

I sat up and looked slowly around.

The hammock rope creaked.

And the frog was chirruping again.

The smell persisted.

I felt the need for a cigarette, but feared the smoke would drift into the open windows and disturb Jessie and her mother.

I turned my head and glanced in at them. The hammock creaked again – and I uttered a whispered curse.

The smell grew stronger.

Again I felt impelled to glance in at the window.

I did so – and this time my gaze steadied.

Something had moved in the space between the two beds – something grey and of no definite shape. A humped shadow-mass that settled out of sight on the floor.

Mrs. Nevinson began to move restlessly in her sleep. I could hear her sigh.

Jessie slept on peacefully.

I remained where I was, my gaze on the space between the two beds. My heart seemed to beat at a distance – perhaps amidst the shrubs by the river's edge where that frog was chirruping now in leisurely but steady insistence. I felt the moist gaze of the moonlit jungle upon my tingling back, as though out of their aloof silence the dense walls of foliage were trying to communicate a warning to me to rush away back to my room, to leave this spot as quickly as I could and not pry further into matters that were beyond this known scheme of living.

But I did not move, determined to witness what was happening in the room.

The strange smell gradually faded, but I noticed that Mrs. Nevinson's restlessness was increasing. After a moment I heard her moan. Her face kept wincing in a troubled manner. More than once her hands would pluck feverishly at her hair or she would make a dismissing gesture as though to ward off some unseen insect that might have been worrying her. This gesture would be accompanied by a look or irritation or fear. There was an air about her, even in her sleeping condition, of resistance and determination. She impressed me as keeping off from her person some unpleasant influence or undesirable presence not visible to me.

Soon, her body moved without cessation, wriggling and twisting, her arms flailing about and her breath coming in laboured grunts. There was something tortured and desperate about her efforts, as though she were wrestling with a powerful unseen opponent.

When, at length, her frenzy had reached such a pitch that her body began to arch and heave and seemed in danger of tumbling off the bed, she opened her eyes with a gasping cry, then, with a whimper, buried her face into her pillow and grew still, though her back kept heaving from her recent exertions.

I heard her husband call out sleepily from his room, and saw her raise her head as she replied: "The nightmare again, Ralph!"

Throughout all this Jessie had slept on without moving. Even the voices of her parents had not disturbed her.

Stiff and chilled, I sat where I was, unable to take my gaze off the two women. Intuitively I seemed to know that the crisis was not yet over. There was something wrong still, and even though I watched Mrs. Nevinson's breathing grow normal and knew that she had sunk once again into a restful slumber, I could sense a tenseness in the atmosphere. A waiting. The air seemed to contain a malignant vibration.

I began to be aware again of that devilish smell. It grew stronger and stronger, and the air around me seemed to thicken with a pall of evil. I felt a panicky restlessness coming alive within me, and again there was that tingling down my back. The ether seemed alive with baffling apprehensions. The frog had stopped chirruping, but the very absence of its chirruping appeared to signify something important and urgent. The night was livid with insect-churring. A livid, high-pitched rawness that, with the chafing beat of the Petter engine, seemed to bruise my consciousness into a numbed, bleeding silence. I felt as though I were poised within a bubble of buzzing incoherence.

Watching, I saw the thing happen.

In the space between the two beds a humped greyness slowly began to rise into view.

I jerked my head to make sure that it was not my fancy – that it was not a hallucination. And I knew that it was not. I was actually seeing it.

It rose in a shapeless greyish-brown misty mass as though a damp cloud of dust had been spirited up from the floor. But there was too much deliberation in this thing for it to be dust. Leisurely it began to heave itself – almost with a human wriggle – over Jessie's bed. Then I saw it gradually subside and vanish into the girl's sleeping form.

15

As you may recall, I hinted in my prefatory remarks that it was my intention to narrate these occurrences in chronological order and that it was only in deference to the wishes of Mr. and Mrs. Nevinson and Jessie that I did not publish my bare diary notes but decided, instead, to amalgamate them into this narrative form. I am a great stickler for tidiness and routine, and even at the risk of being somewhat annoying, I must once again defer touching on the matter of my Theory in the detailed form promised until I have recorded, for your benefit, what Mrs. Nevinson told us the following morning – that is, on Monday – concerning her dream of the night before.

"Something new has come into it," she said, "though I don't know that it matters much. Everything seemed like the nights before except that suddenly I found myself breaking off from the track and pushing my way through the jungle. The flute-player seemed to have left the track and taken to the jungle, and I had to follow him. The bush was thick, but I managed to go through it somehow. And then that bony hand gripped my arm and whispered. It said this time: 'Eight nights – and then to join us!' And for some reason I began to smell something musky and queer near me – and I could have sworn I saw two greyish furry hands reaching out for my throat. After that I woke up."

I asked her quickly: "You're quite sure the wording was altered? 'Eight nights – and then to join us!'? Was that what you heard?"

"Yes, those were the words," she replied. She sighed and added: "But for Christ's sake don't start cross-examining me about it. I'm not in the mood for that kind of thing this morning, Milton."

I grinned and said, "I'll try not to be a nuisance, but just a question or two, all the same. About this musky smell. Was last night the first time you became aware of it?"

"It must be the same smell I smell in my dreams," Jessie intervened. "A musky kind of goatish smell."

"That's right," said her mother. "There is something goatish about it."

"You haven't answered my question, Mrs. Nevvy," I persisted. "Was last night the first time you became aware of it?"

"I'm not sure – and that's quite honest. I didn't like saying it before, but I have an idea I've been smelling it for the past two or three nights. On waking up from that dream – or just before waking. It's so hard to tell. I thought it must be my imagination, but last night I was sure about it. I did smell it – "

"In your dream – or on waking up?"

She gave me a withering look. "What are you trying to discover now? Why does it matter if it was in my dream or on waking up?"

"It's extremely important," I said.

She shrugged. "Well, it must have been in my dream, I suppose. It couldn't have been actually in the room, could it? Unless you want to hint that Jessie and I are so neglectful of our personal hygiene that we're beginning to smell like goats?"

Jessie turned red and uttered a scream of laughter, and Mr. Nevinson, who had been sucking at his pipe in a rather morose manner, slumped in a Morris chair, also began to shake with laughter.

"You may think it's a laughing matter," I frowned, "but, I can assure you, it's very, very serious. More serious than you imagine."

It was at this point that I deemed it propitious to tell them of my Theory. After their mirth had died down I said: "Look here, sir, I've been thinking this thing over seriously, and I'll swear I've got it this time. I've hit on a theory – and I'm pretty sure it's correct."

Considering, however, that this was about the sixth or seventh time within a week or two that I had "hit on a theory", none of them gave signs of being particularly impressed by this abrupt declaration.

Mr. Nevinson nodded, smiling with an abstracted air as he began to refill his pipe. His wife clicked her tongue and mumbled something about being sick of theories. Jessie hardly seemed to have heard what I said.

"Let's go back to the manuscript," I said, in the manner of a judge summing up (at least, I am sure it must have sounded like that to them). "In the first part of it Mynheer Voorman speaks bitterly of 'the Blacker Ones'. You remember the passage that goes: 'I curse these black wretches, even as I curse the Blacker Ones.' Well, 'black wretches' obviously refers to the rebel slaves who murdered his wife and children. But what does he mean by the 'Blacker Ones'? Mr. Nevvy, in his translation, used capitals, and I think capitals are justified, because I'm sure that what Mynheer Voorman meant was that these blacker ones were not human being but evil entities. Arch-fiends of the nether regions."

I paused here for dramatic effect, but Mr. Nevinson continued to fill his pipe, unruffled, and Mrs. Nevinson had begun to tinker with a clock which she was trying to repair (she had always been good at repairing clocks; it was a hobby of hers). Jessie looked through me with an air of resigned boredom.

I continued. I referred to the "roaming presences" also mentioned in the first part of the manuscript, pointing out that this would indicate that the Dutchman had anticipated being in a state of unrest after death.

"My theory of the matter," I went on, "is this: Mynheer Voorman used to dabble in demonology – "

"Good Lord! What a revelation!" exclaimed Mrs. Nevinson, interrupting.

"Wait a bit," I said patiently. "We've already discussed that, I know, but what I've thought now is that he had reached such a stage in his experiments that he realized that in death he would still be in touch with these devilish entities, and he would have no rest until he could get some human in the physical world to aid him in his struggle against the fiends who had enmeshed him in their influence – "

"What elegant language!"

"But haven't we talked about all that already?" said Jessie.

"Yes, I know," I said quickly, leaning forward. "But hear what

I've got to say now. Suppose I tell you that Mynheer Voorman has succeeded in securing you as an instrument of aggression against the evil forces ranged against him, Mrs. Nevvy, and that the devil-entities have taken possession of Jessie who is to be used against you!"

Jessie shrieked with laughter. "Oh, Milton! I can see you hate me!"

Mr. Nevinson smiled, and his wife retrieved a small brass washer which had fallen to the floor, and wagged her head with a pitying air.

Ignoring their reactions, I went on: "And that isn't all. Suppose I tell you that Mynheer Voorman is leading Mrs. Nevvy towards where the remains he speaks of in the manuscript are buried, and that these demon-entities are determined that she must not reach the spot, because they know that if we succeed in being guided to the spot we'll carry out Mynheer Voorman's wishes, and that, as a result, Mynheer Voorman will be free from their influence.

"And suppose," I continued, trying to make my voice as rhetorical and dramatic as possible, "I tell you that I'm almost certain that when the eighth night after last night is reached in your dream, Mrs. Nevvy, on that night you will find yourself at the spot where Mynheer Voorman's flute and bones are buried, and that on that night your life will belong to the evil forces which are plaguing us – because, note this, Mynheer Voorman is no match for the evil that is pitted against him. He's struggling desperately to free himself. He's trying to get in touch with us and make us understand his predicament – and listen to this! I believe that by accident you happened upon the right spell, Mrs. Nevvy."

"The right spell? Boy, you're talking like one of these medieval alchemists you read of in old books," chuckled Mrs. Nevinson.

"Very good. But listen to me. That Thursday night, week before the last, when you struck a match and attempted to burn the manuscript was a lucky event for Mynheer Voorman. There's something in fire that is friendly to Mynheer Voorman and inimical to the forces opposed to him. I don't know a thing about spells and incantations and all the rest of it, and it's just sheer guesswork, of course, but that's my feeling. Fire is some sort of counteractive. I suppose it may sound funny, but it looks as if

171

these demon things are allergic to a naked flame, and through that act of yours, Mrs. Nevvy, you brought yourself, so to speak, into direct rapport with Mynheer Voorman, and, automatically, at the same time, you became an enemy of the 'Blacker Ones'. It's Mynheer Voorman who keeps guiding you night after night towards where his flute and bones are buried – and it's one of the 'undesirable presences' which arrests you after you've proceeded for some distance along the track, and whispers that warning into your ear. It's evident that they have no power, so far, to stop you entirely from proceeding along that track in your dream, but they do their best to intimidate you and delay your progress. And last night what did you hear? 'Eight more days – and then to join us!' 'Don't you see the significance of the thing? It may sound highly fantastic and absurd, Mrs. N., but you've got to remember that we're dealing with something that's quite outside the realm of the rational and natural. These evil presences know that should you fail to accomplish the mission Mynheer Voorman intends you to, you, like Mynheer Voorman, will have fallen into their power. In other words, you'll join them and become one of them as Mynheer Voorman himself now is – "

"And play aimless tunes on a flute, too?"

Sitting at my typewriter now, I can smile at this sally of hers. But on that Monday morning twenty years ago I could see no humour in it. I was too tense and earnest and grave a young man to realize the utter ludicrousness of my words and of how incredible and farcical they must have sounded.

That is the chief difficulty in making this record – to set down faithfully what happened and what we said and did, and yet to make it sound convincing.

I did not try to scold Mrs. Nevinson for her quip. I simply told her that I meant seriously every word I had uttered. "Really, I'm dead serious, Mrs. Nevvy," I went on. "I've seen more than you and Jessie and Mr. Nevvy know about, and I've been thinking it over carefully. I'm not talking idly. You're in grave danger – and so is Jessie. Mr. Nevvy's will is strong, and he's been able to resist the evil which has been planning to take possession of him – and I believe he'll succeed in continuing to hold out. But Jessie is a different matter. Her will is much weaker than the will of any of the rest of us, and it has surrendered to the assault made upon it by the black influences that surround us in this place – don't laugh! It's no laughing matter. Jessie has been invaded. The invasion is not complete yet, but it soon will be – "

"Invasion!" It was Jessie who interrupted me. But though she had been smiling a moment before, like her parents, now there was only a suggestion of levity in her manner. "What's this now, Milton? I'm being invaded? Invaded by what?"

Mrs. Nevinson threw back her head and shrieked. "Milton, look here, we've got enough to bother us! You'll be the death of me if you don't look out! So it's come to invasion now! The arch-fiends of Satan are invading my dear innocent daughter!"

Her husband, who had been smiling, looked at me and said: "Milton, I can't blame you for doing your best to arrive at some plausible solution, my boy, but I'm afraid it won't help us very much if you let your imagination run riot."

"Very well, sir," I said – and I spoke in the tone of voice I imagined Sherlock Holmes or that character of Poe's, Dupin, might have used. (As you will note, the temptation to laugh at my younger self is irresistible.) "I didn't want to divulge this yet," I told him, " but I can see now that it's absolutely necessary. I can see you'll have to be informed without delay concerning what has been taking place during the past few days and what's going to take place every day for the next few days with increasing force and malevolence."

I spoke in a heavily histrionic voice, and with a gravity that, now I view it in retrospect, seems screamingly absurd. It strikes a false note, I am aware, to emphasize the ridiculous side of things, but I purposely want to do my utmost to retain as much as possible the exact spirit and atmosphere of that morning.

When I told them of the transformation that had been taking place in Jessie during the past few days and of what I had witnessed the night before, their laughter and bantering remarks changed to a shocked dread. They stared at me. They were anxious and credulous now, for they well knew that much as I might concoct theories out of my vivid fancy, I would never invent such incidents as I had just related.

Mr. Nevinson asked me why I had said nothing before, and I

told him: "For one thing, sir, it would have caused you more worry, and I hadn't yet decided whether I could trust the conclusions I'd formed. But what happened last night convinced me that my theory is correct, and I think it's time you were told."

"But why do you say I'm in danger, Milton?" his wife asked me. "Who will harm me?"

I told her what I thought – told her that, so far as I could see, before many nights had passed Jessie would have been completely invaded by the shadow-mass I had watched vanishing into her the night before.

Jessie said nothing – simply sat staring at me with a strained expression.

Now that they were taking me seriously I began to feel uncomfortable, and found myself fidgeting a great deal. Very hesitantly I went on to say that if they took my advice, in future it would be wiser if Jessie and her mother slept apart. And I said I thought, too, it would be no harm if the two of us men sat up to keep watch, taking it in turns.

None of them made any comment.

I could hear Jessie breathing.

The morning was still very young. We had not yet had breakfast. The jungle looked wet and misty, and there was no sunlight. A blue-grey mass of clouds that towered rigidly above the trees obscured it.

We sat in silence, listening to the river's soft swish and gurgle and the sound of the men's voices and laughter from the logies beyond the sawmill.

This was one of the moments to which I have alluded. We were aware of that not-too-sane, aerial feeling of being in the midst of occult events and yet still conscious of the commonplace routine of existence; sensible to the normal around us, yet, within, intelligent of something beyond our control that had intruded upon the accepted pattern of our human actions.

We were still waiting for Timmykins to come and announce that coffee was ready when it began to happen.

The treble notes rose clearly on the morning air, seeming (to me) to come from somewhere just beyond the southern veranda.

16

To you who can skim through these pages in a detached spirit, many aspects of our situation must have seemed clear – that is, of course, viewed on a basis of fantasy – even before the propounding of my Theory. For instance, I am sure that it must have been obvious, at least, that in Mrs. Nevinson's nightly dream-progress along that track there was the possibility, even probability, that we were being shown the way towards the spot where Mynheer Voorman's flute and bones lay buried.

Unfortunately, however, it was not given to us to view matters in such a dispassionate manner at the time when the events were actually occurring. Even I myself, despite my confident opinions expressed on that Monday morning, found during the days that followed that I was not so sure I might not be mistaken. Why should I necessarily be right? I was no expert on occult matters, as I have already said. And again, as I think I have mentioned, too, where could we *begin* to look for this track? It might have been two miles or twenty miles from where we were. It could have been down any of a dozen little creek-tributaries.

That was why Monday passed and then Tuesday and Wednesday, and still no action had been taken to go in search of Mrs. Nevinson's dream-track.

The manifestation before breakfast on Monday convinced Mrs. Nevinson that something fearful was taking place in Jessie. Instead of fixing her attention on her husband and Rayburn she kept her gaze on Jessie, and witnessed with me the fiendish change that took place in the girl. At one point she uttered a cry and pressed her hands to her face, muttering: "My God! My God!" in a voice of distracted horror.

We held several earnest conferences, but we could formulate no definite plan of action. Jessie sided with me in my suggestion to take a trip up the river to search for the track-opening which might or might not exist, but both Mr. and Mrs. Nevinson were against the idea. It would be risky, they argued, to venture out on the river for any length of time. A manifestation might occur, and what would be our plight if the boat were overturned and we were thrown into the water? It would be like playing into the hands of the evil influences at work against us. In the cottage here we could be sure, at least, of a certain measure of safety.

We consulted Rayburn, and Rayburn said that there were many track-openings along the left-hand bank and down creeks. One or two he knew and one or two he did not. Most of the tracks led out to the savannah land between the river here and the Canje Creek (a hundred-mile-long tributary of the Berbice, and a creek only in name) and the Corentyne, and some just petered out into the jungle-belt. Yes, plenty of them that he knew were well-beaten tracks and frequented by Indians and forest-rangers and cattle-men, but there were others that only animals used and that "hardly nobody ever walk on – but dose is just de ones it will be hard to find, sir, unless you move along very close to de bank and look carefully to see where de bush part. Dat might take you a whole day, and even then you mightn't find de right one like what you say you see in your dream, ma'am."

That decidedly put the veto on the scheme, for Rayburn was an experienced bush-man, and we knew that he was eager to help us in whatever way he could.

On Monday night, while on guard duty on the northern veranda – this idea of mine received no opposition – Mr. Nevinson witnessed the horrible spectacle in the women's room. In his usual quiet and undramatic manner he told us about it the following morning, but despite his calm, his face looked older and more haggard than I had ever seen it before.

On Tuesday night, hardly fifteen minutes after I had taken up guard – it must have been nearly half-past two – I began to smell that evil musk. I had been standing by the veranda rail, smoking and gazing out at the brightly moonlit scene, but turned at once and strode across to the window nearest me.

Mrs. Nevinson and Jessie still slept together in their room, but the beds had been differently placed. This northern room, as I have explained before, was a large one, and rearranging the furniture in it had been no difficult matter. Mrs. Nevinson's bed had been shifted to the other side of the room, near the door that opened into the sitting-room, while Jessie's had been left near the window where it had always been. There was a distance of at least fifteen feet between the two beds.

The room, as on the nights before, was lit by a shaded ten-watt bulb. Everything seemed normal, and the two women were sleeping peacefully.

There could be no doubt, however, about the smell. It got stronger with the passing of every second.

I kept my gaze on Mrs. Nevinson, waiting for the first signs of restlessness to begin. A wisp of smoke from the cigarette held between my fingers curled past my head and drifted into the room, and I could have cried out, so tense was the state of my nerves.

Any instant I expected to see that brownish shadow-mass materializing, and the smoke, in its slow coiling progress across the room, proved extremely disturbing; it seemed like a herald of what I knew would soon follow.

A minute or more must have passed, but still nothing happened in the room, though the smell persisted strongly about me.

I began to fidget. I glanced round at the shadow of the hammock on the floor. The moonlight that silvered the veranda took on a sinister look. It seemed cold and inimical – in league with the evil abroad in the night.

Something thumped faintly near me, and I turned, looking this way and that, fear seeming to crush my heart as though in a metallic band.

But there was nothing to see. Nor could I discern anything that might have accounted for that peculiar sound.

Again it came – seemingly not a yard distant – just behind me.

I turned quickly.

Nothing.

The smell persisted. It seemed so dense in the air now that I could feel it clinging to the walls of my throat – a virulent, sickening miasma.

My cigarette, for some reason, sent up thick, rapid coils of smoke. It was not quite half smoked. I continued to hold it between my first and second fingers.

The thump came again – insistent. Just behind me. There was something disembodied in the sound, it now struck me. It might have been produced in mid-air. Intuitively I began to feel it could be nothing physical.

I looked about me, but could discover no cause whatever for the phenomenon. I had a sensation of being stifled. I glanced into the room, but Mrs. Nevinson and Jessie slept on undisturbed. By now, I told myself, Mrs. Nevinson should have begun to grow restless, and there should have been some sign of that shadow-thing.

All at once there seemed to occur some strange convulsion behind me. I felt myself jolted violently as though something soft and furry had charged into me. I heard a dull thump and a tiny, lisping sound.

With a cry, I turned, almost choking from fright.

Only the moonlight met my gaze. The smell was fading.

Then I saw my cigarette. It was lying on the floor. I must have dropped it in my fright. Automatically I bent and picked it up, intending to throw it outside, then saw, to my amazement, and renewed uneasiness, that it was out – entirely black where there should have been a redly glowing tip. It was not even warm to the touch – but dead cold.

I did not stop to ponder this, however, for I heard a sound from within the room, and moving to the window again, I peered in and saw that Mrs. Nevinson had begun to toss and sigh in her sleep – and, yes, it was no imagination; there was a dim wisp of greyish-brown settling out of sight under the bed in which she slept. It was the shadow-horror.

What followed need not be related. It was exactly as on the Sunday night, the only difference being that when Mrs. Nevinson had composed herself for sleep again after awakening from her nightmare, the shadow-mass emerged from under her bed and wreathed and wriggled its way all the fifteen feet across the room towards Jessie's bed. It hovered for a moment, then settled out of sight into the girl's sleeping body.

At breakfast the following morning – or, better, I should say, daylight the same morning – I told them about my experience with the cigarette. I was excited. "I'm sure about it now," I said. "There's something in my theory about fire being inimical to them. So long as my cigarette kept burning that shadow-thing could not pass into the room to do its dirty work. We've got to exploit this factor – "

"Just a minute, my boy!" Mr. Nevinson interrupted me. "Now, let's get this aspect of the matter straightened out. You say that while your cigarette kept burning nothing happened. But did you put it out, or wasn't it, as you say, dashed from your hand and extinguished?"

"Something happened behind me, sir. I don't know exactly what it was. I told you about those queer thumping noises I heard. Well, I felt myself pushed, as if something had collided with me – and the next thing I knew was that the cigarette was on the floor and the smell was fading. Don't you see it proves – "

"It proves that fire is, as you conjecture, inimical to the influences working against us, but it seems also to indicate, I should say, that our enemies are perfectly capable of ridding themselves of the obstructing conflagration, whatever form it takes. In the case of Nell, the match was struck from her hand as she attempted to apply it to the manuscript. In your case, the cigarette was struck from your hand – or at any rate caused to be struck from your hand. What do you think would happen if we placed, as you are suggesting, a lighted lamp or candle on the window sill? Doesn't it seem feasible that this lamp or candle would be knocked aside and the flame extinguished?"

I admitted that this had not occurred to me. I was far too enthusiastic and pleased with myself to think clearly that morning. The thought that I had discovered a weapon with which to fight back and keep the evil at bay predominated above every other, and my emotions rather than my reason took control over my utterances. Jessie, I remember, intervened to accuse her father of wanting to throw cold water on every scheme I devised, but I told her: "No, Mr. Nevvy is quite right. I doubt whether the experiment would help much."

Not a moment later, however, I had another idea and said:

"But look here, sir! I've thought of something else. Suppose we set out deliberately to foil them. Suppose we set out – "

"But isn't it understood that that's what we want to do, Milton!" Mrs. Nevinson cut in impatiently. "Stop making speeches and get down to something – "

"Very well, Nell! Let's hear what he has to say." Mr. Nevinson spoke in a tone that was at once conciliatory to his wife and encouraging to me.

"I was only thinking, sir," I said, a little uncomfortably, "that if we could get another flame going the instant the lamp or candle was put out we might still succeed in foiling them. We could have a shallow pan ready at each window with a rag of waste in it soaked with petrol, and stand prepared to apply a match the instant the lamp or candle was snuffed out. When we come to think of it, it's no difficult matter to put out a lighted match or a cigarette, but I bet you what you like a blazing rag soaked with petrol would give them something to think about!"

Mr. Nevinson smiled and returned: "You speak as though you were referring to tangible human adversaries, Milton – "

"That won't work," his wife snapped. "Why couldn't they extinguish a flaming rag soaked in petrol! We're dealing with supernatural forces – "

"Even psychic phenomena," I parried, "are governed by some sort of law. These things that have been happening to us may seem mysterious but that's only because we don't understand the laws that control them…"

A strenuous argument developed, but in the end Mr. Nevinson settled the matter by pronouncing not only his approval of my experiment but his intention to try it that very night.

In my diary I stuck in two sheets of exercise-book paper, both sides of which are crammed with words on the lines as well as between. It is my description of the events of that night.

17

Please don't imagine that, in a weak moment, I am about to break my resolution, and my word to the Nevinsons, regarding the publication of my diary notes. Consider it a temporary lapse and nothing more if I quote briefly from the scribblings that relate to the events of that Wednesday.

"After lunch – Rayburn brought candles. Mr. N. prefers candles to lamp. Says no sense in having lampshade broken if devil-spooks get violent. Agree. Humour: Man came asking us if we had any soft-grease – meaning soft candle. He keeps chickens, and one of them has developed pip. Soft candle good remedy, he says. Mrs. Nevvy told him no, we have only *hard* candles. Jessie turned red, shrieked with laughter – first really hearty laugh heard her indulge in for days. Believe she suspects smutty innuendo in Mrs. N.'s quip. And shouldn't doubt it. Mrs, N., under air propriety, good sport…

"4.51 – manifestation. Mrs. N. deadly pale. Jessie reached out for Mrs. N.'s throat. I checked her – she snarled horribly, tried to hurl me aside; amazing strength; not her own. For first time – she gave off slightly musky odour. Mrs. N. confirms smelling it, too. All of us horrified. Questioned Jessie matter of routine after manifestation. Still declares she experiences nothing unusual. 'I just feel a little shivery', she said, 'and want to hug myself – that's all. But I don't hear the flute or see that horrible thing I used to see a week ago. I don't feel anything is wrong with me. I can't understand how you say I change like this.' Mr. N., as usual, heard flute and saw demon-thing, but strength of attraction no more powerful than before. Asked him if he thought he could resist following it if not stopped. Replied no, could not;

but for Rayburn he would follow it… Admitted terrific strain on nerves. Fears he might soon break if situation does not improve…

"After dinner – 7.30 – we are in state nerves concerning experiment tonight. Mrs. N. suggesting not bother – might rouse up more horrors, she says. Jessie, too, wavering. Told her about her weak will, and she flew at me like tiger-cat. Why should I insist her will weaker than wills of rest of us! 'You're a fool! A conceited fool!' Mother and father called her to order. Jessie sobbed hysterically. We all consoled her. Felt really soft about her myself, and sorry I tackled her about her weakness. Really believe developing soft spot for her, in spite resolutions to desist from falling in love. Must pull up. Won't do, this. Jessie got laugh on me in dining-room just before dinner when spider crawled from under sideboard and I nearly stepped on it. I leapt ten yards, and yelled. Rayburn rushed in thinking it was another manifestation. Killed spider. Harmless house-spider with egg, but I believe I hate these more than hairy bush ones."

The above was written on Wednesday itself, but what follows I did on Saturday morning.

"At about nine Jessie fidgety. Suggests she should sleep with her father. Afraid to sleep as usual in northern room. Mrs. N. told her not to be coward – her father and I would be on guard whole night on veranda. Jessie still insisted. Argument. Convinced her at last no purpose served in sleeping in father's room. He would not be in there tonight, in any case. Any different room wouldn't stop spooks behaving as on previous night…

"At ten past ten Jessie and Mrs. N. went into their rooms to retire, Jessie's face strained. Could have given her a hug. Must check self in regard these impulses. Both Jessie and mother glanced about nervously. Admit nervy myself. Dropped watch and cracked glass. Mr. N. seemed calm, but underneath I know he was as tense as rest of us."

That is as much as I shall quote. My purpose in giving you this glimpse into my diary is merely to illustrate the state of our nervous and mental balance during the hours that preceded the experiment, and to do this without having recourse to long and wordy descriptions. Now that we come to the point, however, when events are actually about to involve the experiment itself, I must leave my diary and resume the old method of narration.

The moon, that night, rose late, for it was on the wane, and when Mr. Nevinson and I, in pyjamas, went out on to the northern veranda to begin our vigil we were almost startled by the bluish-reddish glow that threw the tops of the trees in the east into sharp and detailed silhouette. But then anything would have startled us. As Mr. Nevinson chucklingly remarked: "I shall soon begin to take fright at my own hand when it scratches the back of my neck."

As we approached the hammock, Jessie's voice asked nervously: "Is that you, Daddy?" And we saw her face appear above the window sill.

"Aren't you asleep yet?"

"There's nothing like sleep in my eyes tonight," she said. She was sitting in bed in pyjamas, her chin resting on her knees, her hands mechanically massaging her feet and toes. In the dim light of the ten-watt bulb her face looked strained and furtive.

From the other side of the room her mother called: "Well, if you two stand there holding a conference with Jessie I don't think I shall ever sleep, either." She spoke a trifle irritably, and turned over in a restless manner.

After advising Jessie to lie down and try to compose herself for sleep, Mr. Nevinson and I made a final inspection of the two candles on each of the two window sills. They were fastened tight in improvised candle-rests made out of cocoa tins, these, in turn, being tacked to the sill to ensure that they did not topple over. The space between them was exactly twenty inches, and in this space, also tacked to the sill, stood a rusty, canteen tin plate containing a piece of waste. Rayburn had attended to this in his usual efficient manner, and he had revealed such a feeling for neatness and symmetry that the window sills, as Mrs. Nevinson had commented when surveying them earlier that evening, looked like sacrificial altars at which we were about to "perform desperate and bizarre rites".

The candles had not yet been lit nor the waste soaked with petrol. We had decided that this should not be done until the two women had fallen asleep, for not only might the flickering flames and the fumes of the spirit keep them awake but there would be no sense in allowing the candles to gutter down and the fumes of the petrol to evaporate when there was no prospect of any activity on the part of the demon-entities. From what had happened on the other nights, we felt fairly certain that nothing could materialize unless the two women were asleep.

On the veranda floor, beneath each window, we had placed a bottle of petrol and two spare candles and a box of matches, and two upright chairs substituted for the deck-chairs which usually were out here, for we knew that our vigil would be a tiring one, and the comfort of a deck chair would be too conducive to dozing.

For more than an hour we paced or sat, indulging in very little conversation. Whenever we did speak we spoke in whispers so as not to disturb the two women. Occasionally we smoked.

Outside, the fire-flies flashed in silence, and the moon rose amid inky rags of cloud that dissolved almost as soon as they appeared above the top of the jungle.

In the pocket of my pyjamas I carried my rather aged but still trustworthy Westclox watch, and when I glanced at it at twenty-five past eleven the sky was cloudless and the moon well above the trees. Mrs. Nevinson was quiet, and seemed asleep, but Jessie kept turning and sighing.

I approached my host, and we had a whispered conference. I told him that it might be wise to light the candles now and keep in readiness by the windows. With Mrs. Nevinson asleep, I argued, there was just the possibility that something might happen. But he shook his head.

"We must wait until we're sure Jessie is asleep, too," he said. "Lighting those candles now would simply attract her attention and dispel whatever sleep may be in her eyes at the moment."

So we waited.

Once we heard the camp-cot in the sitting-room creak, as though Rayburn had turned in his sleep. He had offered to join us in our vigil, but Mr. Nevinson would not hear of him losing his sleep. "We do nothing all day, Rayburn. We even manage to snatch an hour or two of sleep when conditions permit. But you're active all day about the place. Can't afford to lose your sleep."

At ten to twelve, Jessie was still awake. I saw her head appear above the window sill, and knew that she was sitting in bed again. Then she looked out and hissed: "I'm sure I'm not going to sleep tonight. It's no use. I may as well get up and come outside with the two of you."

Her father told her: "You're holding up the party, my girl. What about a cup of Ovaltine? Don't you think that might help?"

"I've had two already – one just after dinner, and one just before getting into bed. It will take more than Ovaltine to make me sleep now."

"Sssh! Not so loud. You'll wake your mother." She sat there hugging her knees.

A frog began to chirrup near the sawmill.

And we could hear the river. I looked round at the lovely, peaceful scene. An insect made a sharp ticking somewhere beyond the kitchen. The fire-flies crisscrossed against the shadows of the trees that lay long and black in the grassy clearing. And the chimney of the sawmill, clear and rigid, glimmered faintly. Perhaps there was moisture on it – tiny drops of cool dew in millions reflecting the light of the moon. The tips of my fingers felt icy.

Jessie yawned and lay back. "I'll try again," she said, and her father nodded and returned: "That's the idea. And don't be too scared. Remember we're out here all the time."

Mr. Nevinson and I paced off silently towards the western end of the veranda, and I murmured: "This is something we didn't reckon with, sir. Suppose she doesn't fall asleep until dawn."

He shrugged. "If she doesn't, I take it she won't have to trouble about being invaded. It's evident the phenomenon can only occur while she's asleep. Though I may be wrong, of course. I'm no authority on the matter, I'm sure."

I glanced at him uneasily. "But suppose it does happen while she's awake."

He came to a halt, and began to drum softly on the rail. Then abruptly he stopped drumming and looked at me. "I simply don't know what to think, Milton. My brain feels numb. Quite numb."

"If I were you, sir, I'd let's light those candles right away – and soak the waste."

He nodded. "Very well. Come on."

185

"We'd better warn Jessie first," I whispered, as we were within a pace or two of her window. I looked in and began: "Jessie, we're going to light – " Then I broke off.

Mr. Nevinson stared at me in inquiry. "What's it?"

I put my mouth close to his ear and whispered: "She's asleep."

"Is she? Odd. We haven't left her more than a minute."

"Yes, it is a bit odd, but she's asleep, anyway."

He leant over the sill and touched the girl's shoulder lightly. She did not stir. Her breathing was deep and regular.

We heard the frog near the sawmill. And for some reason I felt an urge to watch that glimmering chimney. The air seemed to grow very chilly of a sudden, and the dank smell of rotting leaves came to my senses.

"Let's light them, sir," I hissed.

In less than half a minute we had accomplished our task.

The candles burned brightly and with a good steady flame, for we had taken the precaution of initiating the wicks earlier that evening.

The petrol fumes flooded the veranda. We had no fear that the candles would ignite the waste, for we had carried out too many thorough experiments during the course of the day. The distance between the waste and the flames was just right.

As prearranged, we took up our posts, I at the window under which Jessie lay in bed, my host to the west of me at the other window.

But the minutes went by, and only the night moved around us, saturated with its millions of infinitesimal happenings. The moon rose higher above the jungle, the fire-flies grew less brilliant as the shadows in the clearing shortened, the river bubbled and gurgled, at irregular intervals a frog would chirrup near the sawmill, then among the shrubs at the water's edge, and we could hear that insect, in the vicinity of the kitchen, that ticked and stopped, and ticked. Often, above the fumes of the petrol, I would find myself aware of the dank, vegetable aroma of the river or of the jungle, and it would almost seem that there was something purposeful in the triumph of this quiet, cool smell that wended its way from out of the depths of the sluggish water – or from the humid spaces among the trees.

The candle flames began to seem like active eyes, liquid and hypnotic, that would tempt me into falling asleep if I watched them too hard.

I glanced at Mr. Nevinson.

He turned his head at once and met my gaze.

I told myself it must be the cane-borer species. Tick, it went. Tick.

My hand with the box of matches felt clammy and icy on the palm. Between the thumb and forefinger of the other hand I kept rubbing the match which I held ready for the instant when the candle flames would dim and go out.

Tick… Tick…

The two women slept on peacefully. It might have been any normal night after a good dinner and two rubbers of bridge and wireless music, and they had bade friends goodbye and had yawned, laughed over a joke and then gone to bed.

Thoughts and impressions moved in me with a fragmentary agitation – dim and in spurts, perplexing and fraught with this or that significance: a significance here that seemed horrible, a significance there that, elusive though it might be, appeared thrilling in the abrupt alcoves of terror it opened up in my imagination.

Mr. Nevinson beckoned to me.

I joined him at the other window.

He asked me what I thought. Should we leave the candles alight? It was not wise that we should waste them. They were rather thin and might burn down within a couple of hours. I told him it did not matter. We must not be taken by surprise. He nodded reluctantly and agreed with me.

I went back to my post.

We continued to wait, fidgeting, glancing around.

The jungle stared upon our backs.

I had left my watch on the floor – near the spare candles and the bottle containing the petrol. I could hear it ticking – bravely and with a reassuring note of prosaic actuality. Easily outdoing the insect near the kitchen.

Every now and then I would bend and take it up to see the time. When I consulted it at twenty past twelve I had no idea that this would be the last time for many hours that I would glance at it. For it must have been about ten minutes after this that the fumes of the petrol-soaked rag took on an odd, rather musty reek, and I realized what accounted for this.

Another odour had mingled with it.

Out of the corner of my eye I saw Mr. Nevinson fidgeting. Our gazes met, and from the expression on his face I knew that he, too, had detected it.

It began to overpower the petrol fumes now. It grew stronger second by second. It dominated the air. The flames of the candles burned steadily.

Instinctively I looked round at the hammock – at the chairs. A sinister gauze seemed to veil the whole scene about us. The moonlight outside had grown unfriendly. The jungle held ugly threats.

Abruptly the candle flames quivered, dimmed, flared bright again. I could almost feel the air itself shifting unstably. But there was no wind.

The smell was intense now. It clung to the throat.

The candle flames quivered again – and slowly leant away from me. Sent out thin tongues that reached toward the interior of the room. They gave the impression of yielding to a power that kept pressing against them. They spluttered a trifle. Then they righted themselves – but behind me the air thumped. A sound that seemed to vibrate throughout the whole cottage.

18

I turned automatically. But, as on the night before, there was nothing visible.

I rushed to the hammock to get my electric torch which I had left there when we first came out on the veranda. I had hardly clicked it on, however, when Mr. Nevinson pressed the switch on the wall in the vicinity of the window at which he was on guard, and the veranda became whitened with the glare of a sixty-watt bulb.

The light, however, did not help the situation. The candle flames were straining into the room again. Putting out tongues. Then they wavered slightly from side to side. The air seemed to shift in a devilish, distorting quake. I could have sworn that the window altered its shape for a fraction of a second, though this was almost certainly an optical illusion.

There were two thumps in quick succession – aerial drummings that might have had their source anywhere in the space between where I was and where Mr. Nevinson stood by the other window.

We stared at each other, two dumb, baffled humans.

I glanced at the window. Saw that the candle flames were not only reaching out towards the interior of the room but were shortening – dimming. I shouted: "Quick, sir! Quick! Don't you see? They're going down – the candles! Get ready to light the waste!"

I heard Mr. Nevinson utter a puzzled exclamation. "The candles? But I can't see anything the matter with them. They're quite steady."

"No! They're dimming. Mine are, anyway. Aren't yours?"

There was a convulsion behind me. I felt myself jolted by some invisible softness. The candles were steady again.

"Did you see what happened? Something barged into me, sir. Didn't you feel it there, too?"

"No. There was nothing here. Nothing at all. I've heard the thumpings, and that's all, I'm afraid."

"Haven't your candles been wavering and dimming?"

"No. Have yours? Mine haven't – not once yet."

"Not once yet!" I almost shouted. "But how do you mean? Mine have – look! There! There again! They're dimming!"

Mr. Nevinson shot a glance past me and called "Who's that there?" He was looking towards the eastern end of the veranda.

I turned with a stumble and saw a greyish figure in the shadowed section near the pantry door. Then Rayburn stepped into the light. He seemed hesitant and fearful, and stammered: "Sir, I didn't mean – sir, I hear some noises and it wake me, and I come to see what wrong."

"Very well, stay," I told him. "Don't go back to bed yet. It's happening, Rayburn. It's happening."

Rayburn approached, clad in the khaki shorts and greyish flannel shirt he slept in. He pointed and gasped: "Mr. Woodsley, sir, look! Quick! The candles. They going out, sir!"

The veranda shook with a disembodied stamping and rolling.

The candles spluttered and wavered, then steadied.

I darted toward the other window, nearly colliding with my host. "Go to my window, sir!" I told him frantically.

"Quick! I want to see what happens to your candles."

"But mine haven't dimmed, I tell you – "

"Go, sir – or no! Wait! Rayburn, you stay there and watch and tell us when the candles dim there again."

The words were hardly out of my mouth when Rayburn cried: "Yes, sir! Oh, Jesus! Look! They dimming down! They going down!"

The candles at Mr. Nevinson's window burned without the slightest wavering – steadily and clearly.

"I've got it!" I exclaimed. "It's Jessie. I know what it is. It's her presence at the other window there, sir."

"Her presence at the other window?"

"Look here, sir, you stay here and be prepared. Don't move. Keep ready to light the waste if necessary."

"What are you going to do?"

Without answering, I hopped up on to the windowsill, agilely avoided the candles and the plate with the waste, and dropped into the room. In two strides I was at Jessie's bed. I grasped the headboard – a low headboard – for it was a bed of the most modern pattern. I pulled the bed along the wall until it was beneath the window at which Mr. Nevinson stood guard. Then I backed off, waiting. Waiting and watching the window.

I may mention that despite the activity and noise, Jessie and Mrs. Nevinson had both slept on without the slightest sign of unrest – a fact that did not escape me. A fact that was to impress itself upon me even more forcibly within a few minutes.

Rayburn moved over to the other window despite my caution that he should relieve me in keeping guard. I shouted at him to get back, and at the same instant I saw the candles at Mr. Nevinson's window beginning to waver. The flames put out tongues and reached towards me.

Mr. Nevinson uttered a soft gasp.

I called to Rayburn: "What's happening at your window?"

"Everything awright, sir. De candles steady."

"Good." I felt a rush of satisfaction, for I knew that I was right. It was Jessie's presence that acted as a directional draw.

The veranda thundered. There was something angry and frustrated in the ugly stamping and thumping. A new note of aggression.

Without waiting to ponder the matter, I again approached the girl, grasped the headboard and hauled the bed into the central part of the room. My object was to shift her out of range of the windows, if I could, and in my nervous hurry I did not stop to think that the windows commanded virtually every section of the room. There was no getting out of range of them. However, my efforts were not unrewarded. (Could I only have guessed at the moment what a doubtful reward it was to prove!)

The noises on the veranda stopped, and I heard sounds of satisfaction and approval from Mr. Nevinson and Rayburn.

"That's it, young man. I believe you've balked them."

"Push the bed farther in, sir," Rayburn advised.

"What of the candles?" I called, beginning to perspire from my exertions.

"They're steady," Mr. Nevinson called, though I could see this for myself. Only Rayburn's were out of range of my gaze. Rayburn called that his, too, were steady. Everything was all right.

I began to look about the room.

I had hauled the bed to within a few feet of the door that gave into the sitting-room, and, incidentally, almost alongside the one in which Mrs. Nevinson lay asleep. I stood between Jessie and the window, and I wondered whether this circumstance might not also have accounted for the cessation of activities on the part of the influence outside.

We waited, silently on the watch for what was to happen now.

Perhaps two minutes must have elapsed, and still the candles were steady. Still there was no sign of any disturbance on the veranda. And then, in a flash, I saw how by my very efforts to balk the evil I had been foiled.

Happening to glance towards the door in the course of my furtive vigil, I saw curling into the room along the floor, under the bottom of the door, a thin, dirty, greyish-brown wisp. It suddenly billowed up in a wriggling hump and began to squirm its way towards Mrs. Nevinson's bed.

I heard Rayburn shout: "Oh, Jesus God! Look! Look what happening!"

It was too late. The thing had vanished into the gloom under Mrs. Nevinson's bed, and at once Mrs. Nevinson began to stir and sigh in her sleep. With a groan, I realized that I had been a fool to shift the bed so near to the door. Even though the door had been shut and locked, there was no flame before it to act as protection – and this was the result.

In the midst of my confusion and disappointment I thought of another device that might, even at this stage, save the situation.

Mrs. Nevinson had begun to toss in earnest now, so I knew that there was no time to be lost. Bending, I slipped my hands quickly under Jessie's sleeping form and lifted her off the bed. She moaned softly, but I took no heed. Moving to the door, I managed, in spite of my burden, to get the key turned after a moment's fumbling. The knob did not give any trouble, and in a second I was out of the room and hurrying across the sitting-room. I stumbled into a chair and knocked over the bookstand with the magazines before I got to the door that gave into the dining-room.

Into the dining-room, into the pantry, and on to the veranda I hurried. At any instant I expected to feel some furry arm arrest my progress. At any instant I was certain I would hear an angry, scrabbling snarl of demoniac rage beside me in the dark.

Rayburn and Mr. Nevinson stared at me as I approached, but, unheeding, I placed the sleeping girl in the hammock and heaved a breath not so much of relief as of sheer desperation and excitement.

"What have you brought her out here for, Milton?"

"She'll be safer here," I gasped. I pointed shakily to the window. "When it leaves Mrs. Nevvy it will try to wriggle across and get into Jessie. The flames at the window ought to stop it. We'll see. Got to try something. Can't just resign ourselves and let it do its worst."

Without waiting for any argument, I hopped up on to the window sill and returned into the room. In there I watched Mrs. Nevinson in the final frenzy of her nightmare. As her writhings and heavings grew animated to such a degree that I knew they were about to cease, I turned quickly and said: "Be on the lookout there, Mr. Nevvy! Rayburn, stay where you are. Don't move. If those candles threaten to go right out light the waste at once. Watch the candles carefully. Don't take your eyes off them one half a second."

"Yes, sir. I watching dem good," said Rayburn, a breathlessness in his voice.

"Hadn't you better come out here, Milton?" Mr. Nevinson said tentatively. "We may need your help – "

"I want to see what happens in here – "

I broke off, and glanced at Mrs. Nevinson who had just given a gasp and grown still. She sighed, opened her eyes, looked at me and said: "What are you doing in here, Milton? It was the nightmare again." She spoke in a weary, indifferent voice, then turned over and lay still.

I darted to the bed and shook her shoulder. "Don't go to sleep again, Mrs. Nevvy? Wake up! Quick! Get out of bed."

Even as I touched her I heard a slight sound under the bed – a faint scratching or scraping. I shook her again – then backed away with a cry.

Leisurely and with its foul wreathing squirm, the shadow-mist was seeping from under the bed. A monstrous, dirty cloud, it curled and humped its way past my ankles while cold and hot shudders moved through my body. The stench that rose around me sent me reeling. I began to cough and groan.

I could hear alarmed gasps and exclamations from Mr. Nevinson and Rayburn. Rayburn bawled at me to get out of the room quickly. Both of them began to call out stammered advice.

Unheeding, I turned again to Mrs. Nevinson. I shook her, shouting at her to wake. But to no avail. She lay there without stirring.

I have never known such utter frustration as I knew in that moment. I heard Mr. Nevinson calling at me to look out, be careful, it was coming at me, get out of the way, run to the window quickly. Rayburn told me to get to the door, it was circling after me, he said. "Quick, Mr. Woodsley! Quick!"

In a dazed way I perceived that it would be hopeless to try again to rouse Mrs. Nevinson. This was no sleep, I realized. In that desperate instant I remembered how, during our discussions the day before, we had asked her why it was that, even though I had revealed what I had witnessed in the room here, she was never curious, after waking from her nightmare, to watch that shadow-mass wriggle its way across the room to Jessie. Surely she should have wanted to verify the phenomenon for herself. But she had replied that she always felt too tired and immediately fell asleep again.

It was no sleep, though. It was a sort of coma. And Jessie was in a similar plight. That was why she had not awakened when I lifted her from the bed and took her out to the veranda. Even at this instant I knew she was still unconscious in the hammock where I had put her.

This went through my head in a crackling whirl, and it was not until I became aware of a thundering that seemed to occur right at my feet that I understood the reason for the urgent warnings from Mr. Nevinson and Rayburn.

I glanced down to see a thin cloud circling slowly about me, grey and weird and menacing.

I have often read of people being "paralysed with fear" or "paralysed from sheer horror". I don't doubt that such a thing may be possible, but all I can say is that so far as I myself am concerned, my first impulse on seeing that thing was to leap from the spot with all the energy at my disposal – and my muscles did not fail me. I did leap. I leapt away and hurled myself across the room in blind panic, heading for the window at which Rayburn stood on guard. But even as I was in the act of hopping on to the sill there was an eruption behind me, and, to the accompaniment of a shattering clap as though a thousand toy balloons had popped simultaneously in desultory fashion, I found myself jerked backward and sprawling on the floor.

I rose, only to feel something soft and repulsively clammy charge into me and send me stumbling further back into the room.

The horrible realization came upon me that I was trapped – that I was being prevented from leaving the room, a fellow-prisoner of a misty fiend.

I stood still, panting and staring round, searching for the evil shadow-thing. But it was nowhere in view now.

Through what seemed a gauze-like barrier I became conscious of the gestures and voices of my host and Rayburn. They were beckoning to me and calling me to the windows. I heard Mr. Nevinson say something to the effect that It had gone under the bed again – to hurry. Rayburn was offering to grip my hands and help me over the sill.

I rushed towards Rayburn's window again. Mr. Nevinson had crossed over to join Rayburn by the time I got there. I put out my hand to grasp Rayburn's – but the room behind me vibrated with ethereal cracklings, and I pitched backward. The stench, which for some reason unknown, had abated considerably during the past minute or two, swirled into renewed activity and with an augmented density.

My stomach heaved as I stumbled to my feet again.

Mr. Nevinson and Rayburn were both advising me to make

another rush for the window. "The westerly window!" Mr. Nevinson shouted – and I saw him and Rayburn appear at the westerly window – the one that it was Mr. Nevinson's duty to guard.

Almost croaking from fright and bewilderment, I shook my head and waved them back to my window – the window I had been guarding before entering the room – for I saw the candles dimming there; wavering and reaching out towards the veranda. "Hurry back there! Quick! Light the waste if the candles go out! Don't move from there!"

Then I saw it – yes, actually saw it – in action.

It was swirling up – swirling up from the floor and hovering with a baffled shrinking and convoluted squirm before the open window where the candle flames strained away from it.

I saw something else, too. It began to take shape.

For a dizzying second I had a glimpse of a dim, revoltingly squat head punctured with two oval patches of an incredibly pure lapis-lazuli – a perverted apology for eyes. Shape ended here, and the sickly greyish-brown mist trailed, and then looped, itself over the vague travesty of a head which vanished as the whole mass disintegrated to the accompaniment of a deep thumping in mid-air.

The phenomenon kept me standing there numbed with a peculiar wonder. In that instant fear left me, and I was jolted by a feeling of heightened consciousness that approached elation. I had the sensation of being witness to something cosmic.

But there was no time for reflection. The thing had materialized again. I saw it, after its violent disintegration, wreathing itself into being once more – near the dressing-table. It began to move in my direction, wriggling and humping itself in its usual grotesque fashion.

It was at this point that something landed with a rattling clack at my feet, and I looked down and saw a box of matches. I heard Mr. Nevinson shouting: "Scratch a match and see if it won't help to keep it off!"

Without stopping to ponder on how effective such an experiment might be, I bent and snatched up the box.

The thing had just begun to circle round me when I struck a match.

A brown wall of mist leapt before my gaze and I staggered back. The room thundered. I heard a muffled whistling sound, and then a lisp, and the box of matches was slapped from my hand. When I recovered I saw the shadow-mist swirling near the washstand. The box of matches lay on the rug before the wardrobe. I dashed across and picked it up. Then I heard the voices of Rayburn and Mr. Nevinson calling confusedly at me. I was too dazed to make out what they were trying to tell me, but suddenly there was a clatter on the floor and I saw what they had done. It was one of the tin plates which had been tacked to the window sill. The soaked piece of waste lay a few inches beside it.

"Light it, Milton! Try that! I don't believe it can put that out!"

I rushed forward, and, with trembling hands, fumbled the waste into the plate. Out of the corner of my eye I saw the shadow-mass approaching me.

I struck a match and threw it into the plate, backing away quickly.

Whatever it was flung me across the room I never knew. There was a drumming surge of sound in my ears, a shock of movement, and the whole perspective of the room seemed to go awry. I came up with a bump against the wardrobe.

The voices of my host and Rayburn, I now realized, had been joined by those of Jessie and her mother. I heard them exclaiming, glanced at the bed and saw Mrs. Nevinson sitting up, staring around in astonishment and terror. At the window with her father, Jessie was gazing in at me, her lips slightly apart.

But this was not all.

Throughout the cottage there was a high shriek sounding, as though someone were blowing fiercely on a flute. Just one note, alarmed and urgent that quivered on the night air.

Of the shadow-horror I could see no sign, but the candles at the easterly window – the window I had guarded earlier that night – were out.

The waste in the plate which I had lit still flared brilliantly in the middle of the room, near a crumpled rug. The flame gave an added unrealness to the scene. Mrs. Nevinson's face had a sculptured fixity, and the faces of the others at the windows seemed like wax-masks, especially Mr. Nevinson's and Rayburn's which were shiny with perspiration.

All traces of that awful stench had vanished, too.

But the sustained shriek did not cease.

"It's the flute," I heard Mrs. Nevinson murmur. She was very pale.

From the expressions on the faces of Jessie and her father, I knew that they, too, were hearing it. And also Rayburn, for I saw him turn and begin to look slowly and puzzledly about him.

Then something new happened. Around us, aery and incorporeal, there broke out a babble of sounds. Lost, wild voices – the voices of crazed creatures of air and space, it seemed – set up a stammering throughout the cottage. In the room here – then on the veranda – then seemingly in the sitting-room – back here in the room with us.

Abruptly everything stopped – though the silence that came down was not one of peace and relief. The air had a strange tissue tautness – a thin rigidity and an oppressiveness. A kind of occult waiting.

When Jessie sighed and said: "You think it's all over now, Milton?" you could detect the tentative note in her voice indicative of the conviction that she had merely said what she had to reinforce her courage.

Her mother murmured: "I don't think it is – and you know it isn't." There was such fear and despair in Mrs. Nevinson's voice that the rest of us looked at her.

"What do you mean, Mother?" Jessie asked.

"Didn't you have a nightmare, too? Don't you know what has happened?"

Jessie shook her head. "No, I didn't dream anything. Daddy says Milton brought me out here and put me into the hammock. Daddy and Rayburn say nothing happened to me. When Milton lit the waste in there the shadow-thing rushed through the window and went out into the night. It put out the candles, but it didn't enter me as on the other nights. Isn't that what you said, Daddy?"

Her father nodded.

"Well, I don't know," said Mrs. Nevinson, "but whatever

experiments were carried out while I was asleep have precipitated a crisis. I had the most terrible dreams I've ever had." She pressed her hands to her face and began to sob nervously.

When she had succeeded in controlling herself she said: "It happened as if it was real. It wasn't like a dream. I actually felt I was dragged along through the jungle towards the spot where the bones of this Dutchman are buried – and his flute. I knew it was the spot. I saw him. I knew it was he. He whimpered and besought me in – in Dutch to help him. I couldn't understand a word, but I knew it was that he wanted to convey. He pointed to the spot where he wanted me to dig, and wailed and wailed, and – my God! I – I don't know how to believe all this is happening – "

"Wait! Go on, go on," I urged her. "What happened next? Was he alone when he told you this – at least, when he whimpered and behaved as you say he did? Give us the details. It's important."

"No, he wasn't alone." She clicked her tongue and added: "If you treat me like a child, Milton, I won't tell you anything. Why should I want to keep back the details!"

I began to apologize hurriedly to appease her, but she interrupted me and said: "As long as I live I don't think I could ever forget it. The thing that was with him – my God! I never dreamt such evil beings could really exist." Then she sniggered hysterically. "Yes, I know I dreamt it – but I know it really exists. This wasn't an ordinary dream. It *happened* to me – to my astral body or whatever you call it. I really went through that jungle tonight – the spirit part of me."

Mr. Nevinson and Jessie had come into the room now – and in the tenseness, in the urgency that possessed us, Rayburn thought nothing of clambering over the sill, too, and joining the rest of us as we gathered round his mistress.

"It was a horrible, slouching thing that was with him," she told us. "It was daytime, but the foliage overhead threw everything into a kind of twilight, though I could still make the thing out clearly. It had grey, wettish limbs – limbs like flippers – and there was a kind of fur on its body. And it had a squashed-in head with two spaces like eye-sockets. They looked blue – very blue. Ugh! And – and while Mynheer Voorman kept pleading and whimpering and beseeching me to help him dig up the bones and things this horrible creature squirmed and staggered about. It seemed afraid of something in the air around it. It made queer scratching noises – or scraping noises – and it thumped about, and at one moment I saw something flicker like fire near it, and it seemed to break apart into slimy rags – but it came together again. And then after a while there was a big white flash, and it snarled and sprang at me. I smelt that foul, musky smell, and I heard it rasp out something at me. It was the same voice I used to hear in my other dreams. It used English words, and it said distinctly: 'Seven more hours – and he and you will join us forever and forever!' And it gave a kind of slobbering squeak, and I felt it press something against my hip – something clammy and hard. I couldn't see what it was, but I knew it was a flute. It branded me – branded me as that woman up the river was branded."

"Have you looked to see if – if – "

She interrupted me and said: "Yes, I've looked. See for yourself." Without a thought to modesty, she drew up her nightgown and exposed the back part of her right thigh. And we saw it. Bluish and ten inches or so in length.

Jessie gasped: "Yes, that was it. The same thing we saw on Matilda."

"I believe we're doomed," said her mother, her voice a little cracked, wild. "You have it, too. Every one of you. You, too, Rayburn. Examine yourselves and you'll see. This is what the marvellous experiments have resulted in. Oh, my God! Oh, my God!"

One by one we examined our right thighs – and one by one we discovered that weal. Against the deep chocolate of Rayburn's skin it looked black and ineffably ominous. A satanic mark that made us each stare about us, conscious again of the watching stillness of the atmosphere.

19

At this point you will have begun to understand more clearly why, as I have stated in my introductory note to this story, I hesitated for so many years to publish an account of the events I am narrating. You know enough now of our experiences, I am sure, to agree with me that a story like this is not the kind of thing any normal civilized person would care to go rushing into print. If these were times when the psychic was not looked upon as something surrounded with an unscientific aura – that is to say, a subject about which nothing rationally concrete can be stated and hence one to be treated with smiles and gentle waggings of the head – my task would be a much easier one. But the harshness of our materialistic age is such that I suppose we cannot be blamed for scoffing at that which does not conform with the physical laws that drive us on day after day in our blind, itching urge for survival. What can we *prove* about ghosts and ectoplasm and all the rest of it!

As I write, I am weighed down all the while with the depressing knowledge that perhaps not two per cent of my readers will credit a word of what I am now putting myself to so much trouble to do. Indeed, I have already acquired a feeling of shrugging fatality in the matter. So long, I keep telling myself, as I succeed in satisfying myself that I have done a good job in recording every salient and relevant incident with as great a faithfulness as is humanly possible, why should I bother? Smile with the scoffers, but retain my good humour in the serene knowledge that I have been guilty of no prevarication.

And now I shall have to ask you to pardon my 'dignified' and verbose little lecture. Let us go back to Goed de Vries on that

Thursday morning – for it was no longer Wednesday night when we stood around Mrs. Nevinson's bed watching that hallmark of unknown forces that each of us in turn revealed. I can remember how I moved my head cautiously round to look at the clock on the dressing-table.

It said ten past one.

Jessie must have noticed the direction of my gaze, for she exclaimed: "Look at the time! And we've got less than six hours! Oh, my Lord!"

Her mother snapped at her to shut up. "What's the use of harping on it! If we're going to die in six hours' time, well, that's that about the matter, isn't it? What have we got to squeal for!" She sounded light-headed and irresponsible, and I saw her husband give her an anxious glance. There could be no doubt that her dream experiences had taken a lot out of her. On her face was still that fixed expression of horror, as though even at the moment she were witnessing the blood-chilling incidents she had described to us a short while before.

Writing this is, for me, extremely awkward and painful, for it is no easy matter for a temperament like mine to be detached in respect to vivid instances of the past. I find myself persistently wriggling in my chair as I attempt to set down my impressions of our behaviour on that Thursday morning.

I can recall that I broke out almost as nervously and hysterically as Jessie: "But look here, we've got to do something, you know! We're not just going to lounge around in this room and wait for seven hours to run out! I don't see why we should be scared of any damned silly ectoplasmic horrors! We've got to do something about it. We've got to act."

"Very well, Milton. Come, this is not like you. Get a grip of yourself." Mr. Nevinson patted my arm, but I could sense that he, too, was trembling and in a state of jitters. His mouth twitched frequently.

"No, but I mean it, sir," I shouted. "We can't stand around and do nothing! We've got to act and foil the blasted bitches. Light fires all over the cottage. Surround the place with fire. Show them we don't mean to cave in without a fight. I don't surrender. I never surrender. I fight to the last bloody ditch."

"But fight what?" Mrs. Nevinson rapped at me. "Fight air? Fight mist, and flute-sounds, and bumpings in the middle of the air? You're talking like a fool, boy! We're lost! We've tampered with what we had no right to tamper with, and we're lost. Resign yourself to it."

"I refuse to resign myself to anything. Let them come!" I bellowed, as though addressing myself to the unseen outside. "The rest of you can resign yourselves if you like, but I'm not. I'm going out after them."

I was perspiring and hoarse. It was only after Mr. Nevinson and Rayburn had both grasped me firmly and pleaded with me that I found myself gradually calming down, though I shook in every inch of my body. I sank down on to Mrs. Nevinson's bed and pressed a hand to my forehead, swept with a desperate nausea.

Paradoxically, however, it was what happened at this point to unnerve us still further that brought me in a snap to a state of alertness and self-restraint.

The air began to thump.

I sprang up, glancing quickly around, and summed up the situation in a flash. The waste in the plate was no longer alight; the spirit had burnt itself out a few minutes before. The candles at the easterly window had been snuffed out, according to what Mr. Nevinson and Rayburn had said, when the mist-apparition had rushed from the room on my setting the waste alight. And at the other window the two candles were going out, having guttered right down to nothing.

"We've got to light fresh candles," I said – and without waiting for any argument, ran to the window, hopped through on to the veranda and looked around for the spare candles. In the confusion they had been kicked away from where they had been originally placed beneath the windows. I retrieved two, and hurrying to the westerly window, lighted them from the dying flames of the spent ones.

As the flames rose and swelled out, the air seemed to get less tense, less troubled. The thumping ceased, and the sinister oppressiveness, which had become more intense, diminished.

I returned into the room, the eyes of the others upon me.

I saw Rayburn in his grey flannel shirt and khaki shorts,

standing by the washstand, poised as though to grapple with some adversary. And by the dressing-table Jessie was crouching on the stool, her hands pressed together as though cold, her eyes almost watery with fear.

Mr. Nevinson, in his blue-and-green striped pyjamas, sturdy-looking, his head, massive and bull-like, thrust forward a trifle, hovered by his wife's bed, right hand gripping tightly the left wrist. And in bed, in her flimsy pink nightgown, Mrs. Nevinson sat erect and with that sculptured look about her face that had struck me when I glimpsed her after recovering from the ordeal I had gone through earlier that morning.

It is a tableau that has carved itself on a plaque of metal in my memory. No detail of it could ever be corroded away.

During the next half an hour we made an attempt to discuss what should be done to protect ourselves against the danger that we felt certain was approaching. As might be expected, however, we all wanted to speak at once. We all had ideas to express and conjectures and speculations to vent. We all had suggestions as to how we might solve the problem of overcoming the forces opposed to us – and solve it within the few hours that seemed to remain for us.

Our voices made an incoherent chatter in that room. We were like people drugged – drugged with the urgency of survival – and, accordingly, forgetful of proprieties and race and class prejudices. Many times, in the midst of our excited babble, one of us would dart an anxious glance at the burning candles on the window sill. Jessie once cried out that the flames were dimming – then contradicted herself immediately, admitting that she was mistaken. Another time, I remember, Rayburn said that we ought to light candles at the other window, too, but I pointed out that the two at the one window had proven themselves to be adequate, for nothing had happened yet. There had been no more aerial thumpings.

I believe that everything absurd and crazy that could be uttered by human beings was uttered in that room. The most wild and lurid conjectures would be posed, the most far-fetched and utterly impossible suggestions would be submitted for consideration. Lash ourselves to the beds, and burn a candle at every door and window, and lie still and wait. Let us crouch and huddle on the dining-table and set a ring of lamps and candles around us on the floor. Push out into the middle of the river on a raft of timber, Jessie mooted. What about climbing into a tree and chain-smoking?...

Yes, at any other time it would have been as funny as a scene staged by the Marx brothers. But unfortunately, it was only too grim and real – and we knew it, for that strange apprehensiveness – I can think of no other word – still persisted in the air, pressing heavily on our harrowed spirits.

It was no ordinary peril that threatened us but one that was warped and unnatural and sickeningly horrible – a peril from which we seemed to know with a peculiar certainty there would be no slipping out of once we had been overpowered and entrammelled. For ours would be a transducting death; it would be death fraught, paradoxically, with the definiteness of survival – a carrying over of ourselves into forms the very thought of which was so vile that we could not discuss it aloud but could only let it simmer within our shaken consciousness.

We did express it afterwards – but that morning we each of us were too weak with fear to speculate too far, for we could sense the quality of eternity threatening us as though it might actually have been a wavering, tangible swathe of silk that kept brushing our cheeks at intervals. And in some hellishly clairvoyant manner, we could even fathom the details of it – the hopeless slavering and gibbering that would become a part of our functions: the poisonous shadowed recesses of that backwater of existence wherein dwelt entities that slouched and wreathed and exuded dank miasmas of putrefaction.

You need not ask me *how* we were able to become so suddenly acute in our perceptions – so unique in our intuitive sensations. All I can say is that we *perceived* that there was this fearful and stinking pocket of nether-life awaiting us. With probably the same psychic power that creates a series of retrospective pictures in the mind of a drowning man we *knew* what menaced us. And we could sense, too, that unless we fought with all the fury and bitterness and impassioned determination human will could generate, we might as well consider ourselves already as lost creatures who had stumbled off irrevocably into slush and black-ness – into some cul-de-sac, perhaps, existent amid the unex-plored dimensions of our cosmos. By a chance shifting of circum-stances and dovetailing of events – the coming of that manuscript into Mr. Nevinson's hands, Mrs. Nevinson's attempt to burn it, our experiments with lighted candles – we had moved within range of forces that had nothing to do with the forces with which men are familiar, and we were about to dodge out of reach of normal laws and be gone forever into a new and slitheringly revolting sphere of intelligence.

I know this is very odd language for a person who professes to be rational. But too much of me is back there at Goed de Vries for me to write in a dispassionate spirit. Try as I may, I cannot coax my pen into the restraint of understatement. However, I feel safe, at least, in the awareness that if I have conveyed a sense of instability and lunacy, even a falseness and unreality, it is something that I had, in the back of my mind, wanted to do, for only in this way can I succeed in recapturing here a semblance of the atmosphere of that scene.

Eventually, Mr. Nevinson and I did succeed in obtaining some sort of order among us, and, after this, we were able to marshal our ideas much more coherently. We also did our best to speak in turn and not all together in an excited jabbering.

"The first thing we've got to do," I said, "is to run over briefly the incidents of the past few hours and try to get them into perspective." (Mrs. Nevinson sighed in exasperation and ex-claimed: "Oh Lord!" but I ignored her and went on.) "I mean, we don't want to rush precipitately into any foolish action, or experi-ment with something else and then find ourselves further in-volved."

"But I thought you said just a minute ago," Jessie put in, "that our only hope was to try another experiment."

"I'm definitely not agreeing to any more experiments," said her mother. "What's happened should be a lesson to us." She shuddered and began to look slowly around the room, murmur-ing: "My God, what's the matter with the air? It's – it's so alive and – and – " She broke off and none of us tried to ask her to explain what she meant, because we *knew*.

Mr. Nevinson said hastily: "Nell, I do hope you aren't going to prove difficult. We have to try something daring if we're to escape what's threatening us, and I can't see any help – "

"I tell you, I'm not going to be a party to any experiment, Ralph! And I mean that!"

"Sssh! Just a minute, Mrs. Nevvy," I said in a conciliatory tone. "This isn't exactly an experiment. Give me a chance to speak. I've been talking it over with Mr. Nevvy, and he agrees that it's worth attempting."

"Well, let's hear what it is," she said irritably. "And you haven't got to talk like Gibbon's *Decline and Fall* to tell us what you want to say. Say it simply."

I chuckled and began to speak, but I had hardly uttered more than four words when I was interrupted. Interrupted in unexpected fashion.

It was the flute.

The notes rose from the veranda – seemingly just beyond the windows. Clear, leisurely, deliberate.

We all heard it. We all exclaimed, and then fell silent, listening.

Rayburn's lips parted, and Mrs. Nevinson grew rigid, a thumb dug into the hollow formed by her collarbone. This was the first time the two of them were hearing it – in a waking state; for, of course, Mrs. Nevinson had heard it in her nightmares.

On and on it went. The same measure over and over. Exactly as it had sounded during the past weeks.

You will remember I stated that one afternoon I took down the tune, note for note. I promised to quote it, so here it is:

Just that – formless and banal, but to us who heard it, full of a significance that sent sick tremors through our stomachs.

There was no attraction of any sort on this occasion. None of us had the inclination to rush out of the cottage and follow a demon-figure. I glanced quickly at Mr. Nevinson, but he reacted like the rest of us and just stood where he was and listened.

At the window the candles burned steadily.

We could sense no odour. There were no aerial disturbances.

Only that strange, shifty denseness in the air.

Abruptly the flute stopped.

We could hear the river bubbling near the bank.

It was I who broke the silence. I sighed and said: "Well, that seems to put the veto on my scheme."

"How do you mean?" Jessie asked me.

"Well," I said, "what I was about to tell you when it began was that we should take advantage of the next manifestation, when it occurred, and see if we couldn't follow the flute to where Mynheer Voorman's bones are buried. If we could have got there before the seven hours have run out and dug up his bones and flute and had them reburied in the manner he requested we might still have been able to save the situation."

"And why couldn't we still try that?"

"Why? Because the manifestation has occurred already, hasn't it? It's quite probably the last one, and look at the time. It's after two – and six hours is the minimum time between manifestations, as we've proved by experience. Unless it decided to alter its habits specially for our benefit – which I can't see it doing."

"In any case," said Mrs. Nevinson, "it would have been useless. That manifestation means nothing now."

"How do you mean it means nothing now?" I asked.

"Well, we all heard it, didn't we? And we were none of us urged to rush outside and go after any spectral demon. Even Ralph didn't seem affected – and he was the worst, unless you've forgotten. Why didn't Rayburn have to hold him back? It means that the flute is without any power now. Mynheer Voorman can't save us. The other things have got us in their grip – thanks to the candles and petrol and whatnot you and Ralph insisted on experimenting with." She put a hand to her temple, and I could see that she was in a pretty bad state.

"I don't quite agree," I said cautiously and without any conviction in my voice. "It might have helped to lead us to the spot. And I'm certain if we buried the bones and the flute with Christian rites as the manuscript requested we would have stood a chance of being rid of these beastly demon-things. At least, it would have been worth trying. Anyway, there's no hope of that now. The flute is gone for good. We've only got about six hours left – less, in fact."

Jessie stared at me, and I saw her eyes beginning to grow watery.

I heard Mr. Nevinson's breath.

Rayburn's foot lisped along the floor as he changed his posture slightly.

Mrs. Nevinson clicked her tongue faintly.

And then it began again! The flute… On the veranda. Clear, deliberate…

This time I acted. I rushed to the window, hopped through and began to move towards the pantry around the corner.

And the notes moved! They preceded me. They were in the kitchen now.

I went down the kitchen steps, and the notes descended. They were at the foot of the stairway. When I got to the foot they were out on the grassy clearing. I began to advance towards the sawmill – but the notes receded behind me, heading for the river.

I heard Jessie's voice from the veranda, concerned, hysterical.

"Milton! Where are you? Come back! Don't follow it! Come back!"

I uttered a quavering laugh and, standing where I was, looked up at her. "No, I won't follow it. I'm coming up now. No fear! But I've got the hang of it. We're going to balk our nasty friends, the musky ectoplasms. Wait and see!"

I spoke idiotically, hardly realizing that the flute was fading on the chilly air. It trailed off towards the river, moved upstream, and then the old silence came down on the moonlit scene once more, oppressive, watching.

20

When I returned upstairs an argument at once began, and Mr. Nevinson had to shout at us before there was order.

"It's no use behaving like this," he said, flushed and frowning. "We won't achieve anything by squabbling. Nell! Come back here!" His wife had turned off in a huff and was moving along the veranda towards the pantry door. " Do you hear me? Come back here!"

She came back, sulky and haughty. "What is it? I try to make a sensible suggestion, and you shout me down," she complained. "If you don't wish to listen to me you've only got to say so, Ralph – "

"That will do. Sit down here and compose yourself – and try to listen. We have heard enough suggestions from you and everybody else. We have no time for further suggestions of any sort. We're going to act on the plan Milton has told us about – "

"I know! It's always Milton. He must be the only one among us with any intelligence – "

"Mother, shut up! Shut up! Sit down!" Jessie screamed. "We haven't time to waste. Didn't you hear what Daddy said? Sit down and listen."

Mrs. Nevinson sat down.

Rayburn, near the hammock, stared from one to the other of us, bewildered.

For the next few minutes, Mr. Nevinson explained what he had decided was to be done. We had reached a point, he said, where exceptional risks must be taken, and though it seemed a foolhardy plan, we were going to set out within a short while on an expedition into the jungle to make an attempt to find the remains of Mynheer Voorman.

His wife began to speak but he silenced her with a bark, and went on to deal with the details of the proposed trip. He ended up by saying: "Everything may depend, of course, upon whether Milton's conjecture is correct concerning this manifestation. Milton thinks that the flute will keep on sounding at brief intervals for the next five or six hours, and that if we are ready to follow where it leads there is every hope that we shall be taken to the spot where the bones and flute are buried. Milton's theory – and I'm inclined to endorse it – is that a crisis having been created by our experiments with the candles and the petrol, Mynheer Voorman is making his last desperate attempt to communicate his wishes to us, and is appealing to us to hurry if we would save him and ourselves from utter and final transformation into whatever it is we can *feel* is lurking in the offing now, threatening us. It will be no easy matter making such an excursion as we are planning. It will mean probably having to cut our way through sections of the bush when, as we suspect, we are compelled to leave the track, and there may be other dangers of which we are so far ignorant – but it can't be helped. We're desperate people – remember that. We must leave nothing undone that might possibly aid us in keeping off what menaces us. That is why we have to take this rash step."

He then asked us to go inside and get dressed, and when we were dressed to return out here on the veranda.

He was so impressive that even his wife's sulky manner had faded. She rose and went inside with Jessie silently, her face rigid and strained.

As Mr. Nevinson and I and Rayburn entered the dining-room we began to sense a tightening in the atmosphere – and a throbbing – and with an exclamation I fumbled out the matches I had slipped into the pocket of my pyjamas a short while before. I struck one, telling Rayburn to hurry back to the veranda and get a candle. "We've got out of range of the lighted candles," I murmured. "We mustn't forget that a naked flame is essential in our vicinity."

I scratched another match as the previous one began to go out, and then Rayburn came back with two candles and I lit them.

The disturbance had died down the instant I had struck the

first match, and now that the candles flamed into life the air steadied itself, though the heavy apprehensiveness persisted as before, threatening and ugly, a continued reminder that any relaxation or complacency on our part would be a serious mistake.

Twice during the next hour the flute made itself heard, but we proceeded calmly with our preparations for the expedition. Rayburn and I had to make three trips to the sawmill storeroom. We took Dietz lanterns with us as a safeguard against further aerial trouble. By half-past three we were ready on the northern veranda, and were overseeing and discussing the haversacks of food and the spades and cutlasses which stood in a clump on the floor, when the flute again sounded out in the clearing.

Except for Jessie, who started nervously, there was no alarm. A taut calm descended on us. We spoke now in lowered voices and only at rare intervals. There was no argument in us.

"You notice it's irregular and frequent now?" I commented. "The last one was only fifteen minutes ago. The interval before that was seven minutes."

Mr. Nevinson nodded. "We must move off at the next one."

When the notes ceased Rayburn and I went off with two of the lanterns to see about the boat. We returned in less than five minutes, for the craft was just as we had left it when last we had used it for one of our brief outings on the river, two days ago. We could have packed the implements and the haversacks into it in advance, but we wanted to take no chances. For, who knew, the flute might take it into its head to conduct us in some new direction, and we had to prepare for such an emergency.

As Rayburn and I rejoined the others on the veranda Mr. Nevinson told us to sling on our haversacks and make preparations to leave in accordance with what he had told us earlier.

In silence we obeyed, Rayburn and I and Mr. Nevinson each picking up a spade in addition to the lantern and cutlass we already carried.

At a signal from Mr. Nevinson – agreed upon before – we moved off towards the kitchen steps, our foot-treads sounding loud and solemn on the floor, for we all wore thick, heavy boots.

It might have been some sacred religious procession.

We had agreed to leave the lights burning in the cottage.

The moon was overhead, and this side of the cottage was in deep shadow. We paused at the top of the kitchen steps, Mr. Nevinson and I in front, behind Mr. Nevinson Rayburn, behind me Jessie, and behind Jessie her mother.

We stood there listening to the night.

All the old sounds were there, but coming to us through the uncertain veil that had been drawn between us and the normal. The river bubbled at intervals – or gurgled. The frogs chirruped as the whim took them – one near the sawmill, one amidst the shrubs that grew near the water's edge, one farther off near the silent logies. The fire-flies arced and criss-crossed – but feebly, reduced by the moonlight to less than half their usual brilliance.

I could hear Jessie breathing behind me. Once she touched my elbow. And the thick khaki material of the shorts I wore could not muffle completely the ticking of my watch. A brave, lusty ticking. A thread of sanity commonplace and inspiring hope. No fantasy troubled it.

A spade – I think it must have been Mr. Nevinson's – made a clank as it was shifted slightly. It must have collided with the facing of the door.

I heard Mrs. Nevinson sigh.

My host murmured: "Now we go."

The notes of the flute rose from near the foot of the steps.

A soft quavering sound came from Jessie as we began to descend. The chilly morning air shivered through my lungs refreshingly. For an instant I almost believed that there was no more apprehensiveness in the atmosphere.

Our lanterns burned steadily and clearly. Our footsteps made dull clumps on the steps.

I had not been wrong. The notes of the flute shifted, as I had calculated they would have done, towards the river.

We circled the cottage, feeling the wet grass under our heavy boots, exactly as though the actual moisture were penetrating the leather to the soles of our feet (this is an illusion we all of us experienced; it still remains a complete mystery). We moved towards the bank of the river at a point to the north of the small pier alongside which, not ten hours before, the weekly steamer had come to discharge supplies. This was where our boat was moored.

The sound of the flute, however, veered south – upstream. It did not cease as we got aboard the craft, and as we pushed off it came towards us again in the most uncannily intelligent manner, as though to re-establish its former distance between us and itself. I recall that Jessie clutched my arm and muttered: "My God, Milton! Is this really happening to us?"

It was the first time any of us had spoken since Mr. Nevinson had given the word to go at the top of the kitchen steps.

The sky was still indigo in the east as we began to move along the bank in an upstream direction, though I knew that within less than an hour dawn would be breaking. The flute continued ahead of us – leisurely, clear and more deliberate now than ever. A spectral flute guiding us towards the remains of a Dutch planter who had lived in the middle of the eighteenth century!

There are many aspects of our situation that strike an unmistakably humorous note. I am quite certain that had I recorded every phrase we each of us uttered, could such a verbatim report have been possible, these events would have seemed like something out of Gilbert and Sullivan, with music complete! Even as it stands now, so much depends upon one's attitude in viewing our plight. So much depends upon the scope of your individual imagination to encompass the uniquely fantastic nature of these happenings.

Anyway, there it was. Slowly we moved up the river, hugging the bank, Rayburn and Mr. Nevinson and I rowing, while ahead of us, perhaps about twenty yards distant, those spirit notes continued monotonously on the chilly, breezeless air, and around us that psychic pressing quality in the ether itself seemed to warn us that being in the open in no way shunted us out of range of the forces whose influence was focused upon us.

Rayburn sat in the bows, the two women amidships, and Mr. Nevinson and I astern. The tide was in flood, and as a result aided our progress.

Now and then I would ship my oar and flash the beam of my torch on the dense, billowing foliage of the trees that overhung the water. The leaves would spring into individual shape, detailed and clear, with the shadowed spaces behind them probing back into the impenetrable gloom and mystery that simmered in the humid depths. I could glimpse shiny aeta palm berries drifting slowly on the surface of the black water – and mauve wild flowers sometimes. Once, the golden dust of mora blossoms eddied past our bows.

And like a live, intelligent thing, that invisible flute kept on sending its clear notes through the dank, leafy air. Twenty or thirty yards ahead of us always, incredible and weird – a symbol for us of life and death. If it ceased we knew that we were lost; if it continued we could hope.

The stars sparkled up at us from the smooth black water, and the sky seemed more terrible in its immensity as a scooped bowl beneath us than as a dome overhead. Often I had the sensation that we were about to plunge irretrievably down into an emptiness of speckled gloom instead of advancing on a level with the river, and a vague nausea would attack me.

We must have proceeded around two bends in the river when we had the first inkling of the opposition that lay ahead.

Rayburn called: "*Tacooba*, sir! Steer clear! Out!"

A *tacooba*, in Guiana jungle parlance, is any obstruction – chiefly a fallen tree – that occurs along a river or creek. I thought that Rayburn sounded a little puzzled when he uttered the caution, so I called back: "But I don't remember seeing a *tacooba* anywhere near this spot, Rayburn."

"Me, too, sir. But something ahead. Ah can see it."

Almost before the words were out of his mouth I had got my oar shipped and had brought the beam of my torch to play on the water.

We peered ahead, the boat changing course in the meantime.

The flute, for some reason, seemed to become more animated. The notes came faster as though to express alarm – to warn us of subtle peril.

A dark, humped object lay about forty feet – ten points to port approximately – ahead of us. In the moonlight it had the appearance of an old tree-trunk embedded below and rearing its jagged, mossy stump above the water – in short, the commonest form of *tacooba*. We watched it in an anxious, suspicious silence.

The flute moved close along the bank as before, unheedful of our heading out slightly into the stream. Its alarmed animation continued.

Without warning, the *tacooba* moved, heaved up, and began to spread out on the water in a sluggish mist.

Jessie cried out.

Rayburn snatched up one of the four Dietz lanterns – which we had kept continuously alight – and swung it to and fro over the bows.

The air shook, and the ugly mist vanished at a flash, seeming to dissipate amid the white beam of my torch.

The flute became leisurely again.

"Get back into our original course," I warned. "We must keep where the path of the flute moves."

"Don't you think there may be a greater danger of encountering that thing if we resumed the old course?" Mr. Nevinson asked me in a murmur.

I shook my head. "Don't think so, sir. And what's more, I believe we're nearing the track-opening. That probably accounts for the sudden manifestation of that mock *tacooba*. They know we're about to discover the track and they're trying to hinder us in every way possible. We've got to keep close along the bank so as to be ready when the flute turns off into the track-opening. We can't afford to risk missing it."

Mrs. Nevinson took up a lantern and said that she would keep it overside as a precaution against the demon mist's reappearance, and I told her that that was an excellent idea. I would have asked Jessie to do the same, but she was in too nervous a state. She had just been sick over the gunwale, and sat now with her hands pressed to her temples.

We resumed the old course.

The jungle foamed out at us monotonously, glimmering dully in the moonlight – but even after we had rounded another bend there was still no sign of an opening that might indicate a track.

Then Mrs. Nevinson exclaimed and pointed.

"What's it?" asked her husband.

"That clump of manicole palms! I seem to remember it. I'm sure I've seen it in my dreams. It was always just near the track-opening – "

"Quick, boss! Quick!" called Rayburn. "We reach de track! De flute music turning into de bush here!"

In that frantic and dramatic manner we came to the track-opening. The jungle parted abruptly, and across the black gap, with uncertain flakes of moonlight shot through it like petrified fire-flies, the boat was about to drift past. Only swift and adept boatmanship on the part of Rayburn brought the bow round. In the excitement of the moment I caught at the limb of a tree in an attempt to pull the boat into the alcove, but only succeeded in swinging the bow outward again. Rayburn called sharply at me to desist, and dug his oar down into the shallow water near the bank. That saved the situation, and the next instant the bow of the boat grounded softly against the bank.

Had we not planned the details of our landing there might have been hopeless confusion. Rayburn attended to the mooring of the craft while Mr. Nevinson and I sprang ashore. Mrs. Nevinson handed across the spades and cutlasses to the two of us. Jessie, who should have attended to the lanterns, failed us, and it was her mother who had to snatch them up and hand them across.

Meanwhile the flute was advancing up the track, unheedful of our delay in disembarking. Rayburn began to explain that this was a fairly well-used track. Indians and *labba*-hunters frequented it, he said. Like a madman I snapped at him: "Keep your information for later! Get up those spades and cutlasses. Look! Mind my torch there! My God! The flute is going. We can't let it get too far ahead. Quick! Hurry!"

I was trembling, and snatched blindly at two spades when I should have taken up only one. Mr. Nevinson, almost as agitated, swore at me, and we began to wrestle over the possession of a lantern.

At length, we managed to sort ourselves out. Remembering Mr. Nevinson's detailed instructions on the veranda, we took up our positions as planned. Rayburn and I in front, the two women behind us, and Mr. Nevinson bringing up the rear, we set out into the gloom ahead. The ground was soft and spongy with the accumulation of decades – perhaps centuries – of fallen leaves and rotted twigs, and the air around us smelt damp and mossy. The moonlight penetrated in tiny patches here and there, ghostly coins and ragged petals. On either side of us we could feel rather than see the looming trunks of *paraipee* and *awara* palms, hoary and vicious with a multitude of long, sharp spines. The light from our lanterns, if anything, emphasized the mystery and gloom around us.

The sound of the flute, which had gone so far ahead as barely to be audible, began to come towards us again in that uncanny manner noted when we got into the boat at Goed de Vries. Within a few seconds it had approached within what seemed no more than a few feet in advance of us, and this distance it kept.

Jessie whimpered nervously, and I stretched back and gripped her arm. Every instant I feared she would collapse on our hands, but, somehow, she kept up.

Her mother, on the other hand, was as alert and determined and forceful as any of us men. I found my admiration for her bounding up tremendously. Her irritability had vanished, and her eyes glittered with a pugnacious light, wild and decidedly crazy yet very feminine and fascinating.

More than once I heard her grunting and expressing familiarity with what she saw about her, and Jessie, too, once or twice would mumble: "I know that tree. It's the same one I saw in my dreams." Or something to that effect.

We must have proceeded about a quarter of a mile when I noticed that the darkness had begun to take on a strange burnt-umber tint; I was on the point of commenting on this, imagining it to be a new development of the menace that hung over us, when it occurred to me that there was nothing mysterious about the phenomenon. Dawn had broken. Within a few minutes it would be daylight above the treetops and twilight down here.

The very thought of day, even though we would not be able to benefit from the full radiance of the sun because of the denseness of the jungle, was enough to send a quake of hope through me.

"It's getting brighter!" I announced with a kind of flighty fervour. "Dawn is here!" And I was on the point of going on to announce that half our worries were over when our guide the flute began to quaver in that alarmed fashion of a short while before when the mock *tacooba* threatened us.

Ahead of us we heard a loud rustling as of twigs being

disturbed, and Rayburn came to a halt and cautioned: "Dat sound like bushmaster, sir. Stop."

We stood still, listening. Jessie pressed herself against my back, and I could feel her trembling.

The rustlings continued, and there seemed no doubt that it must be some kind of snake. It might be a harmless *camoodie* – a kind of boa – but, on the other hand, it could be a bushmaster, the most dreaded of all creatures in the Guiana jungle. Its venomous bite causes death within ten to fifteen minutes.

We had not been able to bring a rifle, but our cutlasses were sharp, and our heavy boots had been worn on purpose as a precaution against snakes.

The flute, still warning in tone, was gradually increasing its distance between us and itself; and recalling the river incident, I had an idea. I said: "I don't believe it's a bushmaster. It's another ruse to delay us – like that *tacooba*. Let's go on. Don't let it fool us."

From the rear, Mr. Nevinson called "Don't be precipitate, Milton. Careful."

Unheeding, I rushed forward, waving my lantern aloft.

The air, more oppressive now, seemed to hum and oscillate. A harsh, savage lashing broke out near a clump of wild pines on the right of the track. I had a glimpse of the cotton-like webs of bush-spiders that are always to be found woven between the razor-sharp leaves of wild pines.

The noises ceased abruptly.

I came to a halt, knowing the old bush tale that whenever a bushmaster is about to strike it grows quiet and unmoving. I kept playing the beam of my torch along the track, standing there rigid, not knowing what nature of horror to expect, physical or psychic.

I had not long to wait. From among the wild pines I saw a thin greyish-brown mist wreathing. The air vibrated.

Rayburn by now had joined me, and I could hear the footsteps of the others clumping in our rear. The flute was coming back towards us, but it still contained that trilling note of alarm.

The darkness had definitely lightened. The coins and petals of moonlight on the ground were growing pale.

The misty abhorrence still hovered ahead of us, even though Rayburn and I waved our lanterns without cessation. Then I saw that it was beginning to take shape. Mrs. Nevinson cried: "My God! Look! Look at that! I saw it like that in my dream!"

The squat travesty of a head was materializing. Two lapis-lazuli orbs glared in blank malevolence at us. I heard Jessie whimper behind me.

I muttered something to Rayburn and he gave me a quick glance, grunted and fumbled in his haversack. Then he hissed: "Ready, sir!" and flung forward on to the ground what appeared in the beam of my torch to be a ragged, grey spider-like object. Jessie gasped and asked what it was, but knowing it to be only a piece of waste soaked in petrol, I did not answer but took two quick steps forward, struck a match and pushed it toward the waste.

The waste flared up – and the very earth seemed to leap at us in a cloud of mist and stench that sent us staggering backwards. All about us there broke out a cacophonous chatter of voices – vacuous hacking yelps and aerial whimperings and snarls. There was a sort of sizzling, crackling sound, too. A long, sustained flute-note, despairful, cut through the hubbub like a scarlet spear.

Then there was silence. Space seemed to tilt and right itself. Our lanterns were out – like the waste. The twilight had a gun-metal tint – a merging of umber and ultramarine. And the flute had stopped.

I heard Jessie moaning.

Rayburn was muttering: "Oh, God, sir! Oh, Jesus God!"

21

A few supremely terrifying moments have loomed into being in the course of the lives of most of us – moments which have produced such a stunning impact that when reflecting on them afterwards we are inclined to wonder whether they were not of deliberate and perverse invention. It was such a moment we experienced now.

The flute had stopped – the all-important, spectral flute. We had come on this absurdly rash expedition into the jungle under circumstances which, even when we had been amidst the civilized surroundings of a well-equipped modern cottage, appeared grotesquely menacing – and now the one symbol of hope we had had, fantastic though it had been, had vanished. Could any calamity have surpassed this? It was an insane moment.

Fortunately, there was one among us who could weather the immediate shock. Rayburn, despite his muttered exclamations of horror, was the first to recover. I heard the hiss of a match, and saw a lantern glow alight. As the flame steadied, the air began to waver – visibly and audibly – and amidst the jungle there was a crackling: a sound as of slips of paper being crumpled distantly. (It would be interesting to note that, afterwards when discussing it, we each of us differed in our opinions about the nature of this sound. Rayburn likened it to leaves being blown around "as if a wind was making a circling in the bush"; Jessie said it sounded like the hissing of several kettles of water boiling; Mrs. Nevinson heard it as a crunching of twigs and the dried shells of palm-seeds; Mr. Nevinson as "a parchment-like sound".)

It soon faded, and in the meantime I had lit two other lanterns.

The oppressiveness was terrible now. The air tingled with filaments of panic – there is no other way to describe it. There was the inclination to glance about furtively, expectantly. Yet there was no difficulty in breathing. The *air* itself seemed in no way barometrically affected. The oppressiveness, the apprehensive fibrousness, so to speak, existed in the ether. It was something *beyond*. An extraneous density whose vibrations belonged to a dimension for which there is no word.

I can remember how I looked around at the twilit scene of jungle, a feeling of puniness shivering through me so that my very brave human ego might have been wilting within me under the stare of some super-presence. My individuality seemed about to corrode and become less than even these ferns that grew about the base of a *paraipee* palm.

This is how we all felt. Earth dimensions swayed. The Peril was upon us.

But far off we heard a thin trickle of music.

Yes, it was the flute. It was returning.

Space righted itself, and our selves went through a remote adjustment. I shook myself into activity, turned to Rayburn and gasped: "Quick! Another piece of waste! I believe this is our last chance. Our very last!"

What followed is somewhat hazy, but I shall do my best to describe it as accurately as I can.

Rayburn produced from the cocoa tin in his haversack another piece of petrol-soaked waste. He did not throw it down but handed it to me. I jabbed the point of my cutlass into it, impaling it firmly, then struck a match and set it alight.

Mr. Nevinson shouted at me as though just realizing what I was about to do. I have a faint memory of hearing him say: "You little fool! You'll precipitate another crisis!" Then the waste flared at the point of my cutlass, and a roaring whoop of sound eddied around us. The twilight seemed to condense into a single bubble of intensity, and envelop us in a specific gloom, so that nothing but our own persons were visible to us. The jungle vanished, but within the sphere of twilight that enclosed us everything was grotesquely clear. I remember glancing round and seeing the faces of the others like grey-brown masks that had absorbed the hue of the vile crepuscle. I remember groping about me and seeming to feel only slippery emptiness – a kind of tangible etherealized slime that, though it could be sensed as a palpable thing, yet had no substance.

And all the while there was a low howling and shrieking.

We found ourselves moving – stumbling like drunk people along the track, it seemed to us, though afterwards we discovered that it was deeper into the jungle itself, into the very bushes themselves and quite off the track.

How long this journey lasted we were unable to calculate. Time seemed a myth, a meaningless symbol. We lurched on, driven by an incomprehensible compulsion. We had no will in the matter. Our mouths opened and shut as we attempted to yell at each other, but there was no sound. Evanescent twigs and leaves and branches brushed past us, grey and insubstantial; furry softnesses charged into our rushing bodies without injury or pain.

Then as abruptly as we had begun to move, we were halted.

The bubble of twilight billowed away from about us – dispersed in a silent whirl as of monstrous wings flapping off into vacancy. Our voices returned. Mrs. Nevinson shrieked: "It was here! It was here! It was here they brought me in my dream. This is where the bones and flute are buried."

We were standing in a depression, a kind of cave in the jungle. On all sides loomed the gnarled, prickly trunks of palms and wild cacao trees enmeshed with vines and spider-webs. Daylight filtered through the tangled canopy overhead very faintly, and the twilight around us was deep. The ground was not entirely covered with rotted leaves and twigs as on the track. Here and there showed patches of what looked like sand – the reddish sand typical of the higher terrain of the river basin.

But for Mrs. Nevinson's terrified declamation, there was no sound from any of us as we stood there gazing around, our eyes gradually becoming accustomed to the twilight.

The silence was profound, but somehow – and we all knew it – there was no longer any apprehensiveness. No oppressiveness. No threat in the ether. No warped fate hung over us.

A slight crackle made us start. But it was nothing supernatural. It was a salempenter that had darted across the clearing.

The air smelt dank and leafy, but not abnormally so. Everything was exactly as we might have expected it to be, standing where we were in this part of the jungle. I looked at my watch. The time was twelve minutes past six.

Our haversacks were still slung over our shoulders and resting on our backs. Rayburn and I still clutched a cutlass each and a spade. Mr. Nevinson had a cutlass but had lost his spade. Rayburn and I had both lost our lanterns, but Mrs. Nevinson and her husband each had one. But – most astounding of all – our clothes showed not the slightest signs of having been roughly treated. If we had been dragged forcibly through the jungle why had our clothes not been torn? Nothing would have satisfied my feeling for the dramatic and spectacular more than to have been able to state that our clothes were in ribbons. But they were not – it is just a simple fact.

Yet, behind us, we could discern clearly the point at which we had entered this clearing. The vines and ferns gave witness to this only too eloquently. The vines had been ripped and torn aside with considerable violence, and the ferns were trampled and scattered, one or two of them uprooted from the sandy soil. Limbs of mora saplings and of wild cacao trees lay hacked off and strewn about the ground as though recently assaulted by a hurricane.

Fear had left us now. Some strange cool peace seemed to move through the humid air, and the silence was not ominous but restful. There was a suggestion of tiny insects humming amidst the foliage overhead – a dim, lonely, benevolent sound.

It was Mrs. Nevinson who, in a lowered voice – we simply could not bring ourselves to speak in our normal voices – brought our notice to something important. She said: "Do you notice how just where we're standing is slightly sunken? I believe we're on the exact spot where the sluice referred to in the manuscript used to be."

And she was right, for it was only a few feet away, on the brink of the depression, that we discovered a dark-green mossy hump – and when we thrust our spades down there was a hard clink, indicating that under the moss lurked stone – "a large round granite stone (often used as an instrument of punishment for those of the slaves who stole or committed crimes of a serious nature)".

And when we dug "for a short way down", it was as the manuscript had said. The jar was there – green and clogged with the soil of two centuries, but solid Dutch earthenware. The stopper was too tightly embedded in the mouth to be removed; we had to smash the jar.

The flute was there – a simple metal flute about ten inches long – we did not think of measuring it – and the metal had hardly rusted. In appearance it was greyish-blue. There were papers, too – a roll of papers tied with a pinkish piece of cloth or ribbon.

Directly north of this spot, we struck brick after the first few tentative prospectings, hardly eight feet from the granite stone. And here we found fragments of bones and a rusted musket which came up in several pieces, the butt with a mother-of-pearl mounting on which were still clearly visible the engraved letters J.P.V.

We had come prepared. The battered-looking Anglican prayer book from which Mr. Nevinson read the burial service belonged to Rayburn.

We buried everything, save the roll of papers, at the spot where the granite stone had stood, and we replaced the stone.

We were very tired. We sat down and ate, and drank hot cocoa from the flasks in our haversacks. None of us wanted to speak.

We knew that never had we experienced such peace as the peace in that twilight clearing.

We encountered no difficulty in finding our way back to the track. The path we had made through the jungle in our incredible and phantasmal trip to the clearing was too well defined to be mistaken. Ferns and shrubs were trampled (we found dead lizards, and hairy bush spiders in a maimed condition as if crushed by our boots), vines and brambles torn aside, thickets of young cacao trees slashed through evidently by sharp blades, wild pines hacked to the roots, and a clump of orchids we took back with us was found on the ground seemingly cut down from the branch of a young mora tree where the parent plant still clung. We arrived at Goed de Vries at a quarter past nine. Timmykins, who slept in one of the logies downstream, said he came to the cottage at six, and finding us not there, had given us up for dead. He was sitting on the kitchen steps.

POSTSCRIPT

You may or may not read the rest, as you wish, for it is more or less of academic interest. Jessie would call it, I daresay, "the solution of the mystery", but Jessie has, I fear, a rather poor appreciation of the value of words (having been married to her for over seventeen years, I can take these liberties *on paper*), so it may be well for me to state that I have no intention whatever of attempting a solution. So far as I am concerned, what happened to us at Goed de Vries was of supernatural causes. There is no explanation that will satisfy conventional canons of reason – and I cannot help if I am called irrational or unscientific for saying so.

I have already quoted the score of that tune we used to hear, and now I shall quote one or two excerpts from the manuscripts we discovered in the jar with the flute, and leave it to you to form your own conclusions. I cannot think of a fairer way.

Several weeks elapsed, of course, before we were able to translate all that was written on these papers of the Dutchman's, and much of what we hurt our heads over to render lucid proved to be sketchy and unintelligible even to three Dutch scholars from Surinam to whom Mr. Nevinson had the opportunity, a year or two later, to show the manuscripts. On the other hand, such of the matter as we did succeed in shaping together so that it could be understood was of profound interest, and it is from these sections that I am going to quote.

I shall do my best to arrange these quotations in chronological order, for though they do not constitute a diary in the strict sense, these notes of Mynheer Voorman's were often accompanied by dates, leaving the impression that he did make a half-hearted attempt to keep a record of the events relating to his personal activities. I have inserted brief explanatory notes of my own where the text touches on matters of general historical record or where some particular point calls for comment.

P. *27th June, 1762.* (*Letter before date incomprehensible. Pieter ?*)

Jannetje's uncle has written advising that she should return with the children to Middelburg. It does not astonish me. She has been complaining to him that she is not happy on this plantation. This colony depresses her, and, moreover, my flute-playing annoys her. She places no value on my researches. What is it to her whether I add three more keys to the flute? My ambitions as an inventor of a flute of wide range mean nothing to her. But threats of desertion will not hinder me in my purpose... If I have to sell my soul to Beelzebub I shall succeed... The overseers annoy me with their talk of unrest among the slaves. Wijs is a fool. I should have known it.

7th July, 1762.

Still no advance. I failed with the F key and with the semitones, but this will not daunt my spirit. P.J.N. (*More incomprehensible letters.*)

9th July, 1762.

Jannetje again urging to sell the plantation and return to Holland. She brings up instance of day before yesterday, but I tell her that such a disturbance should trouble no one. Laurens Kunckler was absent when it occurred, and the Burgher Militia is capable of handling any such affairs. [*On the 6th July there was an uprising of the slaves on Plantations Goed Fortuin and Goedland in the absence of the owner, Laurens Kunckler, who was at Fort Nassau attending a Council meeting.*] The real reason for her anxiety is myself. She heard me during the early hours of Monday last calling to those of the Dark. Perhaps she would be still more concerned could she know that the Call was answered. W.W. P. Z.

20th August, 1762.

I rapped and heard the F key and the desired semi-tones G sharp and C sharp. I heard them in the Dark, and there was blue.

I admit I am a trifle afraid. Tzz. Prin. Txx.

14th November, 1762. J.

I played them all, but I know that it is not I who played. I know that the Dark is within me. Arak. Arak. Tzz. Txx. P.J.

14th December, 1762. Arak.

The work on this plantation depresses me. I have too much to occupy me in this house. They call upon me several times a day now, and all night. Hail Mary. Pray for me!

29th December, 1762.

Jannetje objects to the candles I burn in my room. But I do not care. I warned her before we were married that I should not give up my religion. Because I am not of the Reformed Church she and her uncle detest me. I do not care, I say. Hail Mary! My candles shall burn. My statue of Mary shall stand.

8th February, 1763.

The folds surround me and there is blue. Tau. Tzz.

12th February, 1763.

The keys are all there, but they still come from the Dark. P.J.T.

20th February, 1763.

They are calling insistently. I will fight them with fire, symbol of my faith, for though errant, I am at heart still a Christian. My church is my rock, and they know this and fear it, they of evil.

22nd February, 1763.

I am Chu and Arak and P.J. and Tzz, but these are one with me. I am the good and they are the bad, trailed from me in evil smoke. [*This is the best we could make of this sentence.*] They tempted me, and I tempted them, and now they roam with me for dark intent, I of them and they of me. Sometimes I see myself as I am, and sometimes I see myself as they are, but it is all one. What is good and what is bad? Concerning this I shall say that it would serve us better to avow that there is that which is naturally beneficent and that which is unnaturally malevolent. If a man shall defy his naturally beneficent urges and turn from his God to unnaturally malevolent practices (*symbols, meaningless letters for two lines*) then shall he emit evil emanations and influences – and these came out of that man himself. And should he persist with concentration upon deeds of greed and ambition, attempting to achieve that which is above him – witness me and my inventing of new keys on the flute – then shall his emanations take unto themselves active and frightful shapes. It is the evil from me that has taken unto itself shapes and odours of frightful nature. It is I myself who plague myself in several forms projected and created by my errant will. These presences bear the essence of me Jan Pieter Voorman. When they call it is I who severally call. The evil I have created calls at the good in me. There are no demons but the demons our own wills evoke. Sometimes I appear before myself as I am, sometimes as They are whom I made. And if I haunt in the Afterlife, I sometimes may appear as my own good self in piteous supplication, sometimes as the evil grey fiends, my familiars, who are one with me. How we shall fence and dodge, They and I, in that Afterlife! They bear my own fears; they fear and revere those things which I, the good me, fear and revere. Holy candles and clean flames they shudder and shrink from, shriek and writhe before, and thunder tumultuously, they of the Dark who are me and who attempt to conquer the good me. (*Follow symbols and letters for three lines and a half.*)

25th FEBRUARY, 1763 (*I note this date specially, for it should be stated that the Berbice Slave Insurrection started on 21st February, on the upper reaches of the Canje Creek, though the insurgents did not reach the Berbice River plantations until the 27th, the planters being taken completely by surprise. Hence on the 25th, Mynheer Doorman would have been unaware of the approaching storm.*)

Farther down into the Dark. Oh, Mary, thy name is now sacrilege upon my foul lips! Farther down into the blue, into the odours of Satan that fume perpetually at an angle beyond this life [*sic*]. Last night I heard them speaking in varied languages – languages I know not and yet which I myself spoke. I heard French and German and English and Italian and other tongues I

230

could not identify. [*Mrs. Nevinson, in her dreams, you will remember, was spoken to in English*.] They babbled about me in a clamour too deafening to describe. They fumed and wreathed and turned in spirals [*symbols and letters for a line and a half*] and the air thundered about me. They extinguished two of my candles, but not the third and the fourth, for before these I knelt in prayer, beseeching the saints of heaven to intercede for me. Today I am a wretched being, for as the hours go by so do I sink deeper into the Gloom. A catastrophe threatens. I sense it in the air. I am a thwarted, craven soul, a human tottering on the edge of ultimate darkness. To whom, to what, must I turn for salvation?

ABOUT THE AUTHOR

Edgar Mittelholzer was born in New Amsterdam in what was still British Guiana in 1909. He began writing in 1929 and despite constant rejection letters persisted with his writing. In 1937 he self-published a collection of skits, *Creole Chips*, and sold it from door to door. By 1938 he had completed *Corentyne Thunder*, though it was not published until 1941 because of the intervention of the war. In 1941 he left Guyana for Trinidad where he served in the Trinidad Royal Volunteer Naval Reserve. In 1948 he left for England with the manuscript of *A Morning at the Office*, set in Trinidad, which was published in 1950. Between 1951 and 1965 he published a further twenty-one novels and two works of non-fiction, including his autobiographical *A Swarthy Boy*. Apart from three years in Barbados, he lived for the rest of his life in England. His first marriage ended in 1959 and he remarried in 1960. He died by his own hand in 1965, a suicide by fire predicted in several of his novels.

Edgar Mittelholzer was the first Caribbean author to establish himself as a professional writer.

OTHER NOVELS BY EDGAR MITELHOLZER IN THE PEEPAL TREE CARIBBEAN MODERN CLASSICS SERIES

Corentyne Thunder
ISBN: 9781845231118; pp. 248; pub. 2009, price: £8.99

Ramgolall, an old Indian cow-minder, has punished himself with work and self-denial to save money and has built a sizeable herd. His first daughter is the long-established mistress of a well-to-do white planter. Their son, his grandson, Geoffry, light-skinned and ambitious, seems destined for success. But when Geoffry becomes involved with Kattree, his daughter by a second marriage, Ramgolall's world begins to fall apart.

This classic work of West Indian fiction, first published in 1941, is much more than a pioneering and acute portrayal of the rural Indo-Guyanese world, both the pretensions of the rising middle class keen to display their talents in mastering aspects of European culture and the lively energies of the villagers with their curry feasts and drumming; it is a work of literary ambition that creates a symphonic relationship beween its characters and the vast openness of the Corentyne coast.

This new edition features an introduction by Mittelholzer scholar Juanita Cox.

A Morning at the Office
ISBN: 9781845230661; pp. 210; pub. 2010; price: £9.99

From four minutes to seven, when the aspiring black office-boy, Horace Xavier, opens up the premises of Essential Products Ltd in Port of Spain in 1947 and leaves a love poem in the in-tray of the unattainable, high-brown Nanette Hinckson, to noon when the poetic Miss Jagabir is the last to leave for lunch, the reader is privy to the interactions and inner feelings of the characters who make up the office's microcosm.

Expatriate English, Coloured Creoles of various shades, Chinese, East Indians and Trinidadian Blacks (and a sympathetically presented gay man), all find ample scope for schemes and fantasies – and wounded feelings when they think their positions on the scale of colour and class are being incorrectly categorised, or when those at the bottom are reminded of their position.

Enlivened by the inventive device of "telescopic objectivity" and a humane comedic touch, Mittelholzer's classic novel of 1950 challenges the present to declare honestly whether his news is old.

With an introduction by Raymond Ramcharitar

The Life and Death of Sylvia
ISBN: 9781845231200; pp. 366; pub. 2010; price: £12.99

When Sylvia Ann Russell's louche and philandering English father is murdered in scandalous circumstances, she soon discovers that for a young woman with a black mother, 1930's Georgetown is a place of hazard. This is a world where men seek either respectable wives from "good" families, or vulnerable young women to exploit. Here the fall from respectability to prostitution at the Viceroy Hotel can be all too rapid.

The Life and Death of Sylvia is a pioneering and affecting novel of social protest over the fate of women in a misogynist world – and a richly imagined study of character that inhabits Sylvia's psyche with great inwardness. But Mittelholzer's ambition extends beyond character and protest. His goal is to present Sylvia's individual fate as cosmically meaningful, both when she redeems herself by reclaiming her own story through writing, and by making her story part of the larger patterns of sex and death, creativity and decay, sound and silence that he composes in this onwards surging "Georgetown symphony" of life.

With an introduction by Juanita Cox

Shadows Move Among Them
ISBN: 9781845230913; pp. 358, pub. 2010, price £12.99

When Gregory Hawke, a burnt-out case from the Spanish civil war, seeks refuge at the remote utopian commune his uncle, the Reverend Harmston, has set up among the local Amerindians one hundred miles up the Berbice River, he finds a society devoted to "Hard work, frank love and wholesome play".

Apparently free-thinking and ecologically green before its time, Gregory finds much in Berkelhoost to attract him, particularly when his pretty cousin Mabel shows an unmistakeable interest. But there is an authoritarian side to the project that alarms Gregory's democratic instincts and it is this which makes it impossible to read the novel, first published in 1951, without seeing elements of prophecy – of the fate of the People's Temple commune at Jonestown in Guyana in 1978.

No such dreadful end awaits the generality of the communards, but in this most inventive of Mittelholzer's novels there are darker notes beneath the generally comic tone.

With an introduction by Rupert Roopnaraine

All books available online from <u>www.peepaltreepress.com</u>